# Praise for *Little Stalker*

"An offbeat, surprisingly sweet story about voyeurism, celebrity, obsession, and writer's block . . . *Little Stalker* is a treat—hilarious, richly textured, subtly insightful, and undeniably twisted."

—*The Boston Globe*

"Compulsively readable . . . *Little Stalker* is an affecting meditation on the connections we make—with others and with ourselves—as we age, from a writer whose work is maturing, quite beautifully."

—*Salon.com*

"Hilarious and poignant. Despite some serious attention-deficit problems, this protagonist is an endearing figure." —*The Seattle Times*

"A smart and hilarious read; you'll fall in love with Belle's neurotic heroine Rebekah Kettle as she struggles to make ends meet, unearth her father's secrets, find love, and manage a bizarre obsession with a movie director." —*People Style Watch*

"There are only so many good novels about single women living the big-city life, and Jennifer Belle's novels are among the best, the most human and genuine. Her first-person narrators are solitary female *flanuers* in continual drift through the pretty and gruesome parts of New York, and it's always a treat to be in on their streaming monologues as they . . . generally afflict their humanity on an otherwise indifferent world." —*Venus*

"Deliciously sardonic . . . You have to admire a writer who can create a character who is monumentally neurotic, yet oddly appealing nevertheless. Jennifer Belle has brilliantly done so with the protagonist—no, let's call her the heroine, because she's earned it— of *Little Stalker*." —*The Hartford Courant*

*continued . . .*

"'A lighthearted romp through New York' [is] precisely what Belle delivers. That it comes with a skewering as well makes it just that much more fun." —*New York Daily News*

"Twisted and tender . . . Will keep you hooked to the last page."
—*Cosmopolitan*

"Belle suffuses this story with genuine sweetness."
—*The Indianapolis Star*

"A funny and rich plot." —*The Sacramento Bee*

## Praise for *High Maintenance*

"Hilarious." —*The Boston Globe*

"Razor-sharp, deadpan observations and dazzling prose—by turns utterly hilarious and heart-wrenching." —*San Francisco Chronicle*

"Irresistible." —*Newsday*

"Looking for a good laugh? Enter the world of twenty-six-year-old Liv Kellerman. . . . Her nutty sagas will have you rolling on the floor."
—*Cosmopolitan*

"Stylish, funny . . . Belle's unpretentious humor and clean prose style are in an entirely different neighborhood than your average single-in-the-city author." —*Minneapolis Star Tribune*

"An outrageous, hilarious account of one woman's journey to find herself, the 'Loft of her Life,' and a man worthy of sharing apartment space in New York City . . . wicked and twisted . . . uproariously funny." —*The Tampa Tribune*

"Addictive and captivating . . . The same wisecracking, fierce yet vulnerable point of view that made *Going Down* so special is taken even further in *High Maintenance*."
—*Time Out New York*

"Satisfying. Even non–New Yorkers will be sucked in as Liv navigates her way through heartache and the city."
—*Mademoiselle*

"Sharp, incisive, and laugh-out-loud funny."
—*The Baltimore Sun*

"Just buy the damn book."
—*The New York Observer*

"Belle has created another unforgettable narrator—funny, self-absorbed, a little damaged."
—*Kirkus Reviews*

"Hugely funny."
—*New York Daily News*

"Liv's wackiness gives this unruly novel moments of great humor, but in the end the book is as much about the peculiar landscape of the New York housing market—the snooty upper-class clients and the real estate agents who kowtow to them—as it is about a young woman finding her own independence."
—*The Washington Post Book World*

"Belle deftly mines real estate as a metaphor, especially in Liv's affair with an impulsive architect, and her clients and fellow brokers are both terrifying and hilarious by turns."
—*Entertainment Weekly*

"In this latest New York romp . . . Belle draws both Liv and the idiosyncrasies of the Manhattan real estate market so well that one can't help wondering just what is fiction (Belle did a stint as a broker herself) and what may be biography. . . . Belle's skewed take on life in the big city keeps the smirk-per-page ratio high . . . offbeat observations . . . hilarity and pathos."
—*The Denver Post*

"[An] amusing . . . humorous real-estate romp with Manhattan views."
—*US Weekly*

*continued . . .*

"If you think the Hub housing market is tough, take a look at this tale of high-stakes real estate—and sexual—wheeling and dealing. Belle knows the world she depicts."   —*Boston Herald*

"Like a hot fudge sundae . . . delicious. Gutter-mouthed, smart-ass Liv, she's a Becky Sharp for our time."   —*Gotham*

"You'll feel right at home with Belle's . . . follow-up to her racy debut, *Going Down.*"   —*Glamour*

"Brimming with Gotham references, weird but lovable characters and typical urban scenes, [*High Maintenance*] is a witty and engaging tale of love and real estate in Manhattan. . . . Belle's tongue-in-cheek style and laugh-out-loud antics keep the pages turning . . . fresh and invigorating."   —*Publishers Weekly*

"This work continues in the same tradition of Belle's highly praised first novel, *Going Down*, with equal parts hilarity and pain . . . in turns funny and poignant."   —*Library Journal*

## Praise for *Going Down*

### (for which Belle was named Best New Novelist of the year by *Entertainment Weekly*)

"A witty, gritty, and thoroughly convincing first novel."
—Nick Hornby

"A rollicking debut."   —*The Village Voice*

"A funny, sad, nasty little gem of a novel."   —Jay McInerney

"An exceptionally funny writer."   —*Time*

"A kind of twisted version of *Gentlemen Prefer Blondes* . . . Delightfully, sickeningly, hilariously enthralling."  —Tama Janowitz

"Imagine Holden Caulfield's sister, Phoebe, growing up and turning tricks to study acting, and you have Bennington Bloom. . . . Alternately vulnerable and self-possessed, Bloom is the main attraction of this book, but there are others: a riveting plot with menacing undercurrents and creepy details, a cast of colorful minor characters, and a happy but not sappy ending. *Going Down* is loaded with comical ironies . . . a wonderful, aberrant, compulsively readable novel."

—*Entertainment Weekly*

"The best thing about Jennifer Belle's appealing first novel is Bennington Bloom, the near-tragic yet fantastically winning narrator . . . Belle has created an oddly affecting character whose self-reflexive candor and wry observations add up to an astringent, darkly comic view of New York life."  —*Elle*

"Belle combines very funny, sharply written prose and superb grasp of narrative in her debut novel. . . . The arresting combination of her caustic wit and insightful observations makes for a wickedly hilarious sense of humor evoking Dorothy Parker. . . . Belle's riotous, vivid debut has the energy and gritty appeal of New York City itself."

—*Publishers Weekly*

*Also by Jennifer Belle*

*Going Down*

*High Maintenance*

*Little Stalker*

**FOR CHILDREN**

*Animal Stackers*
(illustrated by David McPhail)

the
Seven Year
bitch

Jennifer Belle

RIVERHEAD BOOKS

New York

**RIVERHEAD BOOKS**
**Published by the Penguin Group**
**Penguin Group (USA) Inc.**
**375 Hudson Street, New York, New York 10014, USA**
Penguin Group (Canada), 90 Eglinton Avenue East, Suite 700, Toronto, Ontario M4P 2Y3, Canada
(a division of Pearson Penguin Canada Inc.)
Penguin Books Ltd., 80 Strand, London WC2R 0RL, England
Penguin Group Ireland, 25 St. Stephen's Green, Dublin 2, Ireland (a division of Penguin Books Ltd.)
Penguin Group (Australia), 250 Camberwell Road, Camberwell, Victoria 3124, Australia
(a division of Pearson Australia Group Pty. Ltd.)
Penguin Books India Pvt. Ltd., 11 Community Centre, Panchsheel Park, New Delhi—110 017, India
Penguin Group (NZ), 67 Apollo Drive, Rosedale, North Shore 0632, New Zealand
(a division of Pearson New Zealand Ltd.)
Penguin Books (South Africa) (Pty.) Ltd., 24 Sturdee Avenue, Rosebank, Johannesburg 2196,
South Africa

Penguin Books Ltd., Registered Offices: 80 Strand, London WC2R 0RL, England

This is a work of fiction. Names, characters, places, and incidents either are the product of the author's imagination or are used fictitiously, and any resemblance to actual persons, living or dead, business establishments, events, or locales is entirely coincidental. The publisher does not have any control over and does not assume any responsibility for author or third-party websites or their content.

The author gratefully acknowledges permission to quote from "The Tongue," from *Lucy* by Jamaica Kincaid. Copyright © 1990 by Jamaica Kincaid. Reprinted by permission of Farrar, Straus and Giroux, LLC.

First Riverhead hardcover edition: May 2010
First Riverhead trade paperback edition: May 2011
Riverhead trade paperback ISBN: 978-1-59448-516-9

The Library of Congress has catalogued the Riverhead hardcover edition as follows:

Belle, Jennifer, date.
   The seven year bitch / Jennifer Belle.
   p.      cm.
   ISBN 978-1-59448-755-2
   1. Motherhood—Fiction.   I. Title.
   PS3552.E53337S48    2010        2010000147
   813'.54—dc22

For Andrew Krents

and our sons,
Jasper and Shepherd

. . . and for Carmen

*Mariah was forty years old. She kept saying it—"I am forty years old"—alternating between surprise and foreboding. I did not understand why she felt that way about her age, old and unloved; a sadness for her overcame me, and I almost started to cry—I had grown to love her so.*

—from *Lucy* by Jamaica Kincaid

*Part One*

# In Bed
# with the
# Trents

# 1

As I walked along Waverly Place to meet my friend Joy for dinner, I saw a girl in her twenties leisurely crossing the street, and something about her brought that whole decade of my life back to me. I had never seen this girl before, but I knew her. I knew that what she was doing now was just getting through the years until she had children. She was planning, as she walked, what she was going to do that night to ward off loneliness. She wasn't thinking of it that way, but that's what she was doing.

She planned a trip to Italy with her girlfriend, calming herself with the knowledge that one day she'd be going on a honeymoon there instead. And she sewed a tail onto the back of her leggings on Halloween to go to some party, sure that one day she'd be zipping her child into his dragon costume. And on dates, she looked into the eyes of the stranger across the table from her, wondering if this would be the man to give her children. Once one had asked me if I would like to go for a drive in the country to look at the "foilage." And I knew I did not want a man who pronounced *foliage* "foilage" to be the father of my children.

Of course not all girls felt this way—I knew plenty who didn't want children—but this one did, I could tell. And until it happened, she would look in toy store windows, planning for some future Christmas, stuffing a stocking that wouldn't be hung for ten or even twenty years.

Watching women walk down the street, I could tell which had children and which didn't. It wasn't a judgment, just a fact. Women with children were always in just a little bit of a hurry and women without weren't.

And I, I realized right then, really loved being in a hurry.

As I entered Pastis, I tried to shake off the fight I'd just had with my husband, Russell. He had thrown out my can of Diet Coke before I'd finished it, and I had blown up because it was always happening. The house could be a complete mess—he hadn't cleaned anything or washed a dish in our whole marriage—but for some reason he would take it upon himself to throw out my soda. "I was enjoying that!" I had screamed like a lunatic. I tried to remind myself to be happy that I had the kind of husband who could stay home with the baby while I went out to dinner. He was the publisher at a small press he had started himself in our living room called Trent Books. He was a lawyer, and one day, right after we were married, his best friend, Ben, sent him a novel he had written. Russell read it and called me from his office.

"Ben's book is so fucking great," he said. "I'm leaving the firm. I'm going to start a publishing house and publish it."

"What's it called?" I said, thinking he was on track to make partner in less than three years and that his friend Ben was an idiot.

"*Shoes and Socks*," Russell said.

"*Shoes and Socks*," I had said, and something in my voice when I said it—"*Shoes and Socks*?" or "*Shoes and Socks*!"—infuriated him and put a wedge between us. He never felt I was behind his publishing venture and rightfully so, even though he loved it more than anything in the world.

"Obviously, you're gonna have to carry us for a bit. But I'm okay with not having my own office. I'll work out of our apartment," he had said, never thinking it might be a sacrifice for me to live in an apartment filled with boxes, desks, and office equipment. Plus, "carry us for a bit" was an understatement, as Russell believed for some reason that "all authors deserved to be paid for their hard work." The truth was I had personally funded *Shoes and Socks* and countless other similar masterworks.

I didn't know why I got so angry at Russell all the time, but I did, and I hated myself for it. But not as much as I hated Ben and the other volatile, desperate, impoverished, needy, ungrateful authors who made up Russell's list and called at all hours and slept on our couch when they were on their "book tours" in New York.

This was Joy's first time back in New York since she'd moved her perfume company to LA—she still had a small shop on Mulberry Street but her factory and flagship store were in LA—and I tried to savor the anticipation of eating steak with béarnaise sauce and complaining with her about our husbands, and that's when I realized that I just couldn't picture myself married to my husband in five years.

*The Seven Year Bitch*

We'd been married for five years, and I couldn't really remember those. I tried to imagine where I'd be in five more years, and I came up blank. I couldn't imagine us on a trip or in a better apartment or even in the same apartment. I suddenly couldn't even picture the apartment we lived in now. It was as if I were wiped out, an amnesiac from some Danielle Steel novel, a ghost.

Joy was already seated at our table, furiously writing on note cards. I still hadn't written a single thank-you note for all the presents I'd gotten for my son, Duncan, when he was born, even though he was almost one. The note cards had a photo of her three sons sitting with their backs to a fire that was burning in a slightly tacky modern fireplace.

"You're amazing," I said. "Sending Christmas cards in November."

"They're to my kids' teachers. You know, Christmas thank-you notes and gift."

"Of course," I said, trying to sound nonchalant but feeling that all-too-familiar panic that there was yet something else I didn't know you had to do now that I was a mother. I had thought naively that one day getting my child into school, and *to* school every day except for weekends, would be enough, but now there were notes and gifts. You had to have a note card with your child's photo on it, and I still hadn't sent out a birth announcement. I couldn't even imagine what the gift might have to be.

"Right, of course, a gift," I said, as if I knew all about it. "You mean like money?"

"Money's a little crass don't you think? I usually go to the big Nike store on Wilshire and get everyone hundred-dollar gift certificates." She stopped writing cards long enough to reach into her purse. "Here, I brought you something."

"Thank you!" I said, taking the small Chanel box from her.

"I'm sorry I can't be at Duncan's birthday party."

"Me too," I said. "And I'm sorry I couldn't be at Ethan's." Ethan was her third son, who had just turned two, and I'd sent a tiny bathing suit to go with their new pool.

By the size of the box Joy had handed me, I could tell it was a silver spoon or cup, and I loved things like that although I didn't know Chanel made baby stuff. I opened the box and pulled out a large pot of cream. "Chanel Precision," I read out loud.

"Eye cream," she said.

"You mean wrinkle cream?" I asked. "Is this a new thing for diaper rash?"

"It's for you," she said. "You dab. Morning and night." She made a demented tapping motion, not around her own eyes but around mine.

"You know this isn't LA," I said. "New Yorkers don't use wrinkle cream." I tried not to let the corners of my eyes move as I said that. I had never said the words "wrinkle cream" in my entire life.

"Right," she laughed. "And according to you, real New Yorkers don't drive and no one in New York wears sunglasses."

"All true," I said.

"Well, I just thought I'd get something for you instead of the baby. After I had Ethan the last thing I wanted to look at was another burp cloth. How boring."

Most of the baby gifts, especially the clothes I'd received, were dog related for some reason that I couldn't figure out. They were

*The Seven Year Bitch*

all fuzzy with little round ears on the hood or they had pictures of dogs and hydrants on them. Why did people want to dress up their babies as animals? I wanted my baby to look like a baby.

"I left Harry," she said.

"What? When?" I asked, shocked.

"Three weeks ago."

"Why didn't you tell me? Are you okay? Are the boys . . ." I was so upset about her boys I couldn't finish the sentence. I hadn't gotten over my own parents' divorce even though it happened when I was twenty-five and already out of business school.

"We're fine," she said brightly. "I tried to tell you on the phone, but one of the boys always seemed to be with me and the timing just wasn't right." She looked cheerfully down at her menu. "Let's see, is today *jeudi* or *vendredi*? Yay, lamb."

"Where's he living?" I asked.

"With his mother, if you can believe it." We both took a moment to snicker at the thought of it.

"What happened? Why did you do this?" I asked. I had a split-second image of trying to explain to Duncan why his father didn't live with us and grimaced from the pain of it, which I was sure caused a lot of wrinkles. I could never have that conversation.

"Well, once I got the idea to do it, it all spiraled very quickly. Come on, we've talked about this a hundred times. You should do it too," she said, her voice filled with excitement.

"Joy, I can't leave Russell now."

"Why not?"

"We don't have the money for two households," I said, surprising myself by saying something out loud I had actually thought through.

"He could stay with Marlon."

"Marlon wouldn't take him," I said, again surprising myself. "He's really sick." Marlon was a bitter old man who had been something of a mentor to Russell ever since he was a kid. He was the father of Russell's best friend since childhood, a sort of father to him too. Marlon had rented a one-bedroom apartment in Hell's Kitchen after his wife had thrown him out of their Westchester home. He inexplicably had a set of twin beds in his bedroom and sometimes when I was at my angriest at Russell, I imagined the two of them sleeping in those beds Ernie and Bert–style.

"He could live in your country house and commute into the city when he has to see a client." I had thought that through too. "You should do it when you get home. You've been married for five years. You shouldn't put this off another minute."

"I can't leave Russell tonight! I'm having a huge party on Sunday to celebrate Duncan's first birthday. And I got fired today."

"What!" she said. "Why?"

"In case you haven't heard, a few people are getting fired on Wall Street. They dissolved our entire department. Of course Russell and I were totally prepared for it. . . ."

"You must feel terrible," she said.

But I felt euphoric and I didn't know why. When Mark, the managing director, had called a meeting for everyone on the desk and told us what we had been expecting to hear every day for weeks, there were baskets of muffins and croissants on the conference table and the freshly baked, just-out-of-the-oven butter smell reminded me of something, but I couldn't figure out what it was. I sat there breathing in as deeply as possible, and then I realized it was just like the smell of my baby's shit.

*The Seven Year Bitch*

Whenever I watch new parents on TV and in the movies gagging and cringing and protesting and avoiding the diapers, I don't understand it. I love the smell of it. I press my face to the back of Duncan's pajamas and breathe in, like a teenager sniffing glue.

"I'm just not sure what I'm going to do," I said. "When Careena shows up at eight on Monday, I suppose I should tell her we don't need a nanny anymore."

"Well this is perfect," Joy said. "You can come to LA with the baby and stay with me as long as you need to. We'll get you on your feet again, teach you to drive, find you a place of your own. I have a lawyer who can help you, a hairstylist, everything you need. Even sunglasses."

She reached across the table and held my hand in her much softer one.

"You can do this," she said, with the seriousness of Harriet Tubman leading the Underground Railroad. "Two words: *Jet Blue. New life.* And you won't have to take his abuse anymore." Throwing out my Diet Coke hadn't exactly been abuse. Forget wrinkle cream, the way she was talking was making me feel like I had two black eyes and a fat lip.

"I'm not ready for that," I said. I would never be ready to do that to Duncan, I thought, but I didn't want to hurt Joy by saying that out loud.

"You'll see. I'm telling you. Once the idea occurs to you, and I know it has, then it all spirals quickly."

"But the boys," I said. "Ethan and Jake and—"

"The boys," she said, looking me straight in the eye, "are just fine. And yours will be just fine too."

*Jennifer Belle*

I noticed she was doing a slight tapping motion around her eyes as she spoke. "Just." Tap, tap. "Fine." Tap, tap.

At my wedding, right before she marched down the aisle just ahead of me, she'd whispered to me, "I have a car waiting in case you change your mind." And now I imagined a new scenario, five years later at my son's first birthday: a birthday cake with its one candle burning down while the birthday boy and his mother were thousands of miles away in a Jet Blue aircraft.

"You're going to be thirty-nine, Izzy. In four months you're going to be thirty-nine. Which is forty, which is fifty. This is your chance."

"Wait, am I going to be thirty-nine or am I going to be fifty?" I said, beginning to get extremely annoyed.

"I think that a happy mother is the greatest gift I can give my kids," Joy said. "Instead of someone who's always yelling at their father. Having children raises the stakes, Izzy. You'll see. It's cute that they're dopey and forgetful when you get married, but it stops being cute when they don't pick the kid up when they say they're going to and put their shoes on the wrong feet. Duncan's going to be one, but wait until he's two and then three. I had to remind him to kiss them good night! He turned me into something I didn't want to be," she said. "Seven years of having to nag, and scream, and fight, and be a policeman in my own home was enough for me. It's not that you get a seven year itch. It's that they turn you into a seven year bitch. After seven years you can't take it anymore. I'll never let anyone do that to me again!"

Had he really turned her into that, or had she been like that already? I wondered. And then I wondered, Had I?

I watched her tap herself for the rest of the meal. There was a smile in her fingertips. Each tap was filled with love and urgency as if she were resuscitating a tiny heart. But despite that, or maybe because of it, I couldn't help but notice how radiant she looked. She had lost at least thirty pounds. Not five or ten, but thirty. She was wearing some kind of incredible garment from Africa and the newest Vivienne Westwood bag. In fact everything she was wearing was incredible, no secret spreading milk stains hidden under her jacket every day. "Are you going to live your life in captivity?" she asked me.

There had to be something to this freedom trail, I realized. I just had to board Jet Blue and I'd look like her—thin, happy, wrinkle/husband-free.

"*Joy and Harry are* divorcing," I told Russell when I got home.

"But she just had a baby?" he said.

"Two years ago."

He sat at his desk even though it was after midnight, contemplating a manuscript.

"Where's Harry living?" he asked.

"At his parents'."

"I guess if it happened to us, I would live at Marlon's."

He said "happened to us" as if it were something that required flood insurance, like an act of God. His voice was somber. We were used to finding our mailbox jammed with oversized wedding invitations, thank-you notes with photos of the bride and groom, save-the-dates. We weren't used to being faced with news of divorce.

Joy's announcement startled us to our senses. Instead of inspiring me to leave that night, I clung to Russell, who put both his arms around me, and we lay very close to each other until morning.

I couldn't sleep, thinking of the exit interview I'd had to endure, walking to my office afterward, escorted by security, to find a cardboard box on my desk that I was supposed to fill with my belongings and somehow carry downstairs to the chauffeured car waiting to take me home. Layoffs had been inevitable for months, so anyone in finance who hadn't already cleared out her desk was a fool. In the weeks prior, anyone you saw disappearing into the Wall Street and Rector subway stations was carrying increasingly bulging briefcases. My files and contacts were safe at home with my photos of Duncan and my dog, Humbert, and enough tape, markers, Post-its, and paper to get us through elementary school.

At my exit interview, I'd sat across from Mark, and Flavin, an executive vice president in charge of special projects, and Merry, a horrible HR drone who was there to make sure I wouldn't sue the company.

"Now you can spend some time with your baby," Mark had the nerve to say to me.

"And you too," I said because he was every bit as laid off as I was and had his own baby.

"You have a good package," he said. It was good. Enough so that Russell and I wouldn't have to worry for a long time.

"I'm sure you have a good package too," I said.

I was forced to sign a nondisclosure agreement and listen

*The Seven Year Bitch*

to Merry tell me how my benefits were continuing and that I should make good use of the outplacement counseling they were providing for an entire year.

I had floated out of the exit interview, completely free, except for the security guard. And I thought about what someone had told me about the people who jumped from the towers on 9/11. They'd had so much adrenaline coursing through them, they may have even thought that they could fly.

# 2

On Sunday I woke up more excited than I had ever been. Duncan was one. I had survived the hardest year of my life. Duncan was still alive. We had made it. I nursed him for what was supposed to be the last time. I ran all around the apartment setting everything up, accepting deliveries, helping the caterer, opening stacks of plastic cups and the first dozen bottles of wine.

Russell's only job was to make sure the batteries in the video camera were charged so we could capture Duncan tasting his first cake.

I had never understood the word "congratulations." At my graduation from business school when people said it, I shrugged, thinking I had done what hundreds of others had done right along with me, and it hadn't even been that hard. At my wedding and after Duncan's birth I couldn't understand why people were congratulating me. Getting married and having a baby didn't seem like my achievement; it required no skill; anyone could do it; most people did. I'd found those acts almost embarrassing really—banal, bourgeois, clichéd. Getting married was like posting a public announcement to the world that you were going to be having sex with this one person for the rest of your life, and having a baby was like an announcement that the sex had been had. But now, as the mother of a one-year-old, I understood. I deserved all the congratulations I could get. I had never felt more proud or happy in my entire life.

I took Duncan's outfit from Makie out of its black tissue paper and put him on his changing table. I peeled off his shit-filled diaper and breathed it in. It would never smell like this again, I realized. Now he would no longer have breast milk. He would have regular milk, and birthday cake, and more and more regular food, and things like little boxes of raisins and juice boxes and grilled cheese sandwiches and Chef Boy-ar-dee and I would never smell this same smell again.

Then I flung open my front door and let all the congratulations come pouring in.

When the party was over and Duncan was passed out in his crib, still in his clothes like a frat boy, I turned on the video camera to replay some of the day's big moments. The tape started with Duncan, still unable to walk on his own, cruising around the coffee table grasping a balloon. Not since Albert Lamorisse made *The Red Balloon* had there been anything as perfect captured on film. Then there I was guiltily nursing Duncan because when I'd refused him for the first time ever he'd cried and banged on my breast like it was a TV he was trying to get to work, turning my nipple like it was the knob on an old, broken-down black-and-white. Then I appeared with the gigantic cake and everyone sang and then . . .

*Jennifer Belle*

Suddenly, the scene cut to a close-up of Russell in our bedroom, drinking from a plastic cup. "Make sure you don't tape over anything. Izzy will kill me," he said.

"I won't," I heard his friend Ben say. "So how does it feel to be the father of a one-year-old?"

"I actually think having a child was a big mistake," Russell said. "Irresponsible really. If you want to have a happy marriage, don't ever have a kid. Actually, don't ever get married."

"Come on, man, it's your kid's birthday," Ben said off-camera. The camera was still close in on Russell's face.

"Well this is what I have to drink to get through the day." Russell held up his cup and the camera zoomed in on what looked like scotch. I knew it was scotch because Russell's voice went up several octaves when he drank scotch, so he sounded like a woman. I begged him not to drink it in front of anyone.

"So this is the day I'm going to kill myself." The camera zoomed in on Russell's face. "This is the window I'm going to jump out of." The camera zoomed in on the window and then out the window and down six floors to the street below. I heard Ben cackle and the sound of clinking ice.

Then Ben said, "That's really dark, man," and suddenly we were back to Duncan with cake all over his face licking frosting from my fingertip, my cheeks lit with pleasure.

I'd hired two belly dancers for the entertainment because Duncan's favorite things were long hair and big breasts, and as they shimmied and undulated on the videotape, I shimmied and undulated too, with rage. As one threw her spangled scarf around my totally embarrassed father and the guests cheered and sipped champagne, I wondered how I would possibly avenge

*The Seven Year Bitch*

Russell's turning my child's first birthday video into a live suicide note.

As the other danced with Duncan in her arms and he tried desperately to free her left breast from her sequined bra, I wondered if my other birthday gift to him might be a broken home. How could a day that was so joyous for me be so traumatic for Russell? He'd been joking, I was almost probably certain. But what if he hadn't been and I really did find his body splattered on the sidewalk one morning, answer the buzzer to find Rashid, the handyman, complaining that there had been a mess from my apartment? And, even worse, what if I hadn't watched the video, just set it aside and played it for Duncan one day?

"That's dark, man," I said out loud to myself. "That's really fucking dark, man."

# 3

The next night our neighbor Sherry's daughter came over to babysit, and we went to a benefit gala at Capitale. As soon as we got there I realized that the word *gala* on the invitation was a bit of an exaggeration, but it still felt good to be out. I had been laid off but life still went on. I perused the silent-auction options. There were theater, sports, and concert tickets, dozens of country houses, Swiss chalets, and Italian villas, every kind of spa treatment, five private yoga classes, five couples therapy sessions, five dog training sessions, your portrait painted, your makeup done, your apartment designed, your event planned, your photograph taken by a million different photographers, LASIK surgery, one round of in vitro fertilization, a vasectomy, dinner with Philip Seymour Hoffman, dinner at Jean-Georges, Gramercy Tavern, and Rao's, dinner with Gabriel Byrne served by Moby, and a scarf knitted for you by Uma Thurman.

"Here's mine," I said. "'Asset allocation analysis by a chartered financial analyst. Are all your eggs in one basket? Let Isolde Brilliant help you to attain your dreams.'"

They had punched up my copy with the "eggs in one basket" and "attain your dreams" part.

The benefit was for the private school that I hoped Duncan would go to in four years when he was ready to start kindergarten, even though I had been rejected from it myself when I was four. When Russell told me on an early date that his aunt was actually the head of admissions at that very school, my heart almost stopped. I knew it was the closest you could come in New York to dating royalty. And to my utmost joy, on the day Duncan was born, she'd come to the hospital with a tiny school T-shirt and proclaimed him accepted.

In a moment of madness, to show my enthusiasm, I'd called the benefit committee chair and offered my services. I'd thought of donating a week or two at our country house but when I started to think about its selling points—inflatable kiddie pool, wind chimes, tire swing—it didn't seem like it would compete with the other houses that were being auctioned off with their twelve bedrooms, ocean views, and vineyard. I'd also thought of offering myself as a lactation consultant but then I couldn't imagine putting another woman's tit in another baby's mouth or slathering lanolin on someone else's nipple.

The prizes were grouped in categories, and mine was on a table with a placard that said "Death and Taxes" with a little drawing of a coffin on it.

Whenever I saw a coffin, I always thought about the Grim Reaper. I thought about the Grim Reaper a lot actually—black cloak, curved scythe, the whole nine yards. And whenever I thought about the Grim Reaper, for some inexplicable reason, I thought about fucking him.

In a certain way it would be like fucking a cartoon character. I thought about the Grim Reaper like some men thought about Jessica Rabbit. I supposed Jessica Rabbit symbolized physical perfection that no real-life woman could come close to, but the Grim Reaper symbolized a kind of perfection too. Death was my idea of the most romantic love. He came to you, he chose you, and, no matter what the circumstances, you had to go with him, like being pulled down a wedding aisle on a black conveyer belt. There was no fighting him. It was what I always thought love would be, a man would know I was the one and prove it to me, until I had no choice but to love him back. He would fuck me from behind on the way to wherever it was he was taking me and I would grab his balls to see what he really had under the cloak.

The printed card next to my prize stated there was a $150 minimum opening bid. The bid sheet attached to the clipboard on the table was blank.

"You have to bid on me," I told my husband.

"What? Absolutely not. I'm not paying a hundred fifty dollars to have you manage your own portfolio. We should bid on that."

He pointed to a prize to have your last will and testament written. We had been putting that off because we couldn't agree on who would take Duncan. "I don't even know why you donated something," Russell said. "I didn't want to come here in the first place."

"You should have donated something," I said. "You should have donated your filmmaking expertise. A unique video of your child's birthday party slash suicide note by an amateur filmmaker."

*The Seven Year Bitch*

"Will you drop that already, it was a joke. At least I remembered to charge the batteries, you didn't even give me any credit for that."

I wrote Russell's name and phone number on the first line of my bid sheet and listed his bid as $150.

For the rest of the evening I checked back to see if anyone else had bid, and finally there was another name on the second line: Gabe Weinrib, $500.

I rushed back to my husband. "Someone bid on me," I said.

"That's great," he said.

"You have to outbid him."

"Why?"

"I don't want to analyze this man's assets!"

"You have to," he said like a pimp. "That would be a ridiculous waste of money. I'm not going to bid on my own wife."

"Your own wife is exactly who you should bid on." We went back to our table. "I don't have an office anymore. Where am I supposed to meet with him, at Starbucks?"

"Have him come to the house."

"I don't know this person. You want me to be with him in our apartment?"

"It's a risk I'm willing to take," my husband said.

I wished I had never done this.

I looked around nervously, wondering who in this sea of people was Gabe Weinrib. Every man there suddenly seemed so sleazy, even if they were all perfectly nice fathers. An announcement was made that the silent auction had come to an end, and I noticed that all the clipboards had been removed. Why had I done this to myself? I wondered.

*Jennifer Belle*

"I wonder where we pay for our prize," Russell said.

"What prize?" I asked.

"I bid on the five couples therapy sessions. One hundred and fifty dollars. Not bad, thirty dollars a time. That's less than we paid for ballroom dancing."

The reason he'd probably brought up the ballroom dancing classes we'd taken before our wedding was because it had been *like* couples therapy. We'd had terrible fights during each class, and Lou, our instructor, had to mediate and say things like "She *wants* to dance with you, man. That's why she's marrying you." If it hadn't been for Lou we might not have gotten married.

"I'm not going to go to some quack from an auction," I said, realizing of course that I was being slightly hypocritical as this Gabe Weinrib guy was probably right now handing over his credit card.

"I will not be attacked!" Russell said. "You always complain that I don't take the initiative and here's something positive that I did for us."

"Bidding on the romantic weekend in the Hamptons or on dinner at Jean-Georges would have been positive for us, tickets to David Letterman at least, not bargain-basement couples therapy."

"I can never do anything right in your eyes."

"You should have bid on the vasectomy."

"You're right about that," Russell said.

We went home and paid our neighbor Sherry's daughter ninety dollars.

*The Seven Year Bitch*

# 4

I had put off telling Careena that I had lost my job because Russell and I hadn't decided what we were going to do, but just when I was getting ready to make a decision, she quit. I didn't know she had quit until it became clear she wasn't showing up and I called her on her cell. "Are you going to make it here today?" I asked her.

"Sure," she said. There was silence on her end.

"You sure you're coming in?" I asked.

"Sure I'm sure."

"When will you be here?" I asked, trying to keep my voice upbeat.

"I'm leaving now," she said.

"Because if you're not coming in you should just tell me."

"Well," she said. "I no gonna work for you no more."

"Why?" I asked, alarmed but resigned like when I used to be out there trying to date. Dating had actually prepared me quite nicely for the misery of having a nanny.

"I had a dream about you," she said.

"All right, Careena," I said, knowing from the stories she'd told me about her life that once she had a dream about a person that was it. "But this isn't nice to do to me with no notice."

"You didn't give me no notice when you gave me that dream," she said.

As soon as I got off the phone I put Duncan in his stroller and walked all the way to Washington Square Park. Some boring community activist type tried to hand me a flyer and get me to sign a petition to fight changes they were making to the park, and as much as I disapproved of anything about the park changing, I kept walking because I hated community activists just as much.

*I swung open the* gate to the big playground, which had always daunted me even though any four-year-old could work its latch. Then I wheeled over to a bench and sat there for a while. Duncan had fallen asleep in the stroller, so the whole exercise seemed suddenly pointless. I could have just stayed home. But staying at home suddenly seemed just as pointless.

This wasn't so hard, I told myself, and I did it all the time. Careena had worked fifty hours a week, Mondays through Fridays, but I was alone with Duncan plenty. I didn't need any help. I was out of work, and—I looked at him sleeping there—he even slept part of the time. Being a full-time mom was going to be easy.

Near the concrete turtles was a row of benches filled only with nannies. I had, without thinking, sat near the gate on the benches occupied by mothers—old mothers like myself who looked as dry and brittle as hay.

When Duncan was twelve weeks old and it was time for me to go back to work, I had sat on this bench with him all bundled up and cried my eyes out. A nanny had approached me gingerly and said, "You need help don't you?" I'd been crying too hard to do anything but nod. She was a total stranger, but I'd looked up into her kind face and said, "Can you help me?," practically ready to hand the baby to her. "No," she had said, "but my cousin can." And that was how I'd come to leave Duncan with not just a total stranger but the *cousin* of a total stranger. But that had only been for an afternoon before I'd come to my senses.

Since it was pointless to stay in the playground I left through the gate and headed to the café I'd been going to since business school and ordered an iced cappuccino.

I loved Duncan and I loved being his mother but I wasn't sure I was prepared to be only his mother. Before we were even married, when Russell and I had gotten our dog, Humbert, I had walked him early one morning, and as I stood on a line for coffee, someone had offered him a dog treat. "I always ask the mommy first," she said, looking at me expectantly. "Oh I'm not his mother," I said, "I'm just his . . . friend," and she looked at me with complete contempt. "You're his *mother*," she had scolded. "Poor dog."

I loved being a mother now, but I wasn't ready for it to be my entire identity. "I'm a mom now," I tried to convince myself. "A SAHM." Many women would kill for this.

Maybe, I thought, I'd wheel over to the Container Store and buy those plastic bags I'd seen on TV that you could fill with clothes and then vacuum all the air out to make them flat as a pancake. I'd stuff them with my Armani suits and Balenciaga and Michael Kors and lay them to rest like a corpse at the back of the coat closet, making all kinds of room for things I could wear in a sandbox.

I had launched a hedge fund, for Christ's sake. I was a CFA. An MBA. Duncan was over a year old. I still hadn't stopped nursing, as I'd planned on his birthday, but I was going to stop one day very soon, and I was, I decided right then, going to find another job. Of course I needed help.

I went to the newsstand to get the *Irish Echo,* where all the nannies advertised. I'd never heard of the *Irish Echo* until a mother at Duncan's Baby Time class had told me that was the best place to look. I couldn't wait until I was home; I opened the paper right on the street like a pervert and read the ads. My heart pounded with expectation like I was reading ads for swingers instead of Irish nannies with apple cheeks and plump arms made for hugging. And of course light cleaning. I went back to the café, circled forty ads, and started dialing.

As soon as I'd left the first message my phone rang and a woman with a thick Irish brogue said, "Is that Isolde Brilliant?" I'd never heard a voice more lovely and motherly and Irish in my life.

"Aye it 'tis," I said, already getting into the spirit of it.

"Hi, Izzy, it's me, Deirdre-Agnes callin' ya," she said.

"Oh, hi, Deirdre-Agnes," I said, disappointed that it wasn't a nanny. Deirdre-Agnes was my friend Edgar's cousin. She had given me her crib before Duncan was born and before I'd ended my friendship with Edgar. It was a beautiful mahogany sleigh spindle crib—she'd insisted we take it—and I was so grateful

*The Seven Year Bitch*

to Deirdre-Agnes for giving it to us, not for the money saved so much as for the fact that it made me feel that I had a sister. After our building's handyman, Rashid, had assembled it and I'd Lemon-Pledged five years of dust off of it from her basement and made it up with the bumper and sheets from Shabby Chic, I'd suddenly called her, paranoid that she might want it back. "What if you want it back?" I had asked. "Oh, I'll never want it back," she had said. "I'm through with having children, believe me. It's yours forever. It held Patrick Junior, and before him my sister Sorcha's three children, and before that all of Aunt Eileen's boys. And ya know what they say?" she'd said. "A crib that holds an Irish babe is lucky for all babes that follow."

"How are you?" I asked. "How's Edgar?" Edgar had been my best friend in business school and for a moment I wondered if she was calling to tell me he was dead. He had been doing heroin in LA, and I'd had to end our friendship after Duncan was born when he'd stolen Russell's grandfather's Emmy award from our apartment. He was always calling the firm and harassing my secretary. But really it was he who had ended our friendship because he couldn't tolerate that I was the mother of someone other than him. A good fag hag didn't lactate apparently. You didn't see Wendy—whom I had always considered the ultimate fag hag—from Peter Pan nursing a baby, flying high over London Town on her way to Neverland. You didn't see Wendy grab her Medela breast pump before she flew out the window. I was no use to him anymore.

"I have great news," Deirdre-Agnes said. "I'm pregnant."

"That's wonderful," I said.

There was a silence as if she was expecting me to say more.

"Are you happy about it?" I said softly, only because she had made that whole speech about not wanting another one.

"Of course! I'm thrilled! So I wanted to make arrangements to get my crib back."

"I thought you said you were through having children," I said, feeling a sense of panic. It was just a crib, I told myself. An old, scratched, squeaky crib.

"What!" she said, her voice darkening. "I would never say a terrible thing like that."

"Well, you did."

"No, I didn't."

"How pregnant are you?"

"Two weeks. My due date is the end of August," she said, her voice sounding almost threatening. "But of course I need to have everything all set up before then."

"Deirdre-Agnes, I'm in the middle of something here. Can I call you back?"

I hung up and called Russell even though I knew he was in the middle of a lunch meeting with an important agent.

"It's an emergency," I said. I had lost my job and my nanny and I really didn't want to lose that crib.

"What? Oh my God, what happened? Where's Duncan?"

"Deirdre-Agnes is having a baby."

"Now?" he said.

"In August."

"So?"

"She wants her crib back."

"Jesus, you really scared the hell out of me," he said. "I'm in a restaurant with someone, can we discuss this later?"

*The Seven Year Bitch*

I didn't even have a chance to tell him about Careena and my new plans to try to find another job, although I knew it wouldn't be easy.

By the end of the day I'd scheduled fifteen interviews for Saturday and fifteen interviews for Sunday. The best ads were the ones written not by the nanny herself but by her employer. These sounded like modern-day slave-trading posts: *Our legal, loyal & reliable nanny of 12 years sks new family. Our loss, your gain*. Not a single nanny, I quickly discovered, was Irish. Or even English. Or even Welsh.

On Saturday, I set a plate of mint Milanos on the coffee table. I unwrapped a new package of legal pads I'd taken from the office, ready to take careful notes about each candidate.

I sat on the couch before the first one arrived, looking at my list of questions, but each question seemed to conjure up a past nanny. Suddenly it was almost as if they were with me, my three former nannies. The three C's—Careena, Carella, and Carellis—or the ghosts of them, like the three witches in *Macbeth*, squeezed onto the couch, talking on their cell phones, each with its own annoying ring tone, waiting for the parade of new nannies.

The first nanny showed up right on time and took her seat across from me in my best Ligne Roset Moël chair. I asked her my first question: "Do you cook?"

"You want me to cook!" she said, making her eyes so wide it was as if I had asked her to take off her blouse. I crossed her off the list.

I crossed the next two off my list right away because one brought her baby with her to the interview and the other had long, decorated nails with pastel stripes.

"You speak excellent English!" I told one enthusiastically.

"I'm from Trinidad," she said.

"Yes, but your English is excellent," I said, nodding my head like a crazy person.

"We only speak English there." She looked at me with unmasked disgust.

I crossed her off my list.

One had an almost contagious case of mush mouth. "Yesh, yesh, thatch nicesh," was her answer to all my questions. I croshed her off my lisht. One, I could have sworn, answered, "Double, double toil and trouble. Fire burn, and caldron bubble," when I asked her how she liked to handle playdates. I crossed her off.

I'd forgotten how much advice these nannies liked to give. "I can tell you had a C-section," one named Marlene said after she'd sized me up. "When they sew you up the air gets trapped in there and your stomach can never be flat again." I crossed her off my list. I crossed off anyone who had a long story about why her bus was late. Or anyone who wasn't the person I'd spoken to on the phone but her friend instead. One of them complained about her last employer, who had worked her too hard. "I was with this child night and day," she said. "I don't know why some people go and have children." I crossed her off. Her children were in Haiti being raised by her parents. Almost all of them had children being taken care of by relatives. "What's that?" one of them asked, pointing to Russell's desk and the towers of boxes all around it. "My husband works at home," I said cheerfully, but she just shook her head no and made a tsking sound I had become familiar with. If I ever went on vacation to Jamaica, I

*The Seven Year Bitch*

imagined I would hear that tsking sound like a sea of locusts when I got off the plane. I blamed Russell-working-at-home for the fact that we'd gone through three nannies in one year. The one who was supposed to be the other family's loss but our gain never showed up.

The last one had a bag of Doritos in her open purse. The last thing I needed was Duncan one day eating Doritos. I crossed her off even though I myself had eaten most of Russell's Doritos the night before.

The next day I took Duncan to his Baby Time class myself. I'd signed up for the class the last week of my maternity leave, so Careena had always been the one to take him, and I'd been too excited to sleep the night before because I was finally going to be the one to take him.

"We're going to school," I told him as I ran, pushing the stroller like a plow.

Sitting in a circle on a rubber mat, I asked all the mothers if they could recommend a nanny. "Be careful," a mother named Dara said. "Our nanny got into an accident and we had no choice but to take in her baby and toddler and dog."

"And dog!" I said. I could not believe what I was hearing.

"An Italian greyhound named Lightning. My husband walks her while I feed the children. I even breast-feed the little one."

"So you're a wet nurse for your nanny!" I practically screamed.

"Basically yes," she said. "And we're still paying her salary while she's in the hospital. What could we do? It sounds terrible, but try not to get one with young children. Just think long and hard before you pick one."

"Excuse me, but I could not help hearing-over," my friend

Gerde said. She had moved from Germany to New York and we had become friends during my maternity leave and sometimes sat in the playground on the weekends with Duncan and her daughter, Minerva, asleep in their identical denim Bugaboo strollers. Having the same taste in strollers and children the same age was enough to make us eligible to be friends for life. And we had both shown up a week early for the first class and stood outside the locked door confused together. She had a short blond bob and dressed like a housewife from the fifties for some reason, in shirt-dresses all the time. She was very particular about what she ate and read too many magazines, so when we got together we always had to walk a million miles to some terrible sandwich shop that had just opened up and wait on a long line for some kind of trendy open-faced thing or little tart. But there was nothing in this world like walking down the street with another mother, our strollers side by side, proudly pushing our cargo, feeling at once as powerful as a God and as small as a worker ant carrying a crumb. Raising children in tandem, even if it was only for an hour here and there, made me feel like the greatest mother, and therefore person, on earth. "Did you say you are wet nurse to your nanny?"

"Well I hadn't thought of it that way, but yes," Dara said.

"I can not even believe it!" Gerde said in her heavy accent. "And you don't mind to change her children's diapers?"

Gerde was the only mother I had ever seen who kept rubber gloves in her diaper bag and used them to change a diaper. Between the rubber gloves and the Purell, she turned museum bathrooms and park benches into some kind of a MASH unit. I was surprised there weren't surgical masks tossed in with the Seventh Generation biodegradable.

*The Seven Year Bitch*

"I don't have a choice."

"Well, of course you had a choice," said a mother I had taken an instant dislike to for no reason other than she was already pregnant with her second.

"No, I really didn't. She's a single mother with a three-year-old and an eight-month-old. No family in this country. I don't mind the diapers but I hate getting up at night with the baby. I haven't sleep-trained him yet. And my husband and I can never go out anymore."

"Who took care of the kids while she was working?" a mother named Polly said, suspiciously. She had a look of pure outrage on her face.

"Her sister, but she was deported right after the accident."

"But where are they now?" I asked, wondering if she had left them in the stroller parking area while she happily sang "Shake, shake, shake, your sillies out." She was there with her own child, but where were the nanny's kids?

"My mother's watching them," she said. "Just be careful who you choose is all I'm saying."

"Well, I had a cleaning lady who vacuumed my father's ashes out of his urn," another mother said, changing the subject. "She said, 'It was so dirty in there, but don't worry, I cleaned it.'"


*Afterward, Gerde asked me* if I would like to go to lunch, and I felt euphoric again. I had been stuffing Duncan into his stroller, trying in a slightly hysterical way to put on his tiny blue suede shoe, and thinking up a plan to give him some kind of food.

Gerde kept going on and on about the nanny.

"Can you imagine something so entirely ridiculous? Changing another child's dirty diaper? Dealing with another child's shit? It is entirely disgusting. I think you should think entirely long and hard before you decide to have another nanny at all."

I could tell she was entirely disapproving of having a nanny at all.

We looked down at our menus.

"I will have the Manchego and honey panini, *ja*, and you will have the tuna and salted capers and we will share?"

"Okay," I said, because every fourteen-dollar thing listed sounded equally awful especially without a Diet Coke, which I felt too self-conscious to order because Gerde was entirely against Diet Coke. "Wait, Manchego and honey?"

"It sounds delicious!" Gerde said, with childish enthusiasm, or maybe it was touristy enthusiasm, everything tasting so exotic when you were far from home. "They make the bread right here in those ovens."

If I were German I wouldn't go around saying the word "ovens" in front of Jewish people. I suddenly remembered that one of the great things about going back to work after my maternity leave had been not spending so much time with Gerde. I had forgotten how *entirely* (her favorite word) bossy she was. It was always slightly terrifying being with her. I never felt more Jewish against her yellow-blond Aryan backdrop.

"Rolph and I just take Minerva everywhere with us. Except sometimes at night."

"And what do you do then?" I asked.

*The Seven Year Bitch*

"Well, this is not very American but we leave her safe in her crib and go across the sidewalk to the Indian restaurant and then we take turns checking on her."

"That's illegal," I said.

"Really?" she asked, pretending not to know, her voice going up several octaves.

I actually had no idea if it was illegal or not, but it sounded like it should be. Drinking Diet Coke and hiring a nanny was amoral but leaving your baby to die in a fire was fine.

We gossiped about Dara and the other mothers for a while and then Gerde had to go "start dinner," which I never understood, since dinner, in New York, was everywhere. "Nice meeting you," Gerde said. She always ended our time together like that. She meant "nice seeing you," but I never corrected her because I liked her mistakes. Then we pointed our strollers in opposite directions and rolled off.

I called my mother, who had gone on a date the night before. "I didn't like him," she said. She always sounded furious after a date, as if the man, simply by virtue of not being good enough for her, had actually committed a crime against her.

My mother had divorced my father the year she turned forty-nine, after twenty-four years of marriage, and hadn't had luck since then, even though, no matter her age over the years, she always looked a lot younger than it. "He told me his whole financial situation," she said. "When he was in the hospital with prostate cancer an inexperienced broker refused to sell and he lost everything."

When men got to be seventy you really saw who they were and what they had become, and not until then. They'd either won a Nobel Peace Prize or they hadn't. All those big deals they were working on when they couldn't get off the phone or look up from their *Barron's* and treated you like shit on dates had either panned out or they hadn't. You knew whether they'd won or lost, and the ones on J-Date, the Internet dating service my mother used, had usually lost.

My mother and her friends had divorced their husbands with confidence, only to find themselves desperately trying to date men who were either exactly the same or so much worse than their husbands had been.

"My shrink has someone who can find you a nanny," my mother said.

My mother always spent all of her therapy sessions talking about my problems instead of her own, and her shrink, I had to admit but not to my mother, actually did a pretty good job of analyzing my relationships, dreams, and problems. When my clothes didn't fit after I had the baby, she sent me, via my mother, to a fantastic store in SoHo called Rosebud where I found great clothes. And when my back was constantly hurting, she sent me, via my mother, to an osteopath who cured me. And when I was feeling especially guilty about having so much babysitting at night, she assured me, via my mother, that there was absolutely nothing wrong with getting more help and I would be crazy not to.

"You shouldn't waste your therapy talking about me," I said.

"But you have so many problems," my mother said. "My shrink gave me the number of a woman who she says is the queen of all the nannies. She can find someone for you. Apparently they all go to the same church."

*The Seven Year Bitch*

Tchaikovsky was playing in the background and I could almost see her, the Nanny Queen, pirouetting in the center of all the nannies and one Italian greyhound in pink tulle.

I called the Nanny Queen as soon as I got off the phone with my mother.

"I have someone for you," the Nanny Queen said. "Her name is Shasthi."

# 5

That night, I sat on the toilet with Duncan on my lap, the shower running hot. He'd been stricken with croup, and was coughing like a seal, crying and gasping for air. He didn't look like himself.

Babies, when they're sick, are actually blurry, as if their cells are so new to each other they haven't figured out how to hold their shape.

Holding his hot, limp body in my arms like that at three thirty in the morning was the closest I had ever come to nirvana. No matter what bad things were ever to come in my life, at least I had done that. I had taken care of him. Love had coursed through me, like I was standing under the showerhead being pelted with it. I had never felt love like that, like I was in the thick glass walls of a blender set on "chop." I was almost sad when the moment had to end. My phone vibrated on the edge of the tub—it was the doctor returning my call—and I reached to answer it.

And when Duncan finally stopped coughing, and fell asleep

in my arms, and I put him in his crib, I was almost sorry he was better.

I wished he would cough again and I could call the doctor, and run the shower, and hold him in my arms. Afterward, I lay in my bed with my ears pricked like a mother wolf's, my heart pounding, just listening for him in the New York City silence.

*In the morning,* Russell agreed to take care of Duncan for an hour or two and I walked all the way from our Tribeca apartment to the café I had been going to since business school. I had done all my studying there because it was a short walk from Stern and I loved the Moroccan tagines and couscous they served. I wrapped my hands around my cappuccino like a strangler. The morning news had warnings that tea tree oil shampoo, which I happened to have used to wash the baby's hair every day for the last eight months at the doctor's insistence, was found to cause breasts to grow in baby boys. Duncan didn't have breasts yet, thank God, but I had taken the bottle right out to the garbage room on my way out of the apartment.

"How is my wife?" the cook at the café said, putting a bowl of soup on the table in front of me and taking the seat across from me. His name was Said and I always pronounced it Sigh-eed, which I believed to be correct, even though everyone at the café seemed to say it many different ways, and he always called me "wife," which was a little uncomfortable and off-putting, but I had never stopped him. Now that it had been about eighteen years, it seemed too late to try. It was especially awkward because he had a wife, a bleak, clunky Russian woman who had been his cleaning lady and was still his cleaning lady but now didn't get paid for it.

"I haven't seen you for a long time. No work today?" Said asked.

"No more job," I said.

"This is shit!" he said. He had a thick Turkish accent and when he got excited, which was about half the time, I couldn't understand him at all, but that hadn't seemed to matter in all these years. I just smiled or laughed at what I hoped were the right times, or said, "Hilarious!" and that had always worked. My cell phone rang and I excused myself and answered it. It was Russell saying Duncan had a fever and he needed Tylenol. I told him the Tylenol was right on the bathroom sink and went back to my conversation with Said.

"Delicious," I said about the soup even though it scared me a little. He always gave me free food in addition to whatever I ordered, and sometimes it was something he had improvised that wasn't on the menu.

"Those are meatballs," he said. "You like?"

"*Ummm*, delicious," I said.

"Why I am tired?" Said asked, reaching across the table to poke my shoulder.

I just nodded, unsure of what to say.

"I ask you, 'Why I am tired?'"

"You work hard," I said.

"No, not work! The woman don't leave me alone."

I laughed uncomfortably. "Right," I said. "Hilarious!"

"I am be serious, Isolde. I spend the night with a woman. It is magic, this hotel. Fourteenth Street and the West Side Highway. One hundred dollars for three hours, Jacuzzi, beautiful, clean, magic."

*The Seven Year Bitch*

Again I laughed and said, "Hilarious." We passed that hotel in the car on the way to the country. It would have to be magic to make that hotel clean and beautiful.

"I am not joking. You think I do nothing every year when Cecylia goes?"

His wife went to Russia to live with her mother every summer for four months. The rest of the year, whenever I stopped in she was sitting hunched over an Irish coffee with a very sad, bloated look on her face, saying things like "New York, she is so durr-ty, how can I stand this, Isolde? Tell me, I beg of you." Each year, I couldn't wait for her to go away. And neither could Said apparently.

"You know Cecylia and me, we don't have nothing, no sex," he said.

"*Hmmm*," I said.

"She say I am too big. She told me when we have the sex it hurt her too much. She feel it in her throat."

I had just taken a swallow of coffee as he said it and was about to clear my throat but forced myself not to. My cell phone rang. It was Russell again saying that the baby Tylenol was not on the bathroom sink.

"It has to be," I said. I had given Duncan a dropperful the night before.

"I'm standing right here," Russell said, "and there's no Tylenol."

"I'm sure it's there."

"You can look, look, look for yourself," Russell stuttered. "I'm telling you, I don't know what you did with the fucking Tylenol."

"Do you need me to come home?" I asked.

"No. Stay out. I'll keep looking." He hung up on me in the middle of his own sentence and I went back to Said to hear more about how big he was, if that was in fact what he was talking about.

"I tell you because you are my friend and you would not tell Cecylia. I do this for ten years when she is away."

I tried to look completely neutral, neither approving nor disapproving, which wasn't that difficult because it was pretty much how I felt. I was trying to be less judgmental in general and their marriage had always disgusted me anyway. I knew—because I had brought him food once when he was very sick and she was away in Russia—that they had two little bedrooms. He had one and she shared one with their six-year-old daughter.

"You don't know I do this?"

"What? No," I said.

He let out a hearty foreign laugh and I had to slap his big rough hand five over the table. I had to stop coming to this café, I told myself. I was like an old mountain goat returning to the same patch of grass every day.

His cell phone rang. "It is the woman!" he said. "She wants more of me."

I thought of Cecylia with her mother, sitting in the garden or cooking in the kitchen, while her husband fucked someone else in a hooker hotel. Their little bedrooms held less intimacy than cubicles in an office building. My cell phone rang. "I don't know what to do," Russell said. "I've scoured the entire apartment."

"I'm coming home," I said, relieved to have an excuse to leave even though I had looked so forward to being able to sit in the café again. I paid the check and accepted the quart of chicken soup with rice that Said insisted I bring home to the baby.

*The Seven Year Bitch*

When I got home, I gave Duncan the Tylenol that had of course been right on the sink where I'd said it was and Russell scrambled to his desk in the living room, tripping over Humbert and bumping into strollers in his haste to get to work. I heated up a bottle of milk and Duncan fell right to sleep on my bed. I remembered when we'd first gotten Humbert and had taken him to the vet who'd said he had a terrible ear infection and I paid sixty dollars for drops that the vet said had to be refrigerated and when we got home Russell put the drops in the freezer and I had to go back to the vet a second time and buy the drops all over again.

# 6

By the time Shasthi showed up the next day, I was too tired of my careful list of questions to ask any of them. The minute she walked through the door, I knew she was the one I loved. The second I saw her, I knew I would be willing to give her two weeks' paid vacation and breast-feed her children if necessary.

"May I wash my hands?" she said.

I stood stiffly in the living room, waiting for her to come out of the bathroom.

She was beautiful. She had long reddish hair, the color of pure Indian henna, and dark skin to match. She wore gold jewelry like an Indian gypsy and an apple-green shirt with gold sequins on it. She had normal undecorated nails that wouldn't hurt Duncan's scalp when she gave him a shampoo.

She had come all the way from the Bronx but had arrived right on time. I sat facing her on the couch feeling incredibly guilty for some reason. As far as I was concerned she was hired but I knew

I should ask her some questions first. "Have a cookie?" was all I could think of to say.

"Thank you," she lilted, taking a mint Milano and nibbling on it reluctantly, making me feel a little like I had bullied her into eating it. I felt like a witch luring her into my gingerbread house. I felt grotesque next to her. She was at least six inches taller than me, but I felt like a giant. My lips were pale while hers were painted a shade of purple I had always loved. I always noticed, when I took Duncan to the pediatrician, how fresh and happy the nannies looked and how old and haggard the mothers did. And I wondered for a moment if that would be us. I was already thinking of us as us, I noticed.

I wished I had cleaned my apartment. If she opened the refrigerator she would see an almost empty pizza box in it. When she went into the bathroom to wash her hands she would have found a clump of toothpaste in the sink. I now realized that she had flushed the toilet twice. I cringed, wondering if I'd forgotten to flush.

"How old are you?" I asked and then felt terrible about it. It seemed like a much too personal question to ask, but that was the point of an interview, I tried to remind myself.

Lately age was the only thing I understood about a person. It seemed to matter more than anything else.

"Forty," she said. Her voice was a few octaves too high but still nice. I felt really, really bad I had asked and forced her to admit something like that. No one wanted to have to go around saying they were forty.

"I'm going to be thirty-nine," I offered.

"Okay," she said.

I started slowly nodding again, the way I had nodded at all the nannies. I was dreading mentioning the salary because I was suddenly sure it would be less than she wanted.

"Do you have any children?" I asked.

"No," she said.

For some reason my mind began to race with this information. No children suddenly seemed like an extremely good thing in a nanny, or anyone really. There would be no earaches to rush home to in the middle of the day. Or, if they were being raised far away by relatives, I wouldn't have to wonder how she could care about Duncan and not resent him. Or judge her too harshly for it.

I wondered where she was from. She spoke excellent English but I wasn't going to fall into that trap again. She had an Indian name, and she looked Indian.

"Are you from India, Pakistan, or Bangladesh?" I asked, proud of how the Pakistan and Bangladesh showed off my knowledge of world geography.

"I'm from Guyana," she said.

"Ghana?"

"No, Guyana," she said.

"Is that in Spain?" I asked, cautiously.

"Guyana, no. It's a country bordering Brazil. But I'm of Indian descent."

"Oh," I said, nodding. "Isn't Guyana where Jim Jones killed all the members of his cult?"

"Yes!" she said, pleased that I knew so much of her land.

I showed her around the apartment, rambling about myself and my idea of what light cleaning entailed, which, when I articulated its many components, sounded an awful lot like heavy cleaning. I was feeling guiltier and guiltier. At Richman I'd been notorious for getting the secretaries coffee all the time. She was silent until we got to my bedroom. "I like your curtains," she said, as if she suddenly felt at home.

"So do I!" I said, relieved. "They're made out of saris. From India." The Queen of the Nannies was right—Shasthi was the one for me. "I would love to go to India," I said.

"Me too," she said.

"If you could go anywhere in the world, where would you go? Paris? Rome?" I asked idiotically.

"Home," she said.

"You can't . . ."

"No," she said. "I'm not here legally."

"Can you start tomorrow?" I asked.

"Yes," she said. I suddenly felt sick to my stomach, as if I had forced her to take the job. And if I hadn't, life had. She needed work and I was offering it, so she had to take it, like a mute bride in an arranged marriage. The choice was mine, not hers, and I had made it.

She took a tiny yellow Post-it out of her pants pocket. "Can I ask you some questions?" she said carefully.

"Okay," I said, bracing myself. None of the other nannies had questions.

"Do I get paid for sick days?"

"Yes," I said even though I wasn't sure about that. "And you get two weeks' paid vacation."

"Do I have federal holidays off?" she said in barely a whisper, reading from the Post-it.

I suddenly felt like crying, thinking of this girl writing this question on a Post-it and putting it carefully in her pants pocket and taking the subway all the way from the Bronx and arriving right on time. Thinking of this girl who was a year older than I was but seemed so much younger and was illegal but was concerned about federal holidays. I didn't even know what a federal holiday was, I just took all holidays for granted and even expected presents for them, and didn't cherish them at all. She wanted to go home, and she couldn't. "Sure," I said to the federal holidays. "Just tell me when they are."

"Thank you," she said. "The girl I take care of now just turned thirteen. They don't need me as much anymore. I've been hoping for a little one to take care of for a long time."

*Feeling sneaky, I called* the number she had given me to check her reference. It was just a formality, due diligence, because my mind was made up. I was just checking a reference, not going through her purse, but my heart was pounding. When the woman answered the phone I felt like I was introducing myself to my new sister-wife. We would be sharing Shasthi now. I'd have her thirty hours and she'd have her ten. The other woman—Rachel was her name—sounded cool, almost casual about it.

"Yes, she's always prompt, never calls in sick. She's very cheerful," Rachel said.

What a fool, I thought. She was just handing Shasthi to me on a silver platter. Didn't she know she should be worried? As soon as I got another job, for just a few dollars I could steal her away, have forty hours or even fifty, just for me. One word from me, I was sure, and we'd never have to hear about this Rachel again, or her newly teenaged daughter.

*The Seven Year Bitch*

"Oh, one more thing," Rachel said.

"Yes?" I asked, screwing up my face in concentration, anxious to hear this one more thing.

"She seems to take great care with her appearance. I'm always impressed by how well she puts herself together."

Understatement of the year, I thought. She was beautiful.

She'd worked for Rachel for ten years and I'd only known her for thirty minutes, but I already felt I had a deeper understanding of her than this other woman did. I saw so much more to her than her appearance. As I thanked her and got off the phone, I couldn't help but think there should be more to the ceremony—we should have to sup from the same table or sip from the same cup—but that was it.

"Thanks. Bye."

"Sure. Good luck."

And we had Shasthi.

# 7

In the night, Duncan cried and I went to him. I brought him to my bed and he curled into my lap and then put his lips on mine. I opened my mouth to say something comforting, when he suddenly vomited right into my open mouth. In my confusion, I accidentally swallowed it.

Then he gave his father a merciless shove and Russell woke up the way parents always wake up: annoyed, worried, guilty, angry.

"Your mother's going to take you back to bed."

"I just swallowed vomit. Your father will take you."

After Russell settled Duncan down in Deirdre-Agnes's crib and I brushed my teeth, Russell and I lay in bed. "I wonder why she doesn't have children," I said. "She's forty, you know."

In my mind, I could see the number 40 in the age column on the birth-defects chart in the pregnancy book. I could see the number 35 and the statistics next to it, and the statistics getting significantly worse as the age increased, 36, 37, 38, 39, and then—and this number was printed in an alarming red—40.

Down syndrome: one in three. Or maybe it was one in thirty. Either way it wasn't good.

"I know, you've told me ten times. You've been talking about this all night. What's her name again?"

"Shasthi. Try to remember it," I said.

"Why can't she have a nice name like Myrtle?" Russell had an almost perverted fantasy of having a nanny who was fat and over the age of eighty.

"But why do you think? I know she's married. She said her husband was going to drive her home after the interview. Oh, and she said what he does. Construction. He's one of those guys who hangs on the side of a building like a fly. But I wonder why she doesn't have children. She seems to genuinely like them."

"Let's get some sleep."

"Maybe we shouldn't have a nanny at all," I said. "Actually, I think if it's part time you call her a babysitter. 'Sitter,'" I said, trying that out.

"Stop feeling guilty. You're probably going to find a new job. It's not like we've never had a nanny."

I thought about the portfolio I was supposed to analyze for the man from the auction. I thought about leaving Duncan alone with a woman I had met for thirty minutes.

"I should be the one with him."

"You can't wait to get away from him half the time. I've gotta go to sleep. Stop being obsessed with the nanny."

"Sitter," I said.

I lay in bed trying to sleep but the A. A. Milne poem I had recited to Duncan that night kept playing itself over and over in my head. That sometimes happened to me with a song lyric or something when I was overtired.

It was called *Buckingham Palace* and it was about Christopher Robin going to watch the changing of the guard with someone named Alice. The fact that Christopher Robin goes there with Alice is repeated over and over. Alice just babbles on about the soldier she is going to marry and what she thinks is going on inside the palace, talking to the little boy, and it suddenly hit me. Christopher Robin went down with Alice, not with *him*. A. A. Milne sat at his typewriter while his son was wandering around London with a virtual stranger—someone named Alice—just some girl involved in her own life, saying whatever she felt like to his son. I'd recited the poem a hundred times but I'd never realized before that it was about a nanny. Even the words "they're changing guard" were about being replaced by a nanny. My eyes filled with tears thinking of the fact that I should be the one to show Duncan the changing of the guard.

"You know A. A. Milne was as obsessed with his son's nanny as I am with mine," I told Russell.

"You're crazy."

"I'm his mother," I said, sitting up in bed, still tasting his vomit in my mouth.

"You're a hedge fund manager," Russell mumbled, half asleep.

That, in the end, was probably the real reason to be married, I thought. He still respected me as a hedge fund manager even though I had been wiped out in the blink of an eye. When he looked at me he still saw my unscarred prebirth body, the one I'd had when we met. He still got hard when I took off my clothes to get ready for bed.

*The Seven Year Bitch*

*"We're really glad* you're here," I said as soon as Shasthi came into the apartment.

"It's my pleasure," she said. "Let me go to the bathroom to wash my hands."

A professional nanny, or sitter, I thought, silently congratulating myself for making such a good choice.

I stood there and listened to her flush the toilet twice. When she came out Duncan cruised to her and took her hand.

She picked him up in her arms and started toward his room. I followed after them. "You and your husband don't want children?" I blurted.

She looked surprised and swallowed, as if answering my questions was a part of the job she'd clearly have to endure like vacuuming. "Yes, we do. We've been trying for four years and nothing has happened."

"Have you seen a doctor?" I asked.

"No, it costs too much money."

"No insurance?"

Then I felt like an idiot. Of course she didn't have insurance. She didn't even have a green card. Going to someone like my Dr. Heiffowitz would cost two or three weeks' salary just for the initial exam. A sonogram, day three blood work, progesterone series, a postcoital test to check the viability of her husband's sperm would be out of the question.

I saw the birth-defects age chart in my mind. I felt terrible. "I should get in the shower," I said.

*Leaving my building,* I felt relieved. I was free. Duncan was in great hands. With nothing better to do, I started walking up West Broadway and then MacDougal Street until I got to the southwest corner of Washington Square Park. I walked into the park a few feet, past the chess tables, but was suddenly blocked by a high chain-link fence. I walked, almost running, back out the way I came and up the south side of the park, which was completely fenced off. The only point of entry came after the Indian guy who sold dosas from a cart and I had to enter by the bathrooms. Once I was in the park, the fence blocked my way again, and I was forced to walk on an odd dirt path around the playground like a squirrel. I felt strangely infuriated, the way I did when a block I was walking on suddenly became a film set and some punk with a clipboard told me that I had to cross to the other side of the street or, even worse, wait.

They were planning to move the fountain just a few feet so that it aligned perfectly with the arch, which seemed absurd to me, but I tried not to get too worked up about it. I hated people who lingered on things like that. My son was in great hands and I was free, despite the alarming chain-link fence.

Then I saw a mother pushing a Bugaboo and guilt detonated inside me like it had been hiding in my chest in someone else's luggage. I wanted to be that mother pushing her child in the Bugaboo. I wanted to rush over to her and tell her to take a hike, and take her place, pushing her child wherever they were going. But I *was* that mother, I told myself. All I had to do was go back home and pop my own child into my own Bugaboo. Instead I stood frozen staring at the dump trucks—and what kind of mother of a boy didn't know the names of the different kinds of trucks!—as if I were standing there with Duncan.

I felt guilty that I had a nanny when I was no longer working. I felt guilty that I wanted thirty hours a week to myself instead of enjoying my child enough to want to spend the whole 168 hours a week with him. I felt guilty that I had been fired even though I knew I had done nothing wrong. But when I thought of getting another job, I felt sick with guilt about the seventy hours a week it would require me to be away from Duncan. I felt guilty that I had hired an illegal immigrant as our nanny. Sitter. And the fact that she could never go home again and see her family, when I was free to flit all around the world, froze me with guilt. When I thought of what she must think of me, leaving Duncan with her when I went off to do nothing, I crumbled with guilt. She was in my home giving my child a bath.

How many times a day, I thought, had I sat at my desk and wished I was home with him? And how many times had I stood pushing him in a swing on the weekend, wishing I was at work?

I chose the way of the dirt path, and when I exited, I saw some old ladies from the senior center selling their wares—knitted scarves, crocheted baby blankets, and tiny booties.

After I'd married Russell and before I'd gotten pregnant with Duncan, I'd had a miscarriage. I'd bought a pair of booties just like these. "I'm pregnant," I'd said and handed them to him. "That's terrible," he had said. There was nothing worse, it seemed to me, than a reluctant father. I hadn't counted on his ambivalence. But before I could think too much about it, I had lost the baby.

I realized my problems with Russell had started when I'd handed him those booties.

I held up a beautiful baby blanket.

"That's exquisite. Doris made that," the one who was the leader said. She had soft white hair molded into a helmet and nice blue eyes. She wore a huge rhinestone pin on her lapel, a wasp or a bumblebee or something. "You have excellent taste."

Old ladies liked me. With the exception of my mother-in-law, I had never met a senior citizen I couldn't befriend. As a child, I always wondered why Dorothy couldn't win over the witch or why Snow White couldn't just make the Queen something nice at her school.

"How's business?" I asked.

"Doing nicely, thank you," she said.

I had started at five, selling Kool-Aid on the street, and I'd probably end up just like this, I thought. Actually I kind of liked the idea. I'd be ninety, selling my knitting, and the Grim Reaper would walk up and buy a scarf—black of course—and we'd do it on the steps of the senior center before he took me with him.

"How much is the blanket?" I asked.

"Only thirty-five," she said.

"That's a steal," I said. "I'll take it."

"Doris, you got a sale. That's Doris and Gert, and I'm Marilyn. And you are?"

"Isolde."

"Isolde. You don't hear that name too often with young people. Hat and booties to go with it?"

"No, just the blanket," I said.

She handed me the blanket in a Gristedes shopping bag and I had an incredible urge to pull up a beach chair and join them.

"We'll be here next Wednesday," she called after me as I walked away.

# 8

The next day, when Shasthi came, before she had even set down her quilted gold fake-leather pocketbook, I said, "Do you know how to tell when you're most likely to get pregnant?"

I had meant to just say hello and tell her there were sweet potatoes on the counter for Duncan.

I was wrapped in a towel and hadn't gotten into the shower yet. My heart was pounding but I had no idea why. There was no reason to feel uncomfortable talking about this and I was practically an expert. Russell sat at his desk, talking to someone on the phone about a book jacket.

"Tell? No?" Shasthi said.

I indicated for her to follow me into the kitchen. "You know there's only about forty-eight hours a month, or maybe only twenty-four, when you're able to get pregnant. You know the . . ." I couldn't think of any possible word. "Mucus. That's in the vagina?"

"Yes?" Shasthi said. She seemed interested and open to this. "Let me just wash my hands."

She went into the bathroom and I stood helpless in my yellow towel.

"Where is the baby?" she asked a little suspiciously when she came back in. She seemed to have approached with caution when she arrived, as if she wasn't sure what would have gone on the night before in her absence. It was the way, I realized, I had always entered the apartment when I came home after leaving Duncan with a nanny. Or with Russell.

"He's asleep in his crib," I said. "When a woman is ovulating the mucus is very thin like egg whites."

"Okay," Shasthi said. She looked like she was concentrating, like I was giving her instructions for what to do in an emergency.

"That's how you know you are able to become pregnant."

"Okay. I will try that," Shasthi said, as if it were a recipe for an omelet.

"You should," I said.

I went to take my shower and then got dressed in what I was starting to think of as fatigues—my jeans from Rosebud and a long black jersey that I alternated with a long gray one.

I went back out to the living room. Russell went to the post office and I watched Shasthi run the vacuum. She was tall and tubular, slightly barrel-shaped but not fat. Her legs and arms were thin, but she was thick in the middle, her midriff puffed out a little from her low-waisted jeans and high-waisted sequined shirt. I examined her from my perch at the dining-room table as thoroughly as a midwife. Why couldn't she get pregnant? I wondered. I stared at the caramel strip of exposed flesh until I had practically given her a hysterosalpingogram with my eyes. Fibroids, I diagnosed. I bet she had fibroids.

*Jennifer Belle*

Three years before, I'd had to have a myomectomy to have my fibroids removed before I could get pregnant with Duncan. The doctor had shown me an enormous book of photos of different kinds of fibroids—not exactly what you'd want to have on your coffee table next to the Annie Leibovitz and Georgia O'Keeffe— but they were strangely beautiful planets, red and angry molten cratered moons in the uterus universe. I was sure that's what she had and I suddenly had a violent urge to grab the vacuum cleaner hose out of her hands and vacuum the motherfuckers right out of her.

I'd always felt a little bit guilty about the vacuum cleaner because I'd gotten it for free after 9/11. We lived on Hubert Street, not far from the World Trade Center, and everyone who lived within a certain radius of the towers got a free Eureka bagless provided by FEMA to vacuum up any asbestos or human remains that may have blown in through the window. I needed a new vacuum and I was very excited at the time, but every time there was a new world tragedy like the tsunami in Thailand or Hurricane Katrina and FEMA rolled in their insufficient trailers, I thought of that free vacuum cleaner in the linen closet.

After the myomectomy, when I still couldn't get pregnant, we filed papers to adopt from China. As intent on my mission as a twister on its course, we went to an adoption agency called Spence-Chapin on the Upper East Side and listened to a panel of adoptive parents talk about their experiences in China, Guatemala, Russia, and Korea. We had decided on China and eaten Chinese food every night for a month, while we labored over the essays in the application packet.

I looked at what Russell had written:

*The Seven Year Bitch*

*Our desire for a baby girl and China's current laws in regard to such girls dovetail quite nicely.*

"Dovetail quite nicely? Dovetail! Who the hell uses the word *dovetail*," I had screamed at him one night in Suzy's Chinese restaurant on Bleecker Street where all the waiters already thought we were crazy. "What's wrong with you!"

Another time, at Wo Hop in Chinatown, a Chinese waiter in his sixties wearing the Wo Hop uniform of a formal red Mandarin jacket with epaulets and knotted buttons brought us our menus, and Russell said, "Why can't we just adopt him? He could bring us tea in bed in the morning. Honey, our own little Chinese waiter. It would be so nice."

"That's sick!" I had laughed in spite of myself.

"Our son. I'm so proud," Russell said, taking my hand across the table and looking lovingly at the waiter after he had brought us fortune cookies and bustled off.

When we had finished our application and were eating Chinese takeout at our own dining-room table one night, I'd accidentally spilled my glass of red wine, soaking the application, and we'd laughed at how funny it was that we had worked so hard to make ourselves look like the perfect parents, claiming we'd never had therapy, taken any medications, and even knocked a few pounds off our weight, and in the end were shown for what we were, a couple of boozers.

In the time it had taken to get a duplicate application from Spence- Chapin, I had gotten pregnant.

I'd gone to Dr. Heiffowitz to regulate my thyroid, not to get pregnant, and he'd looked me over and said, "Your medication is wrong. If you cut your pill in half with a kitchen knife and take half every twelve hours instead of a whole one every twenty-four, I see no reason why you won't get pregnant."

I'd been lying on his examination table and when he said those words, "I see no reason why you won't get pregnant," in his quiet Israeli accent, I'd had to fight the urge to spread my legs right then and there and beg him to be the father. Why wait all the way until the end of the day when Russell would finally come to bed, when I could get pregnant right now?

"We're in the process of adopting from China," I said.

"You have a beautiful follicle," he had said and showed it to me on the sonogram screen. "You should ovulate tonight. I don't want to be the one to tell anyone not to adopt a baby from China, but I see no reason why you wouldn't get pregnant tonight." And suddenly, just like that, when he saw no reason, I saw no reason. There was no reason. It was as if a lens cap had been covering my cervix and now it had been removed. I could see Russell's sperm attach itself to my beautiful follicle. I could feel it.

And that night it happened.

Just thinking about the kind blue Israeli eyes of Dr. Heiffowitz, I was moved to tears and I had to turn and wipe my eyes so Shasthi wouldn't see me.

"I'm going now," I said, but she just kept vacuuming, slowly and gracefully, her sequins glinting and rhinestone hair clip casting rays of blue light on the ceiling and on her cider-colored hair, like a statue of the goddess Kali had come to life in my living room and had decided to tidy up.

As I was leaving the apartment my phone rang and I heard Deirdre-Agnes's voice on my answering machine. "Patrick and I are comin' into the city this weekend and we'd like to swing by and pick up our crib." I rushed out before I could hear the end of her message.

*When I got out* on the street my cell phone rang.

"Did she come?" my mother asked. "How is she?"

"I love her," I said.

"It's a miracle. You should always listen to my shrink. I just came from therapy."

"How was it?" I asked, with a perfunctory tone to my voice because I didn't want her to know I was really interested.

"I told her you just got laid off and you're conflicted about doing nothing all day and she had a fantastic idea for you. It's a job."

"I managed a hedge fund," I told my mother, since she seemed to have forgotten. "And staying home with Duncan is not doing nothing all day."

"This is something you can do part time from home. It turns out my shrink does it for extra money."

"Give me a break," I said. I definitely had to go back to work if this was the kind of conversation I was going to be having.

"You judge contests," my mother continued. "Essay contests. Companies advertise essay contests and you read all the essays and pick the winner. My shrink judges them in the car on the way up to her country house while her husband drives, and she thought you could do the same thing. She said it would pay for the nanny."

"Sitter."

"So you wouldn't have to feel guilty."

*Jennifer Belle*

"If it's so great why doesn't she do more of them?" I asked.

"There are some she just doesn't want to do, like motherhood ones. You know, because she can't have a baby."

"I'm actually already working," I said. "I have to analyze a portfolio for someone." The man—Gabe Weinrib—from the auction hadn't called me yet but I supposed he eventually would since he'd paid good money for me. "And why would they hire someone in finance? I'm not a teacher or an editor."

"She said they would hire you. They're hiring ex–Wall Streeters. I suggested Russell should do it, being in publishing, but they only hire women. At least take down the number," my mother said.

"No," I said, taking a pen and my little date book out of my bag. "I don't have a pen." My mother recited the number anyway and I wrote it down. "I'm not writing it down."

Then I got off the phone and went to my gym.

I'd joined the New York Health and Racquet Club on Thirteenth Street between University Place and Fifth Avenue years before when I was at Stern, and I'd never wanted to make the switch despite the fact that it was so inconvenient. I could use any location, and they'd just built a new one with top-of-the-line equipment right near me, but I preferred the one on Thirteenth Street because I was by far the youngest and thinnest member. It had a tiny pool and Jacuzzi and as soon as I saw it, escorted by a peppy salesman, I felt like I had walked into Boca Raton, 1970.

A dozen old wrinkled bosoms floated at the top of the Jacuzzi. Rolls of fat and folds of skin paraded without shame above forests of veins. Pale gray hair glistened in tufted armpits and all around bikini lines. And it was the only hair showing, because

*The Seven Year Bitch*

faces beamed under every manner of pastel bathing cap—the old-fashioned kind with giant yellow flower fringe, rubber appliqués, under-chin straps.

"You know, we uh have a newer location," the salesman said nervously when he'd signed me up. "They have spinning, kickboxing, Pilates, funk, masala bhangra, capoeira, pole dancing for strippers . . ."

"That's okay," I'd said. "I like it here."

"That's a lovely suit, dear," a woman said to me as I headed downstairs from the locker room to the pool. "Where did you get something like that?"

"SoHo," I said.

It was a one-piece (obviously) white suit with blue ticking and a slight iridescent shine. I looked like I had just come from performing in a production of *South Pacific*.

"Your figure looks wonderful in it."

"I just had a baby," I said, not even bothering to hold in my stomach as I slid into the Jacuzzi. Working out with old people was the best-kept beauty secret in New York.

When I got home, there were two messages on the answering machine. The first was from Deirdre-Agnes wanting her crib—the crib she had *given* me—and the second was the call I had been dreading.

"Hi, this is Gabe Weinrib calling for Isolde Brilliant," a man's voice said. "I'm the lucky man who won you at the auction. I'm calling to set up a time to meet." He left his number and I wrote it down on the box of Cheerios in the kitchen. He sounded like the kind of man I usually couldn't stand—lurid, a little goofy, possibly a Wall Streeter, his voice half an octave too high—the kind of man who had strict weight requirements for women. I did not want to sit with this man and give him investment advice.

I called him back from my cell phone and got his voicemail. "Hi, Gabe," I said. "This is Izzy Brilliant calling you back. I'm so sorry but I'm away in Paris for a few weeks. I'll call you when I'm back in New York."

I hung up, relieved that I had put that off for a while. Then my cell phone rang and I didn't answer it in case it was him again. It was him again, and he left a message that he was actually in Paris and we should meet there.

I stared at the phone wondering if I was actually going to have to fly to Paris now to meet with this guy.

I called back and miraculously he didn't pick up and I was able to leave a very perfunctory message that I was leaving for the airport to fly home to New York but that he should certainly give me a call when he was back. Then I said, "Au revoir," hung up, and turned off my cell phone.

# 9

A few weeks later I was standing in Kmart filled with excitement. The vacuum cleaner had broken. I had crouched in front of it, feeling like a farmer with a cow. There was a tumbleweed of black hair and sequins in the canister. To show Shasthi I wasn't wasteful, I'd called a number and talked to a man who'd asked me if I remembered when I'd gotten it.

"September 2001," I'd said guiltily, wishing I had just thrown it out in the first place. In New York there is no better feeling on earth than dragging something out of your apartment into the incinerator room.

In Kmart, I reached in my pocket for the scrap of paper I'd written the model number on and pulled out a pacifier instead. I looked at it in desperate wonder that I was walking around with something as precious as that. I'd had a baby and there was the beautiful proof. My pockets were like other women's pockets; I was complete. I just stood there weeping for joy right in the middle of Kmart.

"*Did you get the* vacuum cleaner part?" Shasthi asked me when I came home.

"No. I got something else," I said.

I handed her the Kmart bag. "It's an ovulation predictor kit," I said. Actually it was five boxes of them, each one costing twice her hourly wage.

I took the bag back from her, ripped open one of the boxes, and unfolded the instructions. I read the instructions to her even though I could have recited them by heart. For at least a year I didn't pee unless it was on one of these sticks. "You hold it under your urine stream," I told her. "When did you get your last period?"

"On the fourth," she said tentatively.

I took my tiny red-leather date book out of my pocketbook and circled the first day of her period. "Start testing first thing in the morning, right away. Don't listen to what the instructions say about waiting fourteen days after your period. Everyone's always telling you to wait. Never wait. That's the first rule of in—" I was going to say *infertility* but luckily I stopped myself. "In getting pregnant."

"Okay," Shasthi whispered, taking serious note of the first rule of getting pregnant.

My heart raced with excitement.

I picked up Duncan and kissed him a hundred times. I realized I had been shy to hold him or kiss him too much in front of Shasthi because I hadn't wanted to flaunt that I had what she wanted. "Bye bye," he said and kissed his own palm passionately.

*The Seven Year Bitch*

It was his way of blowing a kiss, except he didn't blow; he just kept it all to himself.

*When I got home* at the end of the day, I went into my bedroom and I noticed my bed was made.

Sometimes she made my bed and sometimes she didn't. At first I had thought it was a matter of free time—perhaps the baby had napped a little longer in the afternoon—but then I started to realize that she granted me this favor if I had pleased her in some small way, if I let her go an hour early or washed the bottles myself.

Sometimes my bed stayed in a rumpled mess for days, and I stayed up wondering what I had done wrong. Had she said we were out of Dreft and I'd forgotten to pick some up at the store? Had I eaten her yogurt in the fridge?

I didn't know why it mattered so much what she thought of me, but it did. I felt like the groom in an arranged marriage who had lucked out. Big time. And was now wooing after the fact.

Sharing a baby was more intimate than sharing a bed. "I love you," I said to both of them when Shasthi and Duncan left the house to go to the park. I may not have picked the perfect father for my son, but at least I had picked the perfect nanny. Sitter.

*That night I'd asked* Shasthi to stay late so that Russell and I could go to a fund-raiser for a documentary film a friend of mine was editing about a homeless crazy woman who lived in Central Park.

The movie was called *Begging Naked* and I'd actually seen the woman it was about in Central Park a few times. A woman who was her sometime benefactor was being interviewed in her dining room with her big silver coffee set behind her. The homeless woman peeled off her filthy clothes in the woman's house. She was letting her take a shower.

Sitting in the dark theater next to Russell, I suddenly regretted the ovulation kits. It wouldn't work and it would give Shasthi false hope. It was all too much, watching this homeless woman and thinking of Shasthi peeing on those awful sticks, with no chance in hell of having a baby without Heiffowitz.

"Maybe I'll take her to Dr. Heiffowitz," I whispered to Russell. "But what if she gets pregnant? Would she be given Medicare or Medicaid, and, if so, would it cover amniocentesis? Or what if she refused amnio out of fear or for religious purposes? She's forty. What if she has a Down's baby?"

"You'd probably want us to pay for it to go to a special school for eighteen years and then an adult special-needs living environment," Russell whispered back.

*That night I dreamt* I was feeding Duncan on the stoop of the building where I used to live. I was feeding him my milk from a teacup, and when I turned away for a moment, a Siamese cat lifted her leg and pissed in it. I brought the cup to my nose to smell if the milk was still okay, but of course it was spoiled, putrid. I woke with a terrible, foreboding feeling.

"Did you do the ovulation test?" I asked Shasthi, who was taking off her coat the next morning.

"Yes, I got two lines!"

I beamed with excitement. "Did you have sex?" I asked, making my eyes very wide as if that would somehow help make this an acceptable question.

"Yes, we did do it," she said.

"Good!" I said. "That's really good!"

The phone had rung and Deirdre-Agnes's angry voice had come through on the machine. "Look, Izzy, I'm pregnant and I need my crib." I couldn't help think of it as a good omen.

# 10

The next night Russell and I loaded the baby into the car and headed to our country house.

Russell turned on Howard Stern, who said the word *fuck* about ten times in a row.

"Fuck!" Duncan said from the backseat.

I wasn't too upset, because *fuck* seemed to be Duncan's word for *fire truck*, but I pushed his favorite CD into the CD player and we listened to a song called "Daddy Daddy" by Joe the Singing School Bus Driver.

"Okay, he's sleeping," Russell said, putting Howard back on.

"No, he's not," I said, putting Joe the Singing School Bus Driver back in.

"I can't take this anymore," Russell said.

"Why?" I said. "Joe the Singing School Bus Driver is great. Duncan loves it." He put Howard back on again and we had a huge fight right in front of Duncan. My father had always sung kids' songs in the car. It was what all good fathers did.

I turned off the CD and we rode for a long time in silence.

We'd bought the house right after we got married. We had been spending weekends at Marlon's country house but he screamed at us the whole time we were there and then said, "Bless you for your company," when we left. One morning Marlon was at his kitchen table enjoying his coffee and suddenly brown water dripped from the ceiling onto his head and right into his cup. Russell was shitting in the toilet upstairs and had no idea he had caused the flood. "Get out and take your New York City asshole with you," Marlon yelled when Russell came out of the bathroom completely bewildered. I didn't know if by "New York City asshole" he meant me, a native New Yorker, but after that we had no choice but to buy our own house. Still, our house was too close to Marlon's and we always ended up doing favors for him. He had cancer and the doctors had given him one summer to live, three summers ago.

We drove in silence most of the way over the George Washington Bridge and up the highway. When we turned off on 18, Russell said, "I'm going to stop at the Dunkin' Donuts. We should pick up something for Marlon."

Every time I heard the words "Dunkin' Donuts" I thought of a time when, nine months pregnant, I'd been forced to go to La Goulue for lunch alone with Russell's mother. She was interrogating me on the subject of names. What, she had insisted, was wrong with her father's name, Gene?

"We like Duncan," I had said.

"Duncan!" she said. "You have to be kidding. You can't do that."

"Why not?" I asked.

"Dunkin' Donuts! You can't call him Dunkin' Donuts. I never thought I'd have a grandson named Dunkin' Donuts."

I hadn't even thought of that.

"I guess he can always change his name when he's of majority," Russell's mother said. "He only has to be saddled with the name Duncan for eighteen years. That's not so bad. You can lie and tell people Duncan is your maiden name."

Waiting for Russell in the Dunkin' Donuts parking lot, I looked out the car window at two men standing near the entrance talking. They were both gorgeous in different ways. Which one would I want, I thought, if I could choose, as if I were catalogue shopping. One was tall with gray hair. He looked like an academic, replete with faded jeans and sport jacket and leather bag presumably filled with books and students' papers. I pick him, I thought, despite the fact that his thighs were just a little thin in his jeans. The other man was also tall, exactly equally tall, sportier, and had a more boring or familiar look. But then I wondered if he might be the better man. Maybe he was funnier or great in bed. I went back and forth between the two, trying to choose, in a mild panic because they were both so great-looking and it was hard to tell, from such a distance, without even hearing them speak, who was the better man for me. I imagined myself fucking each of them, underneath the brown-haired man, on top of the gray-haired one, having breakfast with them afterward.

I watched as the gray-haired man took out a cigarette and lit it, which should have ruled him out but didn't for some reason. I stared at his just slightly too-skinny legs and then brought my gaze back up to his face. I had looked at his lips and then at the other's and that's when I realized that their lips were very close together and that they were in fact kissing.

Then I watched Russell, through the plate-glass window, carefully pouring what I knew was whole milk into my Earl Grey tea even though I had asked for skim, his face frozen in concentration, a wax bag of chocolate doughnuts for Marlon tucked under his arm.

*When we pulled up* in front of Marlon's house, I saw something hanging from the eaves. "What is that?" I asked Russell.

"I don't know."

"It looks like a dead bird."

"It can't be," Russell said. "It must be a clump of leaves or a branch or something."

I got out of the car and moved toward it. I looked up at it and gasped. Its talons were sharp and knotted and shockingly red. Its black wings were spread. It was headless, yet it seemed to be suspended at the neck. When I looked closely I saw that its head must be stuck inside the eaves, but it seemed impossible, as if the only way that could have happened was if they'd built the house around the bird.

"How could that have happened?" I asked Russell, who was now standing next to me looking up at the bird. I normally would have yelled at him for leaving Duncan alone in the car asleep in his car seat, but we were standing just a few feet away and the passenger-side door was still open.

"Its head must have gotten stuck, but I don't see how," Russell said.

It was an omen—a gruesome symbol outside the home of a dying man.

"Should we tell him?" I asked.

"I don't know," Russell said.

What would he do about it if we did? I wondered. He was much too weak from his chemo treatment to climb a ladder. And if he could climb up, what then? If you pulled the bird down, you would have to just tear its body away from its head or even cut it with a knife. There seemed no other way.

"We could show it to Anya. Maybe she could call someone to take care of it," Russell said.

Anya was Marlon's live-in nurse who had agreed to stay with him in the country for what was supposed to be his last summer (again) in exchange for him paying extra to send her son to a nearby day camp. "I think Anya's been through enough," I said. I couldn't think of a worse fate than being locked up with Marlon in that house with a dead bird as its bowsprit. "I'm not going in."

I got back in the car. A few minutes later, Russell came out still holding the doughnuts and got back in the car. He looked sick to his stomach. Marlon was dead, I thought. I remembered my black suit was at the cleaners, abandoned there since my layoff.

Russell turned the key in the ignition and backed out of the driveway. "Is everything . . . okay?" I asked.

"Yeah, it's fine," Russell said. "If you call walking in on Marlon having sex with Anya fine."

We ate the doughnuts in silence for the rest of the trip.

*The Seven Year Bitch*

*We pulled up to* our house, and, as much as I hated it, I was relieved to see it still standing. It was dark now and Russell always went in first to turn on the lights, check the mousetraps, and check Duncan's room for spiders.

He got out of the car and I watched him sinking deep into the snow with each step. As he walked in the dark toward the house, I couldn't help but wonder what would happen if he were attacked by a grizzly bear.

There were bears in the area; we'd seen them once, a family of three lumbering across the road. There had been a horrifying story in the newspaper about a Hasidic family who filled their baby daughter full of milk and put her out on the porch in a bassinet and a bear came and carried her away. It was winter now, and they would be hibernating, but there had also been an article about their not having gathered enough food and coming out of hibernation early, or maybe it said they weren't hibernating at all. I imagined Russell's piss-pants fear when he saw the bear coming right at him, nosing him, sliding his claws down Russell's face as he looked to the car, to me, for help.

I could survive trapped in the car for at least three days, I figured, if the bear wouldn't leave. We'd already eaten the doughnuts but there was one bottle of water in the car and a few nuts on the floor. I regretted weaning. If I hadn't stopped breast-feeding, I could have made enough milk for the baby to survive for days, or until someone in a passing car saw the bear circling the parked car and Russell's carcass lying on the blood-stained snow, and called for help.

I could hold the funeral at the Frank E. Campbell Funeral

Home on the East Side and afterward, at home, lie curled up on my bed, our bed, as visitors came to sit beside me to comfort me. We had life insurance, now that I thought about it, and I could sell this house if I could find it without Russell. I had never learned how to drive. The Second Avenue Deli had moved but I was pretty sure they would still deliver sandwich platters for the shivah. How many people would come to pay their respects to Russell? I wondered. All those authors would show up and gorge themselves on the free food. I could probably tell the Second Avenue Deli to cater for two hundred hungry mourners.

I felt a shock of cold and realized that all that thinking about nursing had made my milk come back. Even though I hadn't breast-fed Duncan since November and it was now February, milk was soaking through my bra. It was as if to show me that I was right, Duncan and I would be fine.

*The next day we* had no choice but to invite Charlie Cheney, our neighbor who had just returned from Thailand, over for lunch. He kept an eye on our house when we weren't there. We paid him to mow and plow and we called him from the city regularly with requests to remove the peaches we'd accidentally left on the kitchen table or to find Duncan's blankie and ship it to us overnight express. He was an ex-pat Manhattanite who had lost it after 9/11 and left his job as an upholsterer to live in the country full-time and plant a garden containing fifty kinds of garlic. He had various conspiracy theories about the Bush administrations and he was a cousin of Vice President Dick Cheney, but he pronounced his name Chee-ney to disassociate himself.

In the country you were always so happy to see another person, it didn't really matter who it was. I'd always bought Charlie awkward Christmas presents of multiple shirts from Patagonia or multiple pairs of wool socks until I figured out that multiple bottles of Tanqueray and Ketel One were much more to his liking.

I eyed the shower before getting in. Even though it was my shower, in my house, it still wasn't my shower in the city, and I didn't like getting into it. The water smelled of sulfur. The knobs turned the wrong way. Stepping into it I felt as if I were joining the lesbians who had owned the house before us. I hated being naked in the country, which was ironic because we'd bought the house for the same reason all New Yorkers bought country houses—to be naked outside.

When I got out of the shower I heard Russell already talking to Charlie in the kitchen. I got dressed quickly and went downstairs.

"I got you a souvenir from Thailand," Charlie was telling Duncan. He handed him a carved wooden elephant.

Next to him was another souvenir. A young Thai girl, wearing a strange pantsuit as if she had come for some kind of job interview, stood next to him clutching his arm. She had too-short hair that was begging to be longer and a beanstalk neck that led to a hilly enchanted kingdom of cheeks and lips. Despite her jet-black hair and Asian skin, she had the big round rust freckles of a redhead. She wasn't beautiful and yet she was so much more beautiful than anything in upstate New York and so much more beautiful than anyone who should be standing next to Charlie.

"I'd like you to meet my wife," Charlie said. "This is Gra. She cuts my toenails," he said by way of introduction. "She actually cuts and files them."

"Why don't you do that for me?" Russell asked me.

"You want her to do yours?" Charlie said to Russell. "She'll do it. She doesn't mind."

"Hi, Gra is it?" I said. "Did you say 'wife'?"

"Her name isn't Gra but I call her Gra because that's the Thai word for *freckles*. Her name is too hard to pronounce for Americans."

Every time Charlie said the word *Gra*, the woman flashed a look like she was a prisoner desperately trying to tell us something.

"What's your real name?" I asked her.

"She doesn't speak any English!" Charlie said.

Although I didn't speak any foreign languages, I prided myself on having an excellent ear and the ability to pronounce foreign words correctly.

"What's her name?" I asked Charlie. "I want to try to learn it."

He made some strange combination of sounds and Gra shook her head. "I'm telling you, stick with Gra. She likes it. We're very happy."

Gra suddenly knelt on my kitchen floor and for a moment I was afraid she was really ready to cut Russell's toenails, which had always been a source of many fights between us, but then I saw she was petting Hum. Her black eyes were welling up with tears.

"What is it?" I asked.

"She's fine, she just misses her dog," Charlie said. "She had to leave her dog with her mother. It was a Pomeranian. One of those fluffy little rat dogs."

*The Seven Year Bitch*

"You can get a dog," I told her.

"She say: You. Can. Get. Dog," Charlie translated in a strange exaggerated fake Thai accent.

"What are you doing?" I asked.

"I'm learning Thai," Charlie said.

"That wasn't Thai. That was English spoken in a racist accent."

"I didn't speak Thai just now?"

"No," I said.

"I don't even know the difference anymore. It's called Thanglish. *Dog ao te. Pomeranian mai mai.* I told her we could get a dog, but not a Pomeranian. I hate that kind."

She stood up and looked at him as if she had no idea what he was saying. She pointed at Hum and smiled.

"That's Hum," I told Gra.

"Hum," she tried. "Hum. Hum."

"Yes," I said, as excited as Annie Sullivan talking to Helen Keller. It might not be the most useful English word she would learn, but it was a start. As soon as possible, I would teach her important American phrases like "Cut your own disgusting toenails."

"Humdog," she said.

"Come on, Charlie, you can get her a Pomeranian," I said. I could tell my kidding tone hadn't masked my anger. I couldn't stand the thought of her missing her dog like that. Of her long slim fingers touching Charlie's gross cracked toes. I couldn't stop the horrifying graphic thoughts in my head of various Kama Sutra positions— Gra on top, riding his cock, facing away from him and stretching down to cut his toenails with an enormous metal clipper.

Until this moment I had never really looked at Charlie. He had gray hair and lines on the back of his neck like an argyle sweater. He had brown eyes and a raggedy mustache that looked like it'd been around since the seventies. I thought of a report I had just seen on CNN that girls as young as three were used as sex slaves in Cambodia and China. They called oral sex "yum yum"—the same thing I called Hum's food when we gave it to him in his dish—and it showed footage of two little Chinese girls saying, "We do yum yum."

"I'm not getting one of those fur balls."

"She has to live with your big turtle, the least you could do is get her the dog she likes."

"She likes the turtle."

"You hold out for the Pomeranian," I barked at Gra like an agent. I didn't want her to take this deal.

"Well, this is great," Russell said, shooting me a look. "Can I get anyone a drink?"

"She don't need a Pomeranian. She'll have a Jack, Russell," Charlie said, giving Gra a taste of the humor she would be stuck with for the rest of her life. He laughed until we were forced to laugh to stop him. "And yes, I will have a drink. Vodka if you have it. This is a celebration."

"So are you two actually married?" I asked, trying to sound as enthusiastic as a bridesmaid.

"We have to wait for the paperwork to come. And then we want to have a wedding, and we really want you to be there."

"Of course, thank you! We wouldn't miss it," I said. There was no way I was going, but I would give a gift, a Pomeranian perhaps.

Gra stood and started talking excitedly and Charlie seemed to understand her.

*The Seven Year Bitch*

"What's she saying?" I asked.

"I have no idea," Charlie said. "Wait, I think she wants to cook for you. You. Want. Cook. For. Izzy. And. Russell? She's a great cook. She wants to start a Thai catering company here in Woodstock."

I always got a kick out of everyone in our little town, including Russell, thinking they lived in Woodstock. We were at least thirty minutes from Woodstock. Maybe it was because if we really were in Woodstock our house would be worth a hell of a lot more. Or maybe it was because our town was called Kripplebush, which didn't exactly sound auspicious.

Gra reached into a shopping bag, pulled out a photo album, and laid it out on the kitchen table next to the uninspired ham and Brie, lettuce, and bread I had set out for sandwiches.

"Is this your family?" I asked.

"No, it's food," Charlie said. On each page was a glossy photo of a different noodle dish.

"Yum yum," Gra said, and I cringed.

"Maybe Gra can teach Izzy to cook," Russell suggested.

Maybe Gra could cater Russell's funeral instead of the Second Avenue Deli.

"Sure," Charlie said. "Gra doesn't mind. She can cook, garden, clean. I'm the luckiest man in the world."

He knocked back his drink and then another one.

"That's great," Russell said. "I highly recommend married life."

We assembled sandwiches and brought them to the living room to sit in front of the fireplace.

"So how did you two, uh, meet?" Russell asked.

"Well I went there to get a wife and she was the last one I got to interview. She was the *only one*," Charlie emphasized vigorously, "who *insisted* on having a chaperone. I had sex with all the others but not with her. It just wasn't allowed."

"Really!" Russell said. "So you two haven't even . . ."

"Oh no, we had sex right after, but not when her mother was with us."

And what happens when she stops cutting your toenails, I wanted to scream. Or opening Coke bottles and smoking cigarettes with her vagina, or whatever I'd heard about all those girls who did sex shows out there. Then the joke's on you, I thought. Because you'll be married.

"Very good," Russell said.

"You know it was my third trip there," Charlie said. "It was what I promised my sister right before she died." Charlie's sister had died in a car crash while he was talking to her on her cell phone. He was complaining about a woman he was trying to date, and she had said, "You're impossible, Charlie. Why don't you just go to Thailand to get a wife. It's the only way you'll get one to put up with you," and that was the last thing she had ever said to him.

"You guys are very sweet to look out for me like this," Charlie said. "But don't worry, I'm not being stupid. I'm waiting a few weeks before the wedding. And I can get out of it for like a whole year if I don't like what I see before she gets her green card. We're really very much in love. I mean she was a little surprised because I told her we lived in New York and she didn't know I didn't mean the city."

*The Seven Year Bitch*

"Well Izzy and I are very happy for you," Russell said. "Welcome to Kripplebush."

I don't think I had ever heard anything more depressing.

*Sunday night we drove* home to the city. Before going to bed, I brought Thursday's pizza box out to the garbage room so that Shasthi wouldn't see it there in the morning, and I startled our neighbor Sherry as she was throwing out a stack of newspapers. Sherry was embarrassed to be caught in the hall in her nightgown, a short white cotton girlie thing covered in green fireflies.

"I'm throwing out everything I can. There's one of those giant water bugs in my loft," Sherry said, her voice filled with the particular guttural rage all New Yorkers felt when this happened to them.

"Oh no," I said, my whole body tensing at the thought of it but also flooding with relief that it was in her apartment and not mine, although our apartments were only separated by a wall, a stairwell, and an elevator. I really couldn't stand water bugs. It was a challenge I hadn't been faced with yet as a mother. If I saw one, I would normally scream at the top of my lungs and leave the apartment for several days like a prehistoric woman surrendering her cave, but I knew I shouldn't do that now that I was a mother.

"I'm tired of having to deal with everything alone," Sherry said. She was a single mother of a teenage daughter. "I want to get married if for no other reason than this."

"That's the only reason *to* get married," I said.

"How am I going to sleep with that *thing* in my house?" Sherry said.

"Maybe you shouldn't wear that nightgown," I said, pointing to the fireflies. "Maybe he was attracted to you." I immediately regretted saying something so stupid when she hadn't had a date in two years. I had to find a way to help. "Russell will kill it," I said.

I got Russell out of bed and he dutifully went into battle, wearing only his boxer shorts and carrying a rolled-up *New York Post* for a club. Sherry and I stood in the hall waiting. Moments later Russell came out. "I got it," he said. "I hit it with your scale."

When I got into bed with Russell I felt grateful to him. He had barely grumbled, just gotten out of bed and taken care of it like a man. I thought of Sherry sleeping safely next door. I thought of Duncan in his crib and Shasthi somewhere in the Bronx, with pillows under her so her pelvis was tilted upward as I had instructed her to always do after sex for at least an hour.

I was grateful to be married for this if for no other reason.

"Thanks for doing that," I said.

"It was a really big one."

I lay there for a few minutes considering having sex with him, despite the fact that I was so tired and had absolutely no desire to. There wasn't one cell in my body that wanted to have sex with Russell. It was after midnight and the baby would be up by five. I should at least touch him, I thought, try to do something affectionate. I reached over and gently tugged on a small bunch of his hair.

"*Hmmm*, thank you," he said.

He seemed satisfied with that, and frankly sex seemed just a little bit pointless. Now that I knew what it was like to make love and get a baby in the end, doing it just for the sake of doing it sometimes didn't seem worth giving up the sleep for. Russell

*The Seven Year Bitch*

wanted to use birth control, which seemed almost like a bitter joke, considering all we had been through to have Duncan. It seemed wrong to leave Dr. Heiffowitz's office with your beautiful baby boy and rush to the store for condoms. Russell said it felt dangerous to have sex unprotected, but to me it felt dangerous *not* to be unprotected, like we were slapping the face of God.

"I'm tired," Russell said.

"I'm soooo tired."

"You have Shasthi coming tomorrow?"

"Yes."

"She's really great, isn't she?"

"Yes, she's really great. I just wish we could get her pregnant."

"Well, we can't," Russell said.

"I think we should get her a cell phone," I said. I started to get excited thinking of how happy she would be when I presented her with her own cell phone. "It would be good to be able to check up on the baby."

"Do you think we can trust her with it?" Russell asked.

"You're kidding, right?" I asked, completely exasperated.

"No, why? I don't want her calling—where is it?"

"GUY-ana," I said like I was talking to the town fool. "We trust her with our *baby*, I think we can trust her with a cell phone."

"She can't make long-distance calls on the baby," Russell said.


*Our win-a-shrink was an* obese man named Howard Klein who sat in a sagging chair drinking a Snapple with a mobile of winged frogs dancing over his bald head.

"What made you bid on couples therapy at the auction?" he asked.

Russell and I sat squeezed together on the too-small love seat facing him.

I instantly started to cry and as I cried I realized that my tears were not wholeheartedly sad, because Duncan was fine, and as long as Duncan was fine, I was too grateful to be sad. Still the tears poured out of me for no reason.

"What are those? Frogs?" Russell asked, about the mobile.

"Russell, did you notice that your wife is crying?"

"Yes I did."

"Do you want to ask her why she's crying?"

"Not really," Russell said.

"Well, I'd like to know why your wife is crying," the shrink said. "Izzy, do you want to tell us why you're crying?"

"I'm tired," I said. "I get up with the baby at five while Russell sleeps. He never stops reading. He takes agents and authors to lunch every day."

"She's never believed in my work," Russell spit out.

I hated this accusation more than anything. His business lost money every month. We had put thousands and thousands of dollars into it. There were boxes of unwanted books everywhere in our apartment. We couldn't even sit at the dining-room table anymore.

"The way I see it," Howard said, "we each live on our own planet in our own universe. I live in my own world and you have no way of understanding the rules of my world because the rules are completely different from the rules in your worlds." I knew

*The Seven Year Bitch*

one rule of his world was you could eat as much dessert as you wanted to. "That's something I want us to think a lot about. I want you each to start making a list of some things the other can do for you that makes sense in your world. It sounds like one thing Izzy would like, Russell, is for you to wake up at five with the baby, and it sounds like one thing Russell needs in his world is for you, Izzy, to support his work."

The only thing I knew was that I could no sooner support Russell's work than he could wake up at five with the baby.

"Now," Howard continued, "besides working on your lists, I'm going to give you a trust exercise to do together."

"Great!" Russell said, leaning forward to pay full attention to the assignment.

"This is something you can choose to do blindfolded or not blindfolded," Howard said.

If he thought we were going to take turns falling backward into the other's waiting arms, he was crazy, because if one of Russell's authors called on his cell phone I'd be on the floor in two seconds.

He took a sip from his Snapple. "I want you, Russell, to lead Izzy all around your apartment by her nipples."

"What?" I said, trying to think if there was any other word he could have said.

"Yes," Howard said. "Pull Izzy around your apartment by her nipples. She has to follow you. You are the leader and she is the follower. Does that seem like something you two could try?"

I turned to look at Russell, who was just nodding his head like a lunatic.

"I see," Russell said. "Well that's certainly an interesting suggestion. I forgot to ask, why did you put your therapy services up for auction? Do you have a child at the school?"

"Does it matter to you if I have a child? I happen to have a patient who has a child at the school. I myself am not married and have no children. Izzy, how do you feel about letting Russell lead you by your nipples? You know what, don't answer me now. This is a good place to stop."

"But we've only been here twenty minutes," Russell said.

"We don't go by the clock in my practice. I intuitively know when it's time to stop. Is this time next week good for you?"

"Yes," Russell said, and I looked at him in disbelief. He couldn't even say no to this fat nipple-pervert. I was going to have to be the one to stop this.

"We'll have to look at our schedules—you know two worlds, two schedules—and give you a call," I said and opened the door to his office. As soon as I opened the door someone fell in.

"Oh, sorry. Howard, do you have a moment?" He was beet red from embarrassment.

"It's like a Three Stooges movie," Russell said.

I walked quickly down the hall with no one leading me by my nipples.

For some reason I thought of a man I had met once years before when I was single. He was the kind of man I made sure to stay away from, the kind usually named Roman or Camus, with gorgeous curly manelike hair and a thousand girlfriends all trying to follow him to South America, which he was going to do something like "check out." This particular man I was thinking of I had met in a club the same night I'd met Russell. We'd talked for a long time and he'd told me he was leaving for Paris the next evening. He was leaving his wife, he said, and I was horrified to even be talking to him. "Why would you throw away a marriage?" I had asked him, and he'd said something like, "There has to be more heat to a fire than that." I couldn't remember exactly how he'd put it, but it had to do with heat and fire and passion that had left his marriage and something about it had always stayed in my head after that. I couldn't remember his name or even what he looked like exactly, but I remembered this man saying something like that to me, his voice filled with a certainty and a longing that I admired but had also detested at the time. I could never walk away from someone like he did. Even if I wanted to, I could never do it.

*There has to be more heat to a fire than that*, repeated itself in my head.

I wished I'd said it in couples therapy. I almost felt like walking back down the hall and into Howard Klein's office and saying it now.

"You should come with me to Paris," the man had said.

"I'm not going to Paris!" I had guffawed. But a small part of me had thought about it.

"I think we should give it a try," Russell said when we were in the elevator. "It's a trust exercise." He tried to grab my nipples through my shirt. "For the sake of our marriage."

"We don't even kiss anymore," I said. "We never kiss." We didn't even kiss hello or good-bye, even when Russell came back from a business trip. We didn't kiss when we had sex.

"So we'll kiss," Russell said.

*Jennifer Belle*

But we didn't kiss, and when we got out on the street, he looked at his BlackBerry and then called a moronic writer whose first name was just the letter "C" and immediately started talking to her. We walked that way for a few blocks and finally I just signaled to him that I was going to go in the other direction, and he put up his hand to wave to me, and I walked away without him.

# 11

A couple of weeks later I was pushing Duncan in a swing in the playground when my cell phone rang. It was the man—Gabe Weinrib—calling to make an appointment for me to work on his portfolio.

"Is this a bad time, Mizz Brilliant?" he said confidently.

"Not at all," I said, all business.

"So, m'dear, I seem to have won your services."

"That does seem to be the case," I said, thinking this guy sounded like a complete idiot.

"Can I make an appointment to come by your office this week, or could you be persuaded to let me take you out to dinner? My treat of course."

"Um, let me look in my book," I said. I thought of the last time I had seen my office before riding down in an elevator filled with men in suits.

I tickled Duncan's tummy and made him laugh.

"The problem is I'm supposed to go back to Paris on Friday and I'll be there for two weeks," he said.

"Well, I just don't have anything available this week. . . ."

"All right, I was just hoping to lure you out to dinner before I go, just to get the ball rolling, then you could take your time."

I suddenly remembered that he knew I was at Richman and might think he could stop by the office to see me. A restaurant would solve the problem of where to do this.

"Well maybe dinner would be okay. Let's say tomorrow, but I won't be coming from work. . . ."

"How about Jean-Georges then, tomorrow at seven?"

"Jean-Georges?" I said. It was my favorite restaurant. Dinner would cost hundreds of dollars.

"Is that okay with you?" he asked.

"It's great," I said.

"Thank you, m'dear. Lookin' forward to it."

"You have a record of everything you're currently holding?" I said sternly. With all the *m'dears*, he was playing this like it was out of a scene from *Oklahoma!* and he had bid the highest on my picnic hamper.

I smiled at the woman pushing her baby in the next swing.

He laughed. "Yes and I'm happy to put what I'm currently holding in your hands."

Men always got filthy when they talked about their money. I was used to it and I was going to make a comment about throwing a pair of rubber gloves into my purse but I thought better of it. Instead I said, "Why don't you bring along a personal financial statement and a comprehensive listing of assets, liabilities, real estate, investment accounts, bank accounts, business interests, other valuable property, and art if you're a collector." God help me, I thought, and got off the phone.

*The next night I* considered my wardrobe and finally decided on a blue-and-red pinstripe dress with a little stretch to it. The whole effect was really not so bad. The dress pulled slightly at my stomach, where a year and a half before a baby had been, but when I put on tights and the coat that went with the dress, you couldn't really tell. I put on mascara because my mother's shrink said that was all you needed—mascara—and a little lipstick.

"You look so good!" Shasthi said.

I shrugged.

"No, really. I've never seen you like this." She hadn't known me when I used to dress up for work every day.

Duncan walked to me with his confident stride and touched my knee. "Woman," he said. "Woman."

"He notices too! He's never seen you in panty hose."

I put on a pair of high-heeled black boots I hadn't worn since before the layoff. "You should dress like this all the time," she said. "You look like Marilyn Monroe."

"Whoa, you look great," Russell said, looking up from his desk. "Where are you going?"

"On a date," I said.

"Who with?" he asked.

"Gabe Weinrib."

"Oh, the auction guy. Mr. High Bidder. Mr. Portfolio. *Gabe*

*Weinrib.* Sounds like a comedian from the fifties. Where are you meeting him, the Friars Club?"

"Jean-Georges actually."

"You're kidding me!" I knew he was a little nervous. "He's taking you there? Well, enjoy your big date," he said.

"It's your own fault. You should have outbid him," was all I said, before grabbing my legal pad and heading to the door.

"Bye, Mama," Duncan said. He opened his mouth as wide as he could and kissed my knee, taking my whole kneecap in his mouth.

"I love you," I said to Duncan and Shasthi as I walked out the door.

*I got to Jean-Georges* almost thirty minutes late and a tall blond woman led me professionally to a table in the main dining room where Gabe Weinrib was patiently waiting.

"I'm sorry," I said.

He stood up and looked at me. "Is-old-a," he said, saying my name wrong in a very long and drawn-out fashion. Men never knew what to do with my name and always wanted it to be three syllables instead of two. "A pleasure to finally meet you, m'dear." I was hit with a blast of Listerine that brought back all the nervousness of dating.

I slid onto the oversized white upholstered chair as gracefully as possible and he waited until I seemed settled before taking his seat.

He looked at me. "So do I look familiar?" he asked, grinning.

"No," I said. "Why? Do I know you?"

I looked into his eyes and felt myself blushing again. From his name and personality on the phone, I hadn't expected him to be gorgeous. Suddenly all the *m'dears* didn't seem so bad. He was wearing strange and expensive clothes, some kind of weird wool hat that hugged his head and forced me to stare into his eyes and a tight black sweater that made his chest look very hard and his arm muscles look big. It had been a long time since I'd looked at a man close up like that, I thought. I'd looked at other women's husbands not as men but as fathers. I'd lusted after men but only from the safety of my car the way I looked at animals from the monorail at the Bronx Zoo. I'd wanted Dr. Heiffowitz and Dr. Lichter, but there was always a nurse in the room with us. I tried to conjure up Russell in my mind but could only see glasses, manuscripts, and his big glass desk.

For a long time after I got married, I would play a little game with myself whenever I was at a party or something like that. I'd ask myself, "If you were single, is there anyone here you would even like?" And the answer was always "No!" I was happy I had gotten married. Dating had been miserable. There was never anybody anywhere who was remotely interesting.

"So let's see," I said. "I should ask you some questions."

"What is my philosophy about discipline?" he asked.

"What?" I said.

"It's the first question on your pad. I'm all for it as long as it's consensual of course." I looked down in horror at the nanny questions on my pad. "Do you believe in spanking?" he continued. "Absolutely! I'm a big believer. But only if you're a very, very naughty girl."

I tried to turn my pad over but he grabbed it from me. "You want to know how I like to give a bath? I get the water very hot. A touch of jasmine oil. No bubbles. Let's go to my place right now and I'll show you."

"I think I would actually like that," I said, laughing in spite of myself. "But I have a baby. I'm married," I blurted out.

"I know," he said. "I looked you up. You had a 'Vows' column in the *New York Times*. The big one. Very impressive."

If you Googled me, the first thing that came up was a big photo of me in the "Styles" section of the *New York Times* smiling in my black-and-white Reem Acra dress at Chanterelle. The article was framed and hanging on the wall outside our bedroom.

"Thank you."

"The article said you and your husband met at Don Hill's."

"That's right," I said.

I grasped my menu.

"Interesting. So you're married."

"Yes," I said.

"Happily?"

The word hung there for a minute. No, I thought. And then I thought, I love my baby.

"Just married," I said, smiling coolly.

He looked down at my pad again. "And how does your husband handle your tantrums?"

I thought about that. Whenever I fought with Russell he just apologized for anything and everything until I calmed down. He became single-mindedly focused on mollifying me. It was pretty effective actually.

"Can I have my pad back?"

*The Seven Year Bitch*

He handed it over and I turned several pages of the legal pad and folded them over, exposing a blank page.

"You dropped this," he said, handing me a single sheet of paper that had floated down onto the floor. "A spreadsheet of some sort. Looks impressive."

It happened to be a spreadsheet I had created to keep track of the new foods we were introducing Duncan to, but he didn't need to know that.

Something was happening to me and I hadn't even had a single drink yet. Maybe finally loosing myself of my nursing bras had done something to free me. My hips swayed in my seat. I felt every cell in my body yearning, reaching, pulling toward him. I felt my panty hose begin to rip and I had an incredible urge to go into the bathroom and take them off.

This whole thing was a non-issue. Aside from the fact that I was married, he was now my client and I was extremely sensitive to the ethical issues that could arise. I was angry at myself for even agreeing to dinner and for joking with Russell that I was going on a date.

"So, what brought you to that auction?" I asked. "Do you have a child at the school?"

"I'm an alum," he said. "When my family moved to New York I went to the school for a few years. I loved it."

A legacy! I thought. That was almost as good as your aunt being head of admissions. "That's great," I said. "So did you bring the information I asked for?"

"Let's order first," he said as the waiter came over to our table. We had our choice of two tasting menus. "They're both delicious."

"I know!" I said and let him choose. He picked the slightly scarier one, which included a quail's egg and caviar and garlic soup with sautéed frogs' legs. I wondered if I could delicately leap my frog's legs over to his plate without anyone noticing.

"So you don't remember me at all? We met once and I remembered your name. You have a very memorable name."

"I'm sorry, I'm terrible at remembering names."

"We had an interesting conversation."

"We did?"

"When I saw your name at the auction I wanted to meet you again," he said. "You look the same. You have perfectly shaped eyebrows. Well, I obviously didn't make the same impression on you. That night. At Don Hill's."

"Don Hill's?" I asked. I had only been to Don Hill's once in my life. I'd gone with Joy the night I met Russell. So it would have been eight years ago.

"I was there with a mutual friend of ours—Carla Gigante—and she introduced us," he said.

Carla Gigante was a girl I had gone to business school with who had a very old, ugly sugar daddy who paid her tuition and would pick her up after class in a chauffeured Bentley.

"Carla Gigante isn't really a friend of mine," I said.

"Oh, you don't like her?"

"No," I said.

"So maybe that's why you weren't interested when we met?"

I was taken aback by his straightforward question. And it was a good one. Why wouldn't I have been interested in him?

I tried to think back to that night, but I just couldn't remember anything. I sort of remembered dodging Carla Gigante, but

I had absolutely no recollection of this man, who was probably even more gorgeous eight years ago, eight years more gorgeous, and had been clearly very interested in *me*. I remembered wearing something black velvet that no longer fit, and, now that I thought of it, I might very well have been at my most beautiful that night all those years ago at Don Hill's.

It had always been my deepest wish that someone from my past would remember me and wish they hadn't let me go. He hadn't said that exactly, but it seemed close enough.

"I only ask because I really was," he said. "Interested, I mean. I thought we had such a great conversation. In fact, I think I remember I very sincerely invited you to come to Paris with me the next day."

"I remember," I said slowly. "You were married."

"I was bailing out," he said, smiling. "So you do remember me."

"*Hmm*, I believe you said something like, there had to be more heat to a fire than that."

He laughed. "Sounds like something I would say. I don't want to get too maudlin about it, but I consider the moment you blew me off at Don Hill's one of the most disappointing moments of my life."

"Oh come on," I said.

"I'm serious, m'dear," he said.

"Why?" I asked. "As I recall we didn't get along too well. We argued about marriage."

"You said you would never date a man who was divorced."

"I said married."

"You said separated."

"Well it's true if you were with Carla Gigante who I really can't stand, and I'm surprised you can actually, and if you called me m'dear..."

"Oh, you don't like that?"

Luckily the waiter put a tiny plate with three *amuse-bouche* the size of quarters before each of us, which gave me time to think of an answer.

"Carla and I aren't very good friends, you know. We just met that night at a party and I wasn't interested in her at all. You were the first girl I asked out after my marriage ended. I mean it's *no big deal*. I survived the blow. I lived."

What I remembered most, as I stared into his eyes, were all the nights I'd sat around at bars and sushi restaurants with my girl-friends talking about how I would never meet anybody and there was absolutely nobody to meet. We dissected every possibility, my own portfolio so to speak, of the many inappropriate losers I'd managed to sleep with in the nine years after business school and before I met Russell and got married. Night after night, year after year went by and the only people I met were either clients or asshole traders, while my mother's shrink assured me, via my mother, that when I was emotionally ready and open, men would suddenly fall out of the trees. There weren't, however, any trees in the financial district, and if men were falling it meant they had jumped from their office window or, of course, a terrorist attack.

And here was this man Gabe, whom I had completely ignored because of his association with Carla Gigante and possibly a cou-ple of harmless *m'dears*.

"The article about your wedding said you met your husband at Don Hill's. You didn't meet him that night did you?"

"Actually, I did."

"So while I was thinking about you at the airport—hoping you would come running up to the gate at the last minute—you were grooving on this . . . what was his name . . . Rodger?"

"Russell," I said reluctantly. He had gotten a little sarcastic with the running-up-to-the-gate bit and I couldn't tell if he was serious about any of this or not. Or making fun of me even.

"Anyway, luckily a woman on the plane helped mend my broken heart. I remember her name was Su-san-nah. Great little redhead. But I prefer brunettes."

"Well, I'm glad she eased your terrible pain. And I'm glad she didn't care that you were married."

"Yes, she was a lot less judgmental than you, m'dear."

"So if I was so judgmental, why'd you want me to come with you?" I asked.

"I liked you," he said.

"Why?"

"I believe you said something very meaningful to me at the time."

"What was it?" I asked, wracking my brain, trying to think of anything meaningful I could have possibly said.

"You said you liked my hair."

The way he said it made me laugh probably harder than anyone had ever laughed at Jean-Georges.

"That's it? That's why you wanted me to go to Paris with you? I liked your hair. Now I can't even see your hair, you're wearing a hat."

"I came from the gym."

"Take it off," I said.

"No," he said.

"Come on, take it off," I said.

"No. It's not what it used to be."

I stood up and walked behind his chair and took his weird knitted hat off. He reached up and grabbed my wrists but he was too late. His hair was light brown and a little shaggy. It was too long in the back and a small bald spot was starting to reveal itself.

I wanted to touch it, but I stopped myself.

"So what do you think of it now?" he asked.

"Still nice, but you could take a little off the bottom."

I never could have flirted like that if I hadn't been married. Most people thought love was the cornerstone of a marriage, but it wasn't. Flirting was its bedrock. Flirting was marriage's greatest reward. The ring on your finger was a magical golden hoop that protected you from all pain and rejection. The most happily married couples were constantly flirting, I noticed.

"Can I have my hat back?" he asked.

He reached for it and I pulled it away, spilling my glass of red wine on it. I said I was sorry and he laughed and then I laughed.

"Well I still think we could have had a lot of fun in Paris."

I had always loved the idea, in so many books and movies—and let's face it, I watched a lot more movies than I read books—that love was just around the corner, that if you walked down one block instead of another you'd bump into it. Life was out there waiting and a bad sense of direction might be all you needed. What I hadn't counted on was how much good luck I had avoided with this same idea. The good thing was if you made a mistake, and missed love, you would never know it. You weren't supposed to be confronted by it at a five-hundred-dollar dinner.

*The Seven Year Bitch*

"What do you do?" I asked, suddenly wanting to change the subject.

"I play around in finance too," he said. "I'm an attorney. And I've done some writing."

"What kind of writing?" I asked. I hoped he wasn't writing a novel or a screenplay or something, because all the lawyers I met were trying their hand at a legal thriller and they were so pathetic about it. Lawyers could never just admit they were lawyers. Not writers or chefs or watercolor artists. Just lawyers. In the four months since I'd been laid off, half the people who had been laid off with me had called me to say they were working on a Wall Street thriller.

"Well, I'm working on a novel, but I also wrote a New Orleans guidebook, post-Katrina. All proceeds go to charity. I helped out a lot down there after the hurricane."

"I like New Orleans," I proclaimed. As a New Yorker, if I said I liked a place I always thought I was giving it the ultimate compliment. "Where did you live before your family moved here?" I asked.

"The important thing is not where I'm from but that I came to New York as soon as I could," he said, which I took to mean he was from New Jersey. People from New Jersey were always trying to come up with clever things like that to say.

The waiter brought a quail's egg with caviar along with two shots of pepper vodka.

He took off his sweater and his jersey rode up a little over his flat, hard stomach, showing a line of dark hair. To my complete shock, I felt myself get as wet as a teenager.

"Excuse me," I said, standing up. "I'm going to go to the ladies room."

"It's through there."

"Oh I know exactly where it is," I said.

When I got to the ladies room I took a moment to admire the small framed photograph of people ice-skating in Central Park in front of the Dakota. I peeled down my torn tights and sat on the toilet, and that's when I realized I had my period. It was my first period since before I'd gotten pregnant.

Blood was gushing out of me more violently than it ever had. I hadn't gotten my period in so long, I'd forgotten all about it. But there was no way my blood had ever been this red!

Sitting there helplessly in the bathroom made me feel like I was in elementary school, a virgin again, womanly and fertile—able to have a baby. It was like God was giving me a sign. Getting your period after you've had a baby is not unlike getting it for the first time. I was ready to do it again. I was a woman all over again. I could start again, even with someone else.

Jean-Georges wasn't exactly the kind of place with a tampon machine in its bathroom. I knew I didn't have one in my purse or even in my house, it had been so long. I opened my purse anyway and saw a size 4 Huggies diaper. We'd tried both Pampers and Huggies and there was no question but that Huggies were a million times better. When I saw people in the store buying Pampers, I had to stop myself from ripping them out of their hands and insisting they buy the Huggies. So it was with confidence that I opened it and placed it in the crotch of my torn tights as if it were the most normal thing in the world to wear a diaper on a date, let alone a business meeting, and went back to Gabe Weinrib.

As soon as I sat back down at the table our next course arrived, a scallop the size of my cell phone, but I couldn't eat.

*The Seven Year Bitch*

"Now business, m' . . . Isolde," he said. "I believe you wanted to see my assets. I think you'll find me to be very well endowed. Aha! Your eyes just got very wide."

"They did not," I said, but I knew they had. He handed me a packet of the financial papers I had asked for, and once again I had to fight my eyes from getting wide.

He had what amounted to about two hundred million dollars in tax-exempt munis, stocks, mutual funds, a precious metals commodities fund, and hedge funds. He had an apartment on Fifth Avenue, several apartments in Paris, a house in Florida, and the house he grew up in, in New Jersey. He had a Matisse and a Basquiat and his mother's diamond ring appraised at one million dollars.

"Richman Gold's Private Client Groups handles your annual portfolio rebalancing," I said, doing a quick calculation for the second time. Thirty mil in real estate, eighty mil in safe bonds, one hundred mil in a well-diversified portfolio plus a mil in a checking account. "So you didn't need my services."

"I know," he said. "I just thought it would be fun. I remember that night I met you, I asked you how much I should invest in a hedge fund and you said, 'It depends on your appetite for risk.' I think of that line all the time. 'It depends on your appetite for risk.'"

He looked like he was enjoying himself.

I sectioned the scallop with my fork and popped a portion of it in my mouth to sustain myself.

"And I see your appetite was big," I said, looking at the hedge funds. "Wait a minute, you're Arrowsender, LLC?"

When I was considering having my fund buy stock in an IPO, I'd noticed that a huge portion of the privately held stock in the

IPO company was held by one investor with a ridiculous name—Arrowsender. When the company went public, all of the private stock was bought out by the investors. He had made a killing.

"So we don't really have any business to do together," I said, almost disappointed.

"Well that's good because you probably don't sleep with your clients."

"I'm married," I said. "I don't sleep with anybody."

"Happily?" he asked.

I couldn't wait to tell my mother about this so she could tell her shrink. If it were possible for a person to kick *herself* under the table, I would have. We sat there for hours, laughing and joking, and I couldn't remember having so much fun. I knew in the morning I would have to play hooky from Duncan's Baby Time class. After tonight, I didn't think I could eat strange sandwiches with Gerde and hear her German small-town theories about proper fashions for babies. At the end of the night he rejected his chef's tray of desserts. "The chef knows what I like," he told the waiter.

Then Jean-Georges himself came out of the kitchen with a pineapple and a knife and carved it for us, and a waiter followed with a silver boat of whipped cream.

"Is this an anniversary?" the great chef asked.

"This is only the second time we've met," Gabe said.

"Oh, I thought for sure this was your wife," he said.

*"How was your big* date?" Russell asked when I walked in the door.

"I got my period and had to put a diaper in my tights."

"Your period," he said. "I think that's my cue to get a vasectomy."

When Russell had to have a procedure to test his fatty liver, he'd clutched on to me all the way up to Mount Sinai and I'd had to promise him the whole time he wouldn't die. And that was just his *liver*. I didn't think there was much threat in him volunteering for an operation on his penis.

I went into our room and lay down on our bed, still in my clothes and diaper. Russell followed after me.

"Did you have fun?"

"Yes," I said.

"Does that mean you want to go back to work?" he asked.

"I don't know," I said.


*On my way to* Aquacise at the gym, I called Dr. Heiffowitz's office and spoke to his assistant, a woman named Scottie. It was my thirty-ninth birthday and I had that revved-up, birthday, time-is-of-the-essence feeling. "I have a quick question," I said. "My nanny . . . sitter . . . can't get pregnant. But she doesn't have any money and she's here in this country illegally, so I was wondering if . . ."

"Well, I don't know what we can do if she's here illegally. Has she filled out a patient questionnaire?"

"No, not yet," I said. I felt like a complete idiot. It was a mistake to tell Scottie her status, which when I thought about it had nothing to do with it really. Dr. Heiffowitz was a fertility endocrinologist, not an immigration attorney. It must, I thought, be possible to get pregnant without a Social Security number, people probably did it all the time.

"I'd like to make an appointment for her," I said. "Send the patient questionnaire to my address."

Dr. Heiffowitz was such a genius, they might as well send the baby in the envelope along with the patient questionnaire, because it was practically a guarantee he could get you one.

Walking along Washington Square North, I tried not to notice the changes that were being made to the park. Big signs from the Parks Commission had been placed on the ugly wire fence now lining the perimeter, explaining the plans for the beautification of Washington Square Park. One-hundred-year-old trees and burial grounds were being dug up. Someone had tied balloons to the fence and drawn sad faces on them.

A sad face painted on a balloon is the last thing you expect to see on your birthday.

The cobblestones were all gone. A trench had been dug around the park exposing layers of earth that no New Yorker wanted to know about.

I saw the old ladies selling their wares.

"Do you have any hats?" I asked.

"Doris, do we have any hats?"

"Hold on, Marilyn." Doris went into the senior center and came out with a tiny orange baby hat with a green stem, made to look like a pumpkin.

"I meant for a man," I said. "Like a skullcap."

"You mean one of those African-looking things? My rabbi wears one of those instead of a yarmulke. He's very young. Unmarried," Doris said.

*The Seven Year Bitch*

"We'll have it for you next week," Marilyn pushed in. "Custom made. I can have one of my girls do it right away. Any particular colors?"

The one I'd spilled wine on was black and orange and red. I told them what it should look like.

"Your husband is a lucky man."

"It's not for my husband," I said.

"Oh?"

"Just a friend," I said.

"No judgments," Marilyn said, crossing her knitting needles in front of her. "My girls just knit. We don't ask any questions. We don't judge our customers. We're all mothers here. Between the three of us we've done everything under the sun."

The third old lady, Gert, just sat on the steps staring off into space. It was hard to imagine she'd done much of anything under the sun at all.

"We're all divorced," Doris said. "Marriage did not agree with me. It was fine until the children came and then I had to harp on him for everything. Just to get him to come home. I called it 'The Making of the Shrew.' It was horrible."

"You were already a shrew," Marilyn said. "You're still a shrew. The question is which came first, the chicken or the egg?"

Doris laughed. "The answer happens to be, the chicken *and* the egg. I was a spring chicken, and then became a mother, before I was a shrew, believe me. When we were first married, my husband had a harmless crush on another woman in our beach club. She always wore the same purple bathing suit, and she would hang it on a hook to dry after she rinsed it when she came in from swimming. My husband was always bringing her up, saying what nice legs she had and tush, and why couldn't I have a bathing suit like that one. So one day I grabbed it off that hook and I put it on, and I flaunted myself all over the beach right where everyone could see me, and it was the funniest thing. We would always play tricks on each other and have fun. We had a spark. Then, for the children's sake, I had to nag and pester him all the time. He wasn't a bad father and he wasn't a bad husband, but he was a bad father and husband if that makes any sense. He couldn't handle it, both together. I had to do everything—the school, the doctor's appointments, the vet, and the house payments. He turned me into a nag and a pest."

"Maybe if you'd had a nice 'friend' things would have been different," Marilyn said.

All three women looked at me.

"So what about something for you?" Marilyn said. "A nice scarf? I made these here, but I don't want you to think you have to buy one of mine, because all my girls do wonderful work. I just happen to like this one." She held up a purple eyelash number, reminiscent of the purple bathing suit in Doris's story.

"Did you make that one?" I asked.

"I did, but that's not why I'm recommending it. I just happen to like it."

"Well it is my birthday," I said, taking a twenty out of my coat pocket. I hadn't bought myself anything since I'd been laid off and it felt good to do it.

I spent my thirty-ninth birthday sitting in the dining room of the senior center drinking lemon tea and eating lemon pound cake. Then I attended a special seniors' Weight Watchers meeting on the second floor. Why not, I thought. Thirty-nine was forty and forty was fifty.

At home I changed for our dinner reservation. But Russell wouldn't get off the phone. He talked and talked and talked and talked. It was an emergency. A review in the *New York Times* of a book by one of his authors had begun "In this terrible novel . . ." He talked and soothed and strategized. From the other room I heard him say, "It's my wife's birthday," and then he laughed. "I know, I'm in trouble."

Our babysitter sat on the couch reading a book.

"It's a ten o'clock reservation," I screamed. "Ten o'clock. Not six or seven or eight but ten. You can't even get off the phone at ten o'clock on my birthday."

What had become of me? I wondered.

## 12

Everything caused a fight. Everything was a negotiation. Something as simple as dressing Duncan in a sweater turned into a full production of *Who's Afraid of Virginia Woolf?* Blood was always dripping from my chops.

"Here's a sweater for Duncan."

"He doesn't need a sweater."

"What do you mean he doesn't need a sweater? It's cold outside."

"I don't want him to get too hot."

"It's seventeen degrees."

"No, it's forty-two degrees."

"Okay, you win. It's forty-two degrees. Put the sweater on him."

"It's not that cold."

"Yes it is."

"I was out. You haven't been out."

"It's freezing, Russell."

"It's March. I think you're insane."

"I know it's March. But it's cold. It's raining."

"That's what his coat's for. He's going to be wearing a coat."

"Of course he's going to be wearing a coat!"

"So he doesn't need a sweater."

"Is it that you're just too lazy to put the goddamn sweater on him? It's not that hard, you pull it over his head."

"You're really hurting him by doing this in front of him."

"You're hurting him by taking him out in zero-degree weather without a sweater."

"Fine. I'll put it on him."

"Good. Jesus. Moron."

We fought about the mail piling up on the dining table, the clutter, the house filling up with books, and authors, always these terrible authors.

"What's this?" he asked, holding the large envelope from Dr. Heiffowitz's office.

"Probably nothing," I said, taking the envelope into the bathroom with me.


*When she came in* the morning, I waited for Russell to leave the house to deal with a problem with our car, and we sat down on the couch together and went through the questions. My heart was pounding the way it had when I had filled out my own.

"Now. What was the first day of your last period?" I said in a casual, upbeat tone as if it were the most normal thing in the world to be discussing.

"Were you a DES baby? Have you ever had a hysterosalpin-gogram? Traveled to another country? Been implanted with an IUD?"

I explained each question to Shasthi like a police detective reading her her rights.

Now *this* was how to interview a nanny, I thought. Instead of *Do you have references?* it should be *Have you ever been diagnosed with endometriosis?* And instead of *Can you occasionally stay late if my husband and I have dinner plans or theater tickets?* it should be *Has your period ever been late or absent altogether?*

"Number of births, number of abortions, number of miscarriages?" I read out loud.

I was about to write down *none* when Shasthi said, "I've had two abortions."

"Okay," I said, making my voice normal. "You did!"

"When I was in Guyana I had a boyfriend for many years named Jay. I got pregnant with him two times."

"Two times!"

"My family is enemies with Jay's family so they said I had to choose. They told me if I continued with him no one in my family would ever speak to me again."

"So you didn't marry him?" I asked.

"No. I married the man my family had in mind for me. My family is very important to me, you know."

No, I didn't know. This was a tragic story with a terrible ending. It was like Romeo and Juliet without the happy relief of poison.

"Do you ever think of Jay?" I asked, thinking of Gabe Weinrib fucking some woman on the plane to Paris.

"Yes. He is married now."

"So the problem could be your husband's sperm," I said, bitterly. "If you were able to get pregnant twice before." If she had married Jay she would have many children by now. I was happy to pay for Shasthi's doctor's bills but I wasn't sure I was willing to pay the price for her husband's bad sperm. We both seemed taken aback by the force of my hypothesis.

"No. My husband has two big children in Guyana."

I felt crushed. She lived with this man in the Bronx somewhere, his mother in the apartment upstairs, and the strange thing was she didn't seem at all unhappy. The whole family gathered to watch cricket matches from her country thanks to some cable sports package she had ordered. I had to almost admire the ability to enjoy something as stupid as cricket when she was forty and childless.

I tried to imagine her apartment, immaculately neat, the kitchen smelling of a fragrant, spicy fish stew. All the things I had sent home with her in shopping bags—unused wedding presents, and birthday presents, a fifty-dollar candle from Barneys.

I wondered if I was committing some kind of on-the-job sexual harassment, forcing her to divulge her personal abortion stories like that. I tossed the questionnaire onto a pile of papers, trying to seem casual.

"Well anyway we got this taken care of so we can just send it in and then decide what we want to do next."

I went to get the baby from his crib and was alarmed for a moment, seeing some kind of mark on his forehead between his eyes.

But it was just one of her sequins floating there like a bindi.

*Jennifer Belle*

I still hadn't fixed the vacuum and her sequins were everywhere but I liked that they were there. They were a little off-putting in their quantity but cheerful, like the ladybugs that appeared in my apartment each July.

*When I came home* that evening, Russell said, "Notice anything new?" I couldn't see anything new, just a big pile of four seasons' worth of shoes tossed by the front door.

"Poland Spring came with our new water cooler!" Someone in the kitchen burped loudly, and when I looked over I saw it was the water cooler itself, as if it were trying to make its presence known. It was like having a third-grade boy in the kitchen.

Russell presented me with a glass of perfectly chilled water. I had to admit it was delicious. I gulped it down and drank another.

"Now we can gossip by it," he said. He made me walk over to it with him and stand in front of it. "You'll never guess what I heard about the new woman in 3E . . ." he began. It was the first time someone other than Duncan had made me laugh in a long time.

That night we lay in bed talking about the water cooler. "It's saving us money," he said. "I mean we were spending *at least* four dollars a day on water. Probably more. Now it's *less* than a dollar a day."

"And it looks better than I thought it would. I'm already used to it," I said.

"And I already feel we're healthier. I drank water tonight instead of beer."

"I drank more water tonight than I would usually drink in a week."

"And it's great to have the hot-water part too. Tomorrow I can make you tea. I might even have tea too, instead of coffee. I'm really so glad we did it. So, so glad."

"I'm really glad we did it too."

I hadn't heard us this excited about anything in a long time. Not since our conversations about Duncan when he was first born. In fact, I couldn't help but wonder if we were more excited about the water cooler than we'd been about Duncan. What had our life become, I wondered, if we needed something like Poland Spring to bring us together?

"You feeling frisky?" he asked.

Despite those words, I agreed to make love to him to celebrate our new addition as long as he promised to be very, very quick because I was so tired, which he did. He plastered on a condom from my underwear drawer. "You have to take off your nightgown," he said.

"Why?" I complained.

"I want to see you."

"You've seen me."

"I want to see you again."

"I'm too tired. If I take it off it will be inside out and I'll have to find it and then turn it right side in and put it on again in three minutes."

"Not three minutes," Russell said.

"You said you'd be quick."

We argued about it for a while, and in the end I agreed to hike the nightgown all the way up around my neck in a big bunch like an Elizabethan collar. He climbed on top of me, and I helped guide him into me like an air traffic controller with one hand while holding our dog by the collar with the other. I couldn't remember the last time I'd had sex without holding on to my dog's collar and usually reassuring him and even kissing him the whole time. We'd thrown out his crate when Duncan was born to make room for a glider and we couldn't lock him out of our room because the doorknob was broken and we'd be the ones locked in with no way to get out.

Even with my holding him as hard as I could, he broke free, licked Russell's ass, and finally mounted him until I got him in my grasp again.

"I love you," Russell said.

By way of afterglow he brought me a wad of toilet paper and something new: a glass of water.

"What do you think Shasthi is going to think of the water cooler?" Russell asked.

"I was just thinking how excited I am to show it to her tomorrow," I said.

"I think she's really going to love it."

And then I was too tired to speak.

The next morning when Shasthi came we showed her the Poland Spring water cooler.

"Isn't it great?" I said.

"Yes, it's so much better. I have one at home," she said.

Russell and I looked at each other in shock. She'd heard us complaining about wasting money on water and she hadn't mentioned anything. Why hadn't she spoken up about it? I wondered. She'd left our apartment night after night with its refrigerator full and countertops covered with a small fortune of half-empty bottles of water and she'd smugly returned home to her state-of-the-art water cooler. Maybe I was wrong to help her get pregnant and think about doing things like getting her a cell phone when she wasn't concerned about me whatsoever.

Or maybe she just didn't think it was her place to say anything. I hated the thought of her thinking something like that but maybe it was true. Or maybe what she thought we wasted money on was so vast a list, the water was just a drop in the bucket so to speak. When I was pregnant our doorman had once said to me, "Can I ask you a question? Why do you live here? You could live in a whole house in Westchester for the money you spend for your place."

"I could own a whole village in Africa," I had said, stupidly.

"But Westchester is just a few stops on the train," he had said.

Every time I paid my maintenance, I thought of that conversation.

"Well we love it," Russell said, still praising the water cooler.

I wondered if Shasthi and her husband had made love when they'd gotten theirs.

# 13

"This is it," Russell said, stopping in front of an old door in a cast-iron loft building. We were buzzed in and walked up the three steep flights of stairs to our new shrink's office. I always hated the way Russell walked up stairs, with his body bent completely over. The man had no core strength whatsoever.

Corinne, the new shrink who had been recommended by my mother's shrink, was standing at her door watching us. She had limp curly hair the color of cream of tomato soup and seemed to be wearing some kind of baggy pajamas.

"Take off your shoes," she said.

Russell and I were both wearing two different socks.

We followed her through the vast loft to the living room area and she directed us to sit on a lumpy old couch that was covered with a blanket. Questionable upholstery was one of my biggest fears for some reason. I never went to those cafés with strange assorted chairs and couches everywhere. I wasn't one of those people who was phobic about germs, but the idea of sinking into a couch that ten thousand other New Yorkers had sunk into before me didn't appeal to me at all.

I sat on one end of the couch and Russell sat as far away from me as he could while still being on the same couch.

Corinne sat facing us in an armchair covered in a mid-century print, its white stuffing leaking from every seam. Behind her was a ladder that led to a sleeping loft with a neatly made platform bed.

"Do you live here?" Russell asked, although we both knew the answer.

"I do," she said. "I had an office, and I started to ask myself why I was paying all that rent."

So we wouldn't have to see you in your pajamas with your cat on your lap, I wanted to tell her.

I waited for her to ask if it bothered us that she worked out of her apartment but the question didn't come.

"What brings you to therapy today?" she asked instead.

Russell gave some long-winded answer that included use of the word *dovetail*. "Your schedule seemed to dovetail quite nicely with our needs at that moment. . . ." I looked at the beautiful worn kilim on the floor with its vibrant blue center and almost ugly brown border. I couldn't take my eyes off it. The blue was made more beautiful by the brown. If I had a rug like that my life would be better, I thought.

Everywhere in the loft were interesting antiques, run-down and shabby but pleasing. Lamps, armoires, divans, desks. On the surfaces were all things I suddenly felt I needed—just the claw feet from a claw-foot tub or a green glass bud vase. She had a good eye, I thought, something I envied in certain people. If I'd had all those things they'd look like junk and I'd end up taking them all out to the garbage room.

The walls were hung with framed disturbed-looking children's art where diplomas might have been. There wasn't even a single book.

I heard Russell say the word *dovetail* for the second time. I could go my whole lifetime without saying the word *dovetail* and Russell couldn't go a whole conversation without it.

I thought about how Russell might look good in someone else's apartment, but I just wanted to take him out to the garbage room.

After therapy we were supposed to go to my friend's apartment to pay a shivah call. Her husband had died after a five-year battle with ALS. I was dreading it, seeing my friend's grief, seeing his mother there at the shivah of her son.

I started to think of what I would say to Russell's mother if he died.

*"Well, now that Russell's dead I guess I never have to see you again, Ginny."*

*"You never loved my son."*

*"It's really none of your business who I loved. He hated you and so do I. Now get out."*

"So how would you describe the tone of your relationship?" Corinne asked.

"We fight all the time."

"Not all the time," Russell said.

"Yes, all the time," I said.

"No."

"Yes."

We argued about how much we argued for several minutes.

"Would you say you're arguing now?" Corinne asked.

"No," Russell said.

"I think you are arguing," Corinne said.

This gave us pause. It was almost as if there was nothing else to argue about for a moment. "Well, I guess you win," Russell said to me bitterly.

"I always do," I said.

"Not always."

"Yes. Always."

"No, not always."

"Yes. Always. Always. Always."

"What do you usually argue about?" Corinne asked.

"I want Russell to be a man," I said.

"And what does that mean, to be a man?" she asked.

"You know what it means," I said.

"No, I really don't. If someone told me to be a woman I wouldn't know what that meant either."

I told her how I had worked on the stroller for an hour before calling Rashid up to fix it and how the baby had crouched on the floor next to Rashid carefully holding Rashid's flashlight and screwdriver in his tiny hands.

"So being a man means fixing the stroller," she said.

I just stared at her, too emotional from my story to speak.

"That's right," I said.

"So you have a son?"

"Do you have any children?" I asked.

"No," she said.

"You're lucky," Russell said.

"Why am I lucky?" Corinne asked.

"He always says that," I said.

"I've never been married and I don't have any children." Whatever small hope I had that she could help us leaked out of me like her chair's stuffing. I was starting to wonder if there were any married marriage counselors in New York. "Is that important to you?"

I shrugged unconvincingly.

"Sometimes my married clients feel it's helpful that I can offer the single person's perspective."

I had to admit this seemed almost appealing, the single person's perspective. She could remind me how miserable it was to be single and how Russell dovetailed with my need to be married.

"You can remind me how good it feels to sleep in your own bed," I said. I tried not to look at her actual bed as I said it.

"Oh I wouldn't know about that," Corinne said. "There's always a cat on my legs or on my pillow nudging me to lift up the covers."

Russell and I just stared in dumbfounded silence.

"So you argue a lot. Is there anything you agree on?" Corinne asked.

"Well . . . we just got a new Poland Spring water cooler. We're trying to do positive things for our marriage," Russell said. Then he suddenly let out a loud burp. For a minute I thought I was sitting next to the water cooler.

"Russell!" I said, as if I were saying "Duncan!" But Duncan at sixteen months would have known it was funny or different to let out a burp like that in couples therapy. Russell just sat there with absolutely no idea what he had done wrong.

*The Seven Year Bitch*

"What?" he said.

"You just burped. God!" I said. At least, I thought, the giant jug head of the water dispenser was filled with water. Russell's was just filled with air.

"Who cares?" Russell said.

"I do," I said. "And he doesn't even have the awareness that he's done it," I implored Corinne.

"You do seem a little out of it, Russell," Corinne said.

"A little!" I said. I started to shake with tears as Russell leaned all the way over from his side of the couch and pulled tissues from the box for me. "Jesus, I'm sorry I burped," Russell said.

We spent the rest of the session arguing about how Russell forced me to become his mother.

I started to fantasize about Russell's shivah again. I would say to his mother what she said to me when I'd had my miscarriage: *"Oh weh-ell."*

*"I can't believe he's gone."*

*"Oh weh-ell."*

*"It's not natural for a mother to have to bury her son."*

*"It's not natural for a mother not to pay for the food and drinks. Why don't you just get out of my house. No one wants you here."*

"I want a divorce," I said. I hadn't planned to say it, but thinking of Russell's mother made me do it.

"Okay," Corinne said. "Russell?"

"What?" Russell said like a fool. "I know she wants a divorce because her friend Joy got a divorce. But I'm not giving her a divorce. She can't have one."

"He's right," I said. "We can't afford one."

"Why do you think you want to get a divorce?"

*Jennifer Belle*

I was crying too hard to speak. I had been angry at Russell since the baby was born. Since the pregnancy, when he'd spent the whole nine months making sure everyone knew he wasn't the one who wanted it. One man at Lamaze talked about how he had built a totem pole for his son's room while Russell just talked about how he had never wanted children. "That man is building a totem pole for his baby's room," I had told Russell. "What a putz," was all Russell had to say in return.

"What does your son think about all this?" Corinne asked.

"What do you mean?" I asked.

"What does he have to say about all this fighting?"

"Nothing!" I said. "He's only sixteen months old."

"Oh, so he doesn't talk about it?" She genuinely didn't know the answer to this.

"He doesn't talk yet," I said.

"Yes he does," Russell argued.

"He says 'cup,'" I said. "But he pronounces it 'bup.' And he says 'up' for up or down."

"He says 'butterfly' and 'penis,'" Russell said.

"He says Mama."

"And Dada," Russell interrupted.

"He says 'fuck,'" I said angrily.

"So there seems to be a little competition going on here about who knows more about what your son says."

"He says 'woof-woof' and 'Empire State Building,'" Russell said, ignoring what Corinne had just said.

He says "apple-apple" for pineapple, I thought, but didn't say it out loud.

"Well, Izzy, I think you have to start making a list of reasons

*The Seven Year Bitch*

why you want a divorce from Russell. Since you say you can't get a divorce, we have to find ways to make your situation more livable." What was it with these shrinks and their lists? I thought. "Because it seems the only thing you're *not* arguing about these days is the fact that you can't get a divorce. Unfortunately, we're going to have to stop now."

I sat on the couch feeling a lot worse than I had forty-five minutes before. And because Russell had wasted all our time blathering and dovetailing and burping, the session had been useless.

I wiped my eyes and threw the tissues in the antique red fire bucket Corinne had for a wastepaper basket.

"What exactly are we supposed to achieve here?" I asked, too harshly.

"Well, we'll talk about that at our next session."

"I like your kilim," I managed, putting my boots back on.

"Which one? Oh yes, I found that one on Franklin Street. I go out walking early every morning, and I find great things on the street."

New York, I thought, was divided into people who found great things on the street and people who never did. In the past, whenever I found anything on the street and brought it home there was always gum on it or it reeked of dog piss and out it would go to the garbage room. I suddenly felt like going home and putting my clothes in the laundry hamper and taking a shower.

"Where are you two going now? I often suggest that couples go out to lunch together after leaving here, sit and talk for a little while."

"We're going to a shivah," I said. It seemed fitting that while other couples clinked glasses at the nearby Odeon or Walker's or Bubby's, we had a shivah to go to.

When we got to the shivah I started to cry. There was my friend Michelle looking blown apart as if she were made of the same dirt that was covering her husband. It felt wrong taking the elevator up to their loft because I knew they had just put in the elevator at huge expense to accommodate her husband's wheelchair. It felt wrong putting my coat on his electric keyboard and using the new handicap bathroom with the hospital shower. Pushed against their austere wooden bed, which I had always found particularly romantic for some reason, was a metal hospital one. Everywhere you looked there was equipment.

I had imagined Russell's shivah a thousand times but never quite like this. It was so strange that Michelle would never see what her husband would look like old. She never even got to see him have gray hair. When you married someone you expected to get to see them with gray hair.

I was the one there with a husband, yet I was jealous of Michelle's grief, like a woman in Chanel couture jealous of another woman's rags. Each tear seemed like something I would never have, like Harry Winston diamonds. I wanted to feel grief because I wanted to be sure I had felt love.

I watched married couples linking arms. But suddenly the act of walking over to my husband and putting my hand in his seemed impossible. I could no sooner touch Russell than I could walk over and touch one of the other men there. He wasn't mine in the same way he had once been. For just a moment, I longed to cling to him, but I couldn't bring myself to do it. There was no way I could make this marriage work. I rushed back to that bed and sat on the edge of it crying for myself and for Duncan and for the second child I would never have. Then I went back out to the living room, crowded with mourners, to tell Russell we were really through.

"What else do we agree on beside Poland Spring?" I asked instead as he ate a corned beef sandwich from a tray catered by Zabar's like a wild pig.

"Duncan," he said. "We both love Duncan."

That isn't enough, I thought.

"I love you," he said.

"How can you say that after that therapy session?" I said. "You never do anything with Duncan. Most families sit down to a family dinner. You eat at your desk every night. Or you take writers to dinner."

I watched a good-looking man across the room lovingly take the hand of his slightly pug-faced wife and stroke her wedding ring. Tears filled my eyes again.

"I do things," he said.

"What do you do?" I asked. "You don't know how to open the stroller. You took him to swimming once and lost his bathing suit and yours."

"I change him," Russell said. "I change his diaper every day."

"So you change him," I said.

"I like to change him. I know you're not going to believe me, but I love to be the one to change his diaper. I love the smell of his poop," he said.

"Really?" I said, astonished. I had never told him I felt the same way. "I love it too," I said. "I want to dab it on my pulse points."

*Jennifer Belle*

132

"I wish you would," he said.

Maybe that small thing was enough to hold us together, I thought.

"So there," Russell said, like Humphrey Bogart. "We'll always have poop." And the moment was ruined.

# 14

The next day Russell went on a business trip to a book fair in Jamaica, and I did an incredible thing—I rented my own locker at the gym. For $180 I had my own apartment in Manhattan, even if it was only one square foot. Virginia Woolf had never been more right! Number 205 belonged only to me.

I just slammed my credit card down and said, "I'll take it, but I have to be able to reach it. If I can't reach it, I don't want it, the deal's off."

The man behind the desk said I had my choice of anything without a lock on it and I scoured the locker room until I found it, number 205, just above eye level and mine for the taking. I had a sixth sense for real estate. It might not have been a garret in Paris with skylights and a bidet, but at that moment it felt like one. It might not have been a Hamptons beach house, but it was to me. I slapped my lock on it.

I called Joy in LA.

"You wouldn't have had to leave Harry if you'd gotten a locker," I said.

"A locker?" she said. "You mean like at the gym."

"That's right!" I said. "I just rented my own locker. I'm telling you, you should have had a locker."

"Oh, I had a locker. Are you kidding me? I had three lockers, the big kind, at three different gyms, *and* a storage space, and *then* that little guesthouse I rented on North Bronson and then the office in New York and the factory in LA and it wasn't enough. What do you have in it?"

"Nothing yet!" I said. One thing I wasn't going to put in it was diapers, I thought. No plastic farm animals or sippy cups or wipes. I was happy to have those things in my bed and my handbags and my coat pockets but not in my locker. "I'm just going to enjoy it empty for a little while. Just luxuriate in having the space."

"Believe me, once you put your track shoes in there and a mini deodorant you'll see it doesn't solve anything."

But it would. That padlock protected a whole other world. Even the combination was auspicious—19-21-23—which happened to be when I was at my most beautiful.

"I better go," I said. "People are staring at me."

"Where are you?"

"The locker room," I said.

When I got home I read to Duncan and put him to bed.

"Daddy will be home tomorrow," I told him.

Things were so much easier without Russell there to fight with. I didn't have to argue with him about who would do what, who would put him to bed, who would go to him in the night, I'd just do it all happily without thinking too much about it. I brought Duncan warm milk in a sippy cup, and I read him a book called *365 Penguins*, about a family whose uncle, in an effort to save the penguins, sends the family one penguin a day for 365 days. Duncan was asleep by the second penguin, but I finished reading the whole book, fascinated by the idea of these penguins arriving and wreaking their havoc. Those penguins represented the problems in marriage, I realized. Every day a problem arrived at the door, a stinking, slippery, black-and-white fish-eating bird. I really loved that book. How long had it been, I thought to myself, since I'd taken the time to just sit down and read a great book? Even if it was just a picture book for kids.

Our neighbor's daughter came over so I could walk Humbert, and we walked along Hudson Street, past Chanterelle, where Russell and I had our wedding reception. It was beautiful out and Humbert was so happy peeing on everything I kept going all the way to Broad Street and my old office building. I had gone to that building every day and now I would never go into it again. How had I left Duncan's huge open-mouthed kisses each morning and walked right through the open doors of what now seemed like the most unimportant place in the world? What the hell had I been thinking?

I'd done well and it had gotten me nowhere. My first job was covering the package/container industry, which basically meant I studied cardboard boxes, and which made finding an empty one on my desk waiting for me that much more ironic.

Later, after Humbert and I had walked happily back to Hubert

Street and I was enjoying lying alone in bed, Russell called from Jamaica. "How was your day?"

"Bad," I said.

"Anything happen?"

I smiled, imagining putting my sneakers in my new locker, how they'd just fit, happy as rats. No, not rats, I thought, rats held captive in a locker would eat each other. "It's just really hard doing everything myself while you're having a great time in Jamaica."

"Well, you have to get used to that if we're going to get a divorce."

Actually since he was away everything was so calm and easy. When Duncan had called out in his sleep a few moments before, instead of giving Russell dirty looks and wondering which of us should be the one to go to him, I had simply rushed into his room without giving it a thought and comforted him.

"How was it putting Duncan to bed and walking Humbert?"

"It was hard, but I managed."

"I'm sorry," he said.

"Not all of us can have a vacation in Jamaica."

"I'm in Kingston, for Christ's sake, the worst place on earth. You make it sound like I'm lying on the beach at a Sandals or something."

"Jamaica is Jamaica," I said.

"Did Duncan ask for me?"

"No," I said.

"How's the water cooler?" he asked, trying to change the subject to something happy.

"It's fine."

"Did you have any water?"

"Not really," I said.

"You should have some," he said.

When we got off the phone I had the same thought I always had when he went away. I had no idea what his flight number was or what airport he'd be flying in to. If I saw on the news that a New York–bound plane from Jamaica had crashed, I wouldn't know if it was his or not. I would have to wait to hear from him. Or not.

I turned off the light and looked at the shadows the window guards cast around the room. Black bars slid along the ceiling and all four walls, like a cage. The morning we'd had the bars put up, I'd felt proud. "Put them all the way up," I'd told the man. We had enormous windows that opened like doors and I wanted the baby to be completely safe. The man soldered metal to metal, and the dangerous burning construction smell filled the rooms. We'd bought the loft before Duncan, and now, somehow, as if by Grimm's magic, it had rumbled and swelled to hold a child. I felt like the apartment was smiling and the window guards were braces in its gaping happy mouth. The day the window guards went up, I thought they were the most beautiful things I had ever seen. Then night fell, and the shadows were cast, and Russell and I had stood looking at each other in the center of what was now a cage, wondering what we had gone and done.

# 15

In the morning the doorman buzzed up that I had a messenger. "It's probably for Russell," I said. "Just hold it at the desk."

"No, Izzy, it's for you," Terry said.

"Okay," I said.

I waited at the door in my nightgown after making sure my breasts weren't hanging out as usual. When I was nursing I was constantly accepting deliveries topless without realizing it. Every neighborhood delivery man had seen me at least once.

A UPS man wheeled a carton toward me.

"You gonna be here for a few minutes? 'Cause I've gotta get the rest of the boxes out of the truck."

He hoisted the box into the entryway of my apartment. I examined the label: *Claire Contest Co. Box 1 of 12.* Twelve boxes would block the entryway! Russell already had so many stacked in front of the bookshelves there was no room for even one more box. I slit the packing tape with a kitchen knife and found the box to be filled with nothing but essays, thousands of pages of tiny essays, each taking up only a small portion of each page. When I'd called the name my mother's shrink had given me, they'd told me I would make a quarter for every essay I read, and it had sounded like nothing. I'd agreed to do it and signed something they'd faxed to me agreeing to be impartial and providing my Social Security number but I'd had no idea it would amount to anything.

Floating on top of the essays was an instruction sheet.

**Informilk Baby Formula:** In 100 Words or Less Give Us Your Best Job Description for Being a Mom.

**Grand Prize:** $25,000.

**First Prize:** $500 and a case of Informilk.

**(10) Second Prizes:** $250 (awarded as a check) and a case of Informilk.

**(50) Third Prizes:** one case of Informilk.

**Coupon offers:** A one-dollar ($1.00) downloadable coupon redeemable toward the purchase of any Ree Corporation product will be awarded to the first 50,000 completed entries received.

**JUDGING:** All entries will be preliminarily judged by Claire Contests, Inc., an independent judging organization whose decisions are final, to determine the top seventy (70) entries. The seventy (70) entries will then be judged by a panel of experts from Ling Products Division of Lee Corporation, under Claire Contest, Inc.'s supervision, to determine the winners. All judging will be based on the following criteria: (1) originality & creativity of essay—50%; (2) appropriateness of essay to theme—35%; (3) sincerity of essay—15%. In the event of a tie, the tied entries will be rejudged based on the criteria listed above.

I scanned the rest of the rules and lifted the first essay out of the box.

**Jeanne Mae Johnson**
**Mechanicsburg, PA**
*I wake up at five and heat a bottle of Informilk Plus Iron and feed and change the little one. I get the big one dressed and get him to the bus for school. I feed the dog. Then I do the dishes and strip/make beds, do grocery shopping, put away groceries and laundry, iron my husband's shirts. I dust and vacume and empty the dishwasher. I sort and put away toys, wash kitchen and bathroom floors, and Windex bathroom mirrors. I start dinner, meet the big one at the bus, give him a snack. Then I scrub the toilet.*

There, I thought, twenty-five whole cents earned. That was twenty-five cents more than I'd had three seconds ago. I paid

Shasthi twelve dollars an hour, which was forty-eight quarters. I just had to read forty-eight of these essays to cover a whole hour of her pay and eight times that to cover a whole day. My mother's shrink was right once again. While I stared down at the essay, the UPS man carried in eleven more boxes. When Russell returned from Jamaica he would think I was moving out.

This was great! At work we'd always joked about how nice it would be to have a job that was shoes optional and now I had one.

I lifted the second essay out of the first box.

Darla Jackson
Marietta, GA
*Master chef,*
*One woman cleaning staff and ATM*
*Machine*

Since originality and creativity accounted for fifty percent of the score, I started a "maybe" pile because I had to hand it to her for the acrostic form. Unfortunately, of the next seventy essays I read, at least two dozen of them used the equally creative and original acrostic form.

Sue Gustavo
Elizabeth, NJ
*As a mother of three boys, my job is to teach them*
*about birth control and work hard to keep the bath-*
*rooms clean.*

Paula Lawe
Buchannan, NY

*Help Wanted: Full-time mom. Must cook three meals a day, do laundry, dishes, grocery shopping, vacuuming, make beds, and scrub stinky toilets. Must have experience as a chauffeur, psychologist, CEO, accountant, stylist, hairdresser, doctor, soccer coach, milking cow and slave.*
*Hours: 24/7.*
*Vacation days, sick days, personal days: none.*
*Salary: hah hah you thought there was a salary?*

I used that to start a "yes" pile because she was trying to be funny, and so many of them had been so bad I didn't know if in all these boxes another one might be this good. I was supposed to give the company my top choices, ranked one through seventy.

Mary Pestorini
Amelia Island, FL

*My best job description as a mom is to be in a good marriage with my husband. Go to the gym every day to keep myself skinny and attractive, and make time for dates for dinner/dancing/movies and alone time in the bedroom. Also take regular resort vacations without the kids so I can remember why I wanted to be a mother in the first place.*

This person sounded completely out of her mind.

**Karen Ravenhurst**
**Rhonert Park, CA**
*I don't need 100 words to write my job description as a mom. I'm breast-feeding my beautiful daughter Calen, so I just need one word: COW.*

I loved this one, but the contest was for a formula company.

**Erin Henry**
**Portland, ME**
*I hate going to the playground, but I do it every day and I always put a big smile on my face when my daughter looks over at me. I want her to have high self-esteem and know that she is loved.*

"No" pile.

**Julie Longstreet**
**Topeka, KS**
*Job available! Get covered in every bodily fluid imaginable, never wear a shirt that doesn't have spit-up on it, have your body permanently ruined by a c-section, never get a single night's sleep, watch your husband cheat on you. Your Reward: a teenager!*

Yes.

**Colleen Coburn**
**Middle Village, NY**

*Breastfeed the baby, cry, breastfeed the baby, cry,*
*breastfeed the baby, cry, breastfeed the baby, cry,*
*breastfeed the baby, cry, breastfeed the baby, cry,*
*breastfeed the baby, cry, breastfeed the baby, cry,*
*breastfeed the baby, laugh, pump.*

I loved this one too, and I thought in a way it could be used as an advertisement for giving formula, but I put it with the noes.

**Barbara Knee**
**Flint, MI**
*One hundred words is not enough to describe what I*
*do as a mother of a child with autism. Imagine cooking*
*and cleaning and working and holding my child when*
*he has his fits and getting nothing but dirty looks from*
*the whole world.*

I put this one in "maybe" in case there weren't any more like it. But in the next hundred I read, there were at least fifty like it. Autism, cancer, leukemia, GERD, allergies, Down's, wheelchairs and nebulizers and hospitals. And all these mothers—cleaning, cleaning, cleaning. I had never once associated scrubbing the toilet with having a son. I couldn't stop reading them. All these women who thought of themselves as a "mom" and knew what that meant. I studied each name and hometown for clues, the way I had stared at the missing posters after 9/11.

**Mia Lamm**
**State College, PA**

*The Seven Year Bitch*

*Go to the hospital every day and hold his hand while
he has chemo, play his favorite card games with him,
bring his favorite foods when he can eat, enjoy every
second that I have with him because I have never met
anyone braver, wiser, or more beautiful. Job description? I don't need 100 words, I just need one: gratitude.*

I put this in the "maybe" pile even though I preferred the
one whose one word was *cow*. I forced myself to get up and walk
around the apartment.

"The boxes are filled with essays," I told Shasthi. "I'm judging
a contest." She had come in a little while before and was kneel-
ing, bent over the tub, her knees resting on a folded towel, and
swabbing the baby with a washcloth. He loved the bath and he
looked up at me with his hair all slicked back. I felt terrible that I
wasn't the one giving him the bath, but I was also relieved. It was
hard bending over like that and slightly terrifying.

Of course I would never step away from the tub while he was
in it, but what if some unknown psychosis overtook me and I
did? For just a moment. And returned to find him drowned.

"You are going to read all that?" she said.

*Russell came home from* Jamaica a hero because he brought
Duncan a rubber ducky with dreadlocks painted on it to look
like a Rastafarian and a clam shell with a marijuana leaf painted
on it. He didn't kiss me hello.

"Don't forget we have Corinne today," I said.

"Shit," Russell said.

*Jennifer Belle*

I waited for Russell outside Corinne's office for twenty minutes and then, thinking that he might already be up there and that he had not even had the courtesy to wait for me, I buzzed and walked up the stairs. I took off my shoes and sat on my end of the couch. Russell's side was empty.

"Do you want to get started without him?" Corinne asked.

"Are we allowed to do that?"

"We can fill him in when he gets here."

She was wearing a hunter-green sweatshirt, her cat curled on her lap, and her neatly made bed in the sleeping loft behind her.

"I'm the judge of an essay contest for Informilk baby formula," I said. "I'm reading essays from women all over the country about what it means to be a mom."

"Last week you were thinking about what it means to be a man. Now it's what it means to be a mom. It seems you're dealing with a lot of labels."

What did it mean to be a shrink? I wondered. It certainly didn't mean getting dressed and leaving your apartment.

"And what does it mean to be a mom?" she asked.

"Most of the essays are about scrubbing the toilet," I said.

"Is that what it means to you?"

I started to cry. "It means not ruining your son's life by getting a divorce."

"And is that what you would be doing?" she asked, handing me a box of tissues that I hoped she hadn't found on the street. "Ruining Daniel's life?"

"Duncan," I said.

"Sorry, Duncan," she said.

"I just can't stand it anymore," I said. "He's so defensive. If

I say, 'Pass the salt,' he says, 'I, I, I, I, I, I didn't take the salt, I didn't touch the salt. I, I, I don't know anything about the salt.' He was so ridiculous here last week. I couldn't even understand what he was saying and then he started burping."

"He did seem quite flexible," Corinne said.

"Flexible?" I asked.

"Yes, he seemed much more flexible than other men."

"What do you mean?" I asked, feeling hopeful that Russell was flexible and might be able to change.

"The way he was able to sit Indian-style with his knees flush against the couch." She did an awkward, ugly imitation of him, and I suddenly thought I was going to throw up. She made it sound like I was married to some kind of circus sideshow freak, a grotesque contortionist, a rubber man, a rubber band.

"Is there anything about Russell that you like?" she asked.

"I don't know." I wept into the tissues. This was terrible. My marriage was terrible. And I wasn't sure how it had gotten this way.

"When I was in my first year of business school, I did a bad thing," I said, not sure why I was bringing this up now. "It was a public policy class, and I had to write about class-action lawsuits—there was a certain statute a whole section of my class had to write on. I was up late in the law library and I had the statute in my carrel on my desk, and I somehow packed it into my book bag with the rest of my books. I didn't realize I had it until a couple of days later when the professor made a very angry announcement that it had been stolen from the library and whoever had it better bring it back. I was scared. I didn't want to be seen as cheating or getting some kind of unfair advantage, so I tied it in a garbage bag and threw it into the back of a garbage truck. It's the stupidest thing. I really don't know why I did that."

"You felt stuck," Corinne said.

"I had made a stupid mistake."

"Was marrying Russell a stupid mistake?" Corinne said.

"I guess it was," I said.

"And would you like to tie him in a garbage bag and throw him in the back of a garbage truck?"

I didn't say anything. I just cried, feeling sorry for myself that a conversation like this one was what my marriage had come to.

"You know this is going to take a lot of time," she said. "He might never change. He might always come in here and burp and splay his legs all around."

I just sat there continuing to weep. As much as I hated this, I thought, couples therapy was much more helpful without Russell.

"Well, our time is up," she said. "I'll see you next week."


*For the next few* days I noticed a lot of couples giving each other the finger. Men giving women the finger. Women giving men the finger right back. Spring was in the air, and couples were out, sitting on benches in the tiny little area of Washington Square Park that wasn't being blasted. If you wanted romance in New York anymore, if you wanted Washington Square Park and the Twin Towers and couples saying nice, romantic things about each other, you had to watch *When Harry Met Sally*, because that's the only place they were. My movie started with couples giving each other the finger—white, black, Asian, Muslim, Hispanic, young, old, fat, thin—everywhere you looked, a lot of fingers.

I sat in the café and listened to Said talk about his mistress. I watched his wife slumped over her Irish coffee. She wasn't a wife, I thought. She wasn't in a marriage. How strange that she could think she was a wife, and I, a virtual stranger, could know that she wasn't.

Joy called and I told her I was going to couples therapy with Russell.

"Don't bother," she said. "You should do what I'm doing."

"And what is that?" I asked.

"You should come here with me to Kenya."

"What!" I said.

"It's true. I'm in Kenya. I'm buying a farm. I met a man. This is it, Izzy. I have finally met a good man. I'm going to live here half the year and I'm going to bring him back with me to LA for the other half. Today I bought a sheep because it looked like Chanel. I thought it was a goat, but when I got it home to the shamba they said it was a sheep."

"Home to the shamba?" I said. "How are the boys?" I asked, my voice quavering a little.

"They're here. I got PlayStation. They love the goat. Sheep."

"So tell me about him," I said. "The man."

"His name is Chilemba. He's twenty-two. He has a wife, of course they all do here, but he's going to divorce her. You have no idea what fucking can be like," she said. "We're going to Egypt and Mombasa."

"Just be careful," I said, thinking there was no way she was being careful.

*The next week Shasthi* called and said she couldn't come in to work that day because her cousin had died in Guyana. The family was gathering at the airport to see off the relatives who were able to leave the country and go to the funeral. Russell and I had our appointment with Corinne and nobody to leave Duncan with.

"That's fine," Russell said, "because I can't go anyway. I have a meeting."

All morning I intended to call and cancel but at two o'clock I found myself walking toward her loft with Duncan in his Buga-boo. I convinced the men in the pizza parlor next door to let me leave the stroller there, and walked up Corinne's steps holding the heavy baby in my arms. Even carrying Duncan, I walked up stairs straighter than Russell.

"So this is what a baby looks like," Corinne said. "I don't think there's ever been a baby in this apartment. I don't think the cat likes it too much," she said. "He's never seen one."

I put Duncan on the floor and for several minutes we watched the cat's alien eyes follow the baby's every move.

"How are things this week with Russell?" Corinne asked.

"Russell," Duncan said. "Dada!"

"I look at other people's husbands and I wonder why I made the choice I made. He says 'I love you' all the time. 'I love you. I love you. I love you.' But he doesn't notice that I don't say it back."

"I love you," Duncan said.

"I love *you*," I said and kissed him.

"And do you love Russell?"

I didn't say anything.

*The Seven Year Bitch*

"Were there other men you could have married?" Corinne asked.

"No," I said, thinking of Gabe Weinrib waiting for me at the airport.

I put Duncan next to me on the couch and had what I decided was my last session with Corinne. I couldn't keep coming week after week and complaining about Russell. There was nothing she could do for me. I had to figure this one out by myself.

"How was couples therapy?" Russell asked when Duncan and I got home.

"It was good," I said. "Duncan and I worked out all our problems."

Russell bent down to kiss Duncan. "Did you like going to therapy?" he asked in baby talk.

"Yes," Duncan said, nodding and giving us his shy smile.

# 16

Since I paid good money for you and didn't make use of your financial services, I think you should do me this one favor," Gabe said.

I smiled. He had called.

"What favor is that?" I asked.

"Come with me to get my hair cut," he said. "I have an appointment tomorrow at four and I need your help. You can bring Duncan."

"I have a sitter at that time," I said.

"Then bring her too," he said.

"I really can't," I said. "I'm married, Gabe. I can't go all over town watching you get your hair cut." I'd never even gone with my own husband to get a haircut.

"I'll be at a place called Tomoko on East Thirteenth Street tomorrow at four. Please, please, please come."

The next day, walking along Thirteenth Street, I thought

about a movie I had seen as a kid. It was called *The Adventures of the Wilderness Family*, and it was about a mother and father and sister and brother who leave the big city and move to the middle of the wilderness. As a child I had never seen anything so traumatic. There was no phone or television or games, just this family of four alone amongst grizzly bears in some kind of one-room cabin. Our family went to Cape Cod every summer, which was miserable enough, but this was inconceivable.

I hadn't thought about that movie since I was a kid, but now, walking to see a man who wasn't my husband get his hair cut, I suddenly couldn't get it out of my head. That's what I should be doing, I thought, packing up my family and moving us somewhere like that away from all distractions. Dora the Explorer with her intolerable nasal whine was destroying us. The wilderness would be safe compared to that.

Duncan should see me as a mother, cooking more than his oatmeal every morning, protecting him from a grizzly bear with a broom or something when his father was out hunting for our very survival.

I was so involved with thinking about the Wilderness Family, it was a little shocking walking into the salon and seeing Gabe in a barber's chair, wearing a black robe, his eyes closed, while a beautiful Japanese girl massaged his neck.

Since his eyes were still closed, I could leave, I thought, but another beautiful Japanese woman brought me a cup of green tea and, bowing, indicated that I should sit in the chair next to him.

I watched him in the mirror getting his neck massaged. He

was so great looking, I thought, but vulnerable too. Watching him was somehow not unlike watching Duncan sleeping.

The girl pounded on his back with her palms pressed together. Then he opened his eyes and saw me looking at him in the mirror.

"Rieko, this is my friend Isolde," he said. "She's going to help us here today."

He smiled at me.

"What do you think we should do?" she asked.

"Maybe a little shorter in the back, and some layers," I said.

"Here?" she asked.

When it was over, Rieko helped him off with the black robe. He was wearing just a white undershirt until she took his button-down shirt from a hanger and he slid into it. I watched his fingers working the buttons.

"Well, thank you," he said, after he had paid and we were standing on the grungy street outside of Dolphin Gym. It was like my plane had just landed back in New York.

"Should we have an early dinner or a drink? My treat," he said.

"I've got to go home," I said.

"You know, you could be Japanese," he said. "Your black hair." He reached out and touched the ends. Then he grabbed a handful and tugged on it slightly.

I wanted him to kiss me. I looked away. He was a bear threatening my family, and instead of poking at him with a broom, I was praying for the bear to push me up against a building and kiss me.

Maybe antidepressants would cure this. Or I should start

taking Duncan to synagogue. Then I remembered Shasthi really had to leave at five, because she had an errand to run in Queens and she had to be home in time to watch *American Idol.*

"I have to go," I said. "Your hair looks great. Oh, here's a cab." I jumped into the empty cab and headed back to the big city.

# 17

That weekend, up in the country, we went to an antiques flea market, and, looking at metal lawn chairs, I was sure I saw my ob-gyn, Dr. Lichter, at another table looking at old fountain pens.

He was wearing a Boston Red Sox baseball cap, so I couldn't tell if the man I was looking at had Dr. Lichter's bald spot or not. Instead of a shirt and tie and white doctor's coat, he was wearing big, baggy mom jeans and a plaid shirt. Dr. Lichter hadn't been from Boston, I was almost certain, so maybe it wasn't him. But then I remembered he'd gone to Harvard and men were always so strange about sports.

Russell and the baby were several yards away looking at a painted wooden rocking duck.

"You know," the owner of the booth I was at said, "these are called motel chairs. They're the real deal."

I watched Dr. Lichter reach into his pocket and pull out money to pay for a pen.

"They can also be known as tulip chairs or shell chairs, I guess because the back here is shaped a little like a shell. Or a tulip for that matter."

"Dr. Lichter?" I called, but he didn't hear me.

When I was pregnant with Duncan, I had been in love with Dr. Lichter.

"I ate too much ice cream this week," I would say.

"Ice cream makes healthy babies," he would answer, spending endless time with me while a dozen women waited in the waiting room.

"I don't know if I'm ready to be a mother."

"Let me tell you about the Seven Stages of Motherhood," he had said. "They're exactly the same as the Seven Stages of Grief."

"The Seven Stages of Motherhood?" I flirted over the mountain of my stomach.

"Yes," Dr. Lichter had said. "Stage One: Shock and Denial starts when you bring the baby home from the hospital. You're paying a baby nurse two hundred and fifty dollars a day, you think your life can go on as usual—dinner, movies, work. It lasts from two to four weeks. Stage Two: Pain and Guilt. Change is painful, and there is no bigger change. Your psyche is screaming. You feel guilt until you die, but it is never as intense as months two through six. At six months, your time with the baby starts to get a lot more fun."

My psyche screaming didn't sound too good.

"Stage Three: Anger. This is directed at your husband. He's just not biologically wired to be as good with the baby as you. He can sleep through the night. He is feeling no pain, no guilt, not much change. Okay, where are we? Stage Four: Depression, Reflection, and Loneliness is where you lose touch with who you were before you were a mother. That lasts until the third birthday. Sometime shortly after the third birthday, you will have a sort of graduation. It's like getting out of business school or medical school. Then there's Five, Six, and Seven—the Upward Turn, Reconstruction, and Acceptance—and that's when you have another. Got it?" he said.

"Your psyche is screaming?"

"One day," he said wistfully, "we'll discuss all this over a nice cup of tea—oolong tea perhaps."

He was verbose and professorial and bragged that he'd had a part in inventing one of the fetal tests I was taking. He was short, maybe five foot five, and fat, with a big white bald spot and short, stubby fingers that touched me more gently than I had ever been touched. How I had longed to have that oolong tea with him!

I had fallen in love with him when I'd gone in to hear the baby's heartbeat for the first time. He knew I was nervous as he moved the sonogram wand over my stomach. Then I heard it. He turned up the volume on the machine until it sounded as strong and sure as a herd of elephants. Then, using the sonogram wand as a microphone, he started singing Fleetwood Mac to me:

> Like a heartbeat drives you mad
> In the stillness of remembering . . .

I had laughed and cried with relief.

"I have always wanted to do that," he said, and I opened up to him because I loved when men opened up to me like that.

I had a high-risk pregnancy, with low amniotic fluid, and one day when I was thirty-eight weeks pregnant, I'd gone in for my

*The Seven Year Bitch*

routine twice-weekly nonstress test, and the technician administering it said, "You're not going home. You're going to have the baby right now."

I'd called Dr. Lichter and he'd come in the middle of a luncheon at which he was being given an award.

For nine months I'd imagined him fucking me on the examining table. I'd imagined it every way you could imagine it. And I'd imagined that he'd leave his wife, who was a labor-and-delivery nurse, and I'd leave Russell and we'd buy an apartment together and raise the baby he'd deliver in it.

While Russell waited just outside the operating room door in his scrubs, Dr. Lichter told me that the anesthesiologist was going to be giving me my spinal. I'd rounded my back the way I'd practiced in Pilates, and then I screamed bloody murder. "Motherfucker!" I screamed. "Motherfucker!" I had never felt pain like that.

"Something is wrong," the anesthesiologist said. "She has a difficult back."

A machine sounded and a nurse said, "Doctor, it's dropping," and then Dr. Lichter took me in his arms. Right there on the table he held me and he said, "Izzy, look right into my eyes. It's me. Just look at me, look at me." He wrapped his arms around me and pressed his forehead into my forehead, and with his bald spot hidden under his surgical cap and his mouth and nose covered by his mask, all I could do was look into his blue eyes. We stayed like that for a long time, and finally I felt no pain, just his forehead pressed into mine and his arms around me, until he lay me down on the table and a nurse brought Russell in. Just a few minutes later I heard a cry, and he said, "Well, I've never had this happen. He's crying while he's still inside you. We haven't taken him out yet." Then he said, "Now. Look at your son," and he held my baby up over the paper curtain.

When I went for my six-week appointment to check my stitches, I was told that he'd left the hospital and was no longer practicing medicine. "I don't know for sure," a nurse had told me, "but I heard a family member died and he had a nervous breakdown."

And there, here, he was, in upstate New York.

"Dr. Lichter?" I called out again, but he still didn't seem to hear me. People around me had stopped what they were doing to look over at me. "Dr. Lichter?" He looked around nervously for a moment, lowered his baseball cap down over his eyes, and started walking quickly to the parking lot.

I walked as fast as I could after him, but I was holding Hum on his leash and I got tangled a couple of times and by the time I got to his car he had driven away. He disappeared into the upstate air like a bird I had been watching.

# 18

"What did you do today?" Russell asked the following week when we were in the car on our way to the country. Now that it was spring we were going up more and more.

"I had acupuncture," I told him, even though I had taken Shasthi to have it and had waited for her in the waiting room while Duncan napped in his Bugaboo and I read essays. The waiting room had been filled with women all hoping to get pregnant and I read essay after essay about scrubbing toilets by women who were barely holding it together.

My mind was swimming a little bit. I had that half-there feeling, like a part of me was somewhere else, that feeling when you're in the middle of a good book you want to get back to. And then I realized what it was—the essays. I was dying to get back to them.

I took a stack of them out of the tote bag at my feet and a tiny flashlight I had bought, at my mother's shrink's suggestion, for reading in the car.

**Jessica Horowitz**
**Charleston, SC**

*My husband is in Iraq and has never met our daughter. My mother in law helps but when I lie in bed at night and listen to her cry I sometimes don't think I can handle my new "job". I don't have much money to buy an excersaucer or a swing so I end up holding her most of the time. Feed, change, dress, hold, go grocery shopping, send pictures to her daddy, and pray that we don't get that knock on the door.*

**Hope Greenspan**
**Jasper, WY**

*I tried everything to have a baby. Acupuncture, the Atkins Diet, three rounds of artificial insemination, four rounds of invitro fertilization, and three adoptions that fell through because the birth mothers changed their minds. I have also had nine miscarriages. Then a woman who is my hero allowed me to adopt my beautiful son. Her name is Jamie so I named him James. My job as a mom is to make James know how much I love him and how much Jamie did too to give him to me. It's definitely the best job I've ever had.*

**Bethany Ames**
**Spokane, WA**

*Unfortunately I have to work as a secretary for an accountant so I bring my daughter to her daycare at eight so I can be at my desk by nine. Then I pick her up*

*at seven and give her a bath and her bottle, and play*
*with her in the living room. I have post partum depres-*
*sion so I cry but she doesn't know it. She is a very good*
*baby so my job is easy.*

It was hard to read them in the car with Hum on my lap.

"How was Shasthi today?" Russell asked.

"I really think Heiffowitz can get her pregnant," I said.

"Maybe so, but I'm telling you we shouldn't get involved. I think I should have a vasectomy," Russell said. "I'm really thinking about it."

"We might have another baby," I informed him as if I were telling him to expect a delivery from Fresh Direct. According to Dr. Lichter's Seven Stages of Motherhood, I was almost two-thirds to acceptance.

"Well, definitely after the next one," he said. The way he talked about his vasectomy was the way I had talked, as a young teenager, about losing my virginity and getting my ears pierced, like it was a rite of passage he would undergo that all men before him had undergone. Like his Bar Mitzvah. The way he said it, he was like a soldier going off to war, but in this case it was the war of marriage. The war of sex. And in that way, as negative a statement as it was about fatherhood, it was a romantic one too about marriage. A vasectomy implied having sex with abandon. Lots of it, anytime, anywhere. But even more than that, it meant to me security for Duncan that he was enough, and even after we divorced and Russell married a much younger woman, he would not have children with her. It was a kind of vow of fidelity stronger than the bonds of marriage or the cut of divorce. Still, there had been the fatty-liver incident, so I didn't think he would ever do it.

"I want to help Shasthi get pregnant," I said.

"You have to stop with this," he said. "You're always trying to help everyone. You're not a social worker."

"I don't help anyone," I said. "I just don't think it's fair that we have so much and she has so little."

"She doesn't have so little," he said. "Between Shasthi and these inane essays you're really losing your mind."

"They're not inane."

"Yes, they are, I've read some of them. We can't afford to help her. And it's not our job to help her. And she might not even want our help. Maybe she doesn't even want a baby. Maybe she thinks she does, but deep down she's relieved she doesn't. Maybe she likes her life the way it is. This is really a lose-lose. If you get her started with this and she doesn't get pregnant, she'll be miserable. And if she does get pregnant, she won't make a very good nanny, now will she? You're going to find yourself helping your way right out of a nanny. If she really wanted one she would adopt."

"She can't adopt. She's not here legally. She'd have to go back to her country to adopt."

"Well there you go. If she really wanted a baby she would move back to Guyana and adopt. Believe it or not, not having a child is not the worst thing that could happen to someone."

"Yes, it is," I said, finally sure of something in this argument. "For a woman who wants one, it is the very worst thing that could happen."

We pulled up at our house and unloaded everything, and

*The Seven Year Bitch*

then Charlie and Gra came over with an enormous container of noodles too spicy to eat. In just a few short weeks, Charlie had gotten Gra a Shih Tzu named Curry Puff and had also gotten her pregnant.

"You're pregnant?" I said. The last time we'd seen her she hadn't been able to speak one word of English. Now she told us perfectly clearly that she had gotten Charlie to agree to bring her mother over to live with them and be the nanny.

"I can't believe how much English you've learned," I said. I remembered that my mother's shrink always said I said "I can't believe" too much.

Duncan was toddling after a butterfly, which always made the money we spent on the country house worth it.

We watched Duncan walk up the steps onto the deck, take a drink of milk from a glass, and wave to us. It didn't seem like something a baby would do. "I'm be-carefulling," he said. I said the words "be careful" so much, he had turned it into a verb.

"I'm be-carefulling," Gra repeated, memorizing a new vocabulary word.

# 19

Finally the day for Shasthi's appointment with Dr. Heiffow-itz came. As we drove in the cab up the FDR Drive, with Duncan on my lap, she looked out the window at the East River and the red and white–striped smokestacks of Queens, and I looked out at the apartment buildings that overlooked the river, marveling at their balconies and chandeliers.

"How's Rachel?" I asked about the woman I shared her with.

"Oh, I am no longer working there for the longest time."

"Oh?" I couldn't believe she hadn't bothered to tell me this. I had been thinking about asking her to work full-time, and now there would be no problem with it at all. "Why? What happened?"

"When you increased my hours, I asked if I could do all my cleaning in one day instead of coming there two days and she said no, so I just gave her back her keys and I left."

"But you've been with them for years and years!" I said, completely shocked by her indifference. I could almost feel the pain Rachel must have felt when she walked out the door.

"Well, that is the job," she said.

I wanted to ask her if that's how it would be when she left us. If she would ever think of me again, or Duncan. If she would miss seeing his beautiful cheeks and lips and feeling his arms wrapped around her neck. It was almost unimaginable, and yet in a strange way, it might even be a relief if she left and I had to take care of Duncan by myself.

"Look how high that building is," she said, pointing out her window. "You know when I first came to you, I used to go right into the bathroom and throw up from the elevator ride. I'm so scared of elevators." I thought of her going straight to the bathroom each time she'd arrived and flushing the toilet twice. "But now I am more used to it."

The cab drove around the hospital's large circular driveway.

She checked in with Scottie at the front desk and we took seats in the massive waiting room.

Shasthi was resplendent in a long peach skirt strung with sequins, a pale purple peasant blouse, and beaded pointy Moroccan slippers. She always looked rested and sparkling.

I looked at every woman in the waiting room, considering her chances. I hoped each and every one of them was infertile, as if that would somehow improve Shasthi's odds. Two were speaking a foreign language to each other from one of those icy blond countries. The doctor's patients traveled to him from all over the world; there was a block of rooms permanently reserved at the Helmsley.

I felt bad that I had brought Duncan. No one wanted to see a beautiful baby when she was sitting in a place like that. My heart pounded. In just a few minutes I would see Dr. Heiffowitz again.

"Are you nervous?" I asked Shasthi.

"Yes, I am nervous."

Her name was called and we stood up.

Russell was sure what I was doing was wrong. He had basically forbidden it, as if we were in some kind of *I Love Lucy* episode and it was all up to him.

"I'm sorry, the doctor will only see the patient alone," Scottie said.

"Right, of course," I said, laughing at myself.

I remembered our interview, her three questions written on the Post-it in her pocket. I was sure she could take care of herself in there.

"Call me when it's over," I said.

"Follow me," Scottie said.

"Izzy . . ."

"Don't be nervous," I said.

"I want to thank you. Nobody ever talked about this with me before you."

I watched her walk through the doors to the other side, to the capable brilliant hands and mind of Dr. Heiffowitz.

When Scottie returned I approached her desk. "I'm going to pay for my . . . friend," I said.

It was $1,100 for the first visit and series of blood work.

"I'm actually going to pay cash," I said, feeling like Lucille Ball again. If my own Ricky Ricardo found out how much this cost I'd have a lot of splaining to do.

When I got home I was relieved to see a dozen boxes in the hall outside my door. I had finished judging the Informilk contest—pouring over my "yes" folder and reading the essays over and over again until I'd picked my winner—and I hadn't known what to do with myself for the last few days, although I had scrubbed the hell out of my toilet. I was thrilled to get started with this new one.

I put Duncan into the Excersaucer and I dove into the first box. I lifted out the instruction sheet.

**YOURS Cigarettes:** In 100 Words or Less Tell Us Why YOU and YOURS Deserve to be Daring in Diamonds.

**Grand Prize:** .5-karat diamond necklace.

**First Prize:** $500 and a case of YOURS CIGARETTES.

**Leeann Daly**
**Schenectady, NY**
*Me and Mine's deserve to be daring in diamonds because my mother and my grandfather both died of lung cancer from smoking Yours but I am still your most loyal customer and I only smoke Yours even if I have to drive all the way to the Stewarts and that costs more money in gas. Also my birth stone is diamonds and so is my twins (but they are both boys unfortunately for me).*

**Velma Mason**
**Scranton, OH**
*I deserve this because I am the most daring one I wear fierce animal print pants and my boots are h.o.t. and every man look at me irregardless of any 5 carate*

*dimonds and my life been hard. Not able to graduate
from college. I had a baby girl when I was seventeen. I
should of named her "Dimond" but I named her "Vanessa" because all the girls in my family are V's. Vanessa
would like to see her very tired mother be daring in
diamonds. And so would the women in my church. TO.
BE. SURE.*

The next three essays were from women who also hadn't
noticed the decimal point before the five.

**Sarah Washington**
**Youngstown, OH**
*I have diamond stud earrings that I saved up to buy
myself for my fortieth birthday because diamonds are
my birthstone. But let me tell you they are lonely! Sure
they have each other, but they would really love to
have a diamond pendent to keep them company and so
would I. LOL. Please help me be fabulous at forty!*

**Carla Kurtz**
**Seattle, WA**
*Why do I deserve to be daring in diamonds? I am a
loyal smoker for forty years. Like the song says, I am
beautiful. Yours are beautiful. I take care of my husband who has diabetes and my mother who had a
stroke in '02. The stroke took my mother away from me
because she is no longer her self. If I win the diamond I
will give it to her because she is like a diamond.*

*The Seven Year Bitch*

**Jill Evers**
**Egg Harbor, NJ**

*If I win the diamond I will tell my husband that another man gave it to me, maybe a customer at the restaurant, let's say his name will be "Dave." I'll tell my husband he just came in and gave it to me and said, "You are too stunning not to have a diamond around that lovely neck," and that will make my husband so jealous he'll make passionate daring love to me and try to make sure I am still "all his." I'll never tell him the truth of course, it will just be my secret. Mine and YOURS.*

**Susan Karger**
**San Francisco, CA**

*I am a dental hygienist. I love my patients and they love me. The trouble is I can never get them to look into my eyes, if you know what I mean, they are allways looking at me below the neck. I would love to have something shining and brilliant and multi-faceted dangling there so there's a reason for them not to be looking me in the eye. Here's to all us working girls getting the diamonds we deserve!*

**Lorainne Castle**
**Bodega Bay, CA**

*My last name is Castle but I live in far from it. But inside I raise my drawbridge so no one can cross my mote and I take off my heavy crown and eat my royal feast. A simple home meal I make for myself. My jewel*

chest is empty. But my heart soars on a dragon's back.
I know one day I will have something to nestle in black
velvet and wear on a chain close to my thorny heart.

**Pearl Ogulnick**
**Paducah, KY**
*Well I am a school crossing guard keeping the kids safe*
*and I run the firehouse pancake breakfasts and bring*
*information packets to all the schools about fire safety.*
*My husband of forty years is retired but he works with*
*a program to check that child carseats (rear and front*
*facing) are installed properly and he received a com-*
*mendation and a certificate from the Mayor. I try to*
*stay fit but that's not always easy and I work out at*
*Curves but a little glitz and glamour would certainly*
*keep my motivational level at High! Thank you for*
*listening!*

**Patricia Cooley**
**Brimfield, MA**
*I don't know if anyone DESERVES diamonds. For this*
*assignment I looked up the word deserve in the Dic-*
*tionary and it said merits. So do I merit diamonds? I*
*certainly think so but I'm sure there is more deserving*
*people out there. In this country you have to work for*
*what you get. I certainly think my life is hard and I*
*merit a break! So in conclusion, I say gimme a break*
*and gimme a diamond and I will do you proud! Love*
*and thanks, Patricia*

Dorie Ross
Lubec, ME

*Emphysema, heart attack, adult onset diabetes, high blood pressure, breast cancer, glaucoma, stroke, chemotherapy and radiation = what my family has had to put up with. We can survive it all with love and faith! Also, my birthstone is diamonds but I've never had any. Just a simple band of gold when I got married to my wonderful husband. Your health is the most important thing. Praise Jesus!*

I couldn't stop reading them. I stared at each name and U.S. town with curiosity. Each essay told a whole life's story. I was starting to feel like a gigantic map of America with thumbtacks pricking me in a different place with each essay I read. Bloomington, IN, pricked me just above my lip. Eugene, OR, pricked my right wrist. I felt like a maypole with thousands of ribbons reaching out to these women.

I saw their bedrooms in their houses, or trailers, or mansions. I saw their jobs, their commute to work, their diseases. I saw the name tags pinned near their cleavage on their waitress uniforms, their time cards, their mortgages. I saw their personal financial statements. I stood next to them as they fished around in their purse or glove compartment or kitchen cabinet and found their packs of cigarettes, anxious to light up and inhale.

Shasthi was in a doctor's examining room. She was there and I was here and all these women were somewhere out there living each day and trying to get something—a happy marriage, a baby, a tiny, minuscule speck of diamond. In one hundred words or less, I saw the plight of women. In one hundred words or less, I felt the pain of this country. In one hundred words or less, I thought I could find an answer I had been looking for, for a long time.

The phone rang and, thinking it might be Shasthi, I ran to answer it, but it was just Deirdre-Agnes calling about my crib.

Then Shasthi called.

"What did the doctor say?" I said, practically falling off the bed in my excitement to pick up the phone. I was afraid to call her in case Dr. Heiffowitz had given her bad news. The worst there was.

"He said I had fibroids but they are not so big as all that."

"Okay, that's good," I said.

"But he said they could be interfering with the sperm getting to the right place."

"Oh," I said. She was so uncomfortable saying the word *sperm* it came out pinched like *spoorm*.

"Well that's great news," I said. "Because you can have them out." But as soon as I said it I thought surgery like that would be elective and cost ten thousand or two hundred thousand or a million dollars for all I knew.

"But he doesn't think I should have them out as yet."

"Good," I said.

"He thinks I should have . . . wait, I wrote it down. Ar-ti-ficial insemination."

"Did he explain to you what that was?" I asked, feeling my heart thumping.

"Yes, I think so. But Izzy," she said, whining slightly, "he said it cost eight thousand dollars and then you know there is no

*The Seven Year Bitch*

175

guarantee and I might not even become pregnant. So how can I do that?"

I was going to make eight thousand dollars by judging this contest. "I think we're going to find a way," I said.

When she came in the morning, we sat together on the floor of Duncan's room and folded the tiny clothes he had grown out of into storage boxes I had bought at the Container Store. It was a fortune of clothes and a fortune of boxes. Size 0–3, size 3–6, size 6–12, size 12–18 were all history.

Summer was coming, which meant I'd have to go to the Kidini sample sale and buy Duncan all new things—little shorts and tank tops and water shoes.

We would go up to the country every weekend and wade in the stream or go to the lake in Pine Hill or to the disgusting water hole that smelled of sulfur near Marlon's house. I would show Duncan his first caterpillar and mushroom and sand castle and pinecone.

Thanks to Russell's aunt, we had been accepted to a preschool where Duncan would be starting this September, just a couple of months before his second birthday.

I zipped the storage boxes closed, wondering who I would unzip them for again one day.


*That summer*, divorce hung in the air like the dead bird trapped in the eaves outside Marlon's house, still hanging seemingly by its neck. I'd developed a theory about the bird. It had gotten trapped there as a tiny baby and its mother had continued to feed it to keep it alive. It had gotten bigger and bigger, but now the mother was dead and so it had starved to death.

*Jennifer Belle*

Every weekend we drove to the country and stopped by Marlon's house to bring him groceries for what was again supposed to be his final summer. Every weekend I was amazed that the bird was still there.

Shasthi had her first cycle of artificial insemination and had not gotten pregnant, but we had both remained upbeat although the two-week wait to find out the results had been almost unbearable.

Her period had become irregular due to stress, so the doctor was insisting we wait a few months before trying again.

"Do you think we're going to get a divorce?" I asked Russell at night when we were lying in bed after a fight. I had put down my sandwich to help Duncan with something for a second, and he had thrown it out. If I had been one of the authors he was publishing, he would have saved the sandwich for a lifetime, fed it to me bit by bit if I liked, but because I was just me, his wife, he couldn't throw it out fast enough.

"No," he said. "We are never, ever getting a divorce. But you've got to stop with these essays!" He was half-asleep, in his glasses, a manuscript butterflied on his chest.

"Just a few more," I said.

"I can't stand living with these things. God, I hate this. They're everywhere."

"You're one to talk," I said, pointing to the leaning tower of remaindered books by his bed. "I live with the lost Collyer brother."

"Why do you judge these contests?" Russell asked.

"Because I love doing it," I said.

"I suddenly feel like making love to you," he said.

*The Seven Year Bitch*

"No," I said. "I have to finish this stack."

"You can read essays while we do it. Come on. We didn't even get to do it for our anniversary." We'd been upstate for our sixth wedding anniversary, went to the Bear for dinner in Woodstock with Duncan, and then he had crawled into our bed with us. "So we have to do it. Happy anniversary."

He pulled my nightgown up around my neck and then got up and fished around in my sock drawer looking for a condom.

"I can't believe we're all out of them," he said.

"Well I guess we can't do it," I said, pulling my nightgown back down and straightening my "yes" pile.

"Wait, I got one at the Jamaica book fair—it was in a gift bag. Here it is," Russell said. I heard the wrapper being torn open. Russell slid it on with his back to me, and when he turned around, a big black cock was coming at me.

"Sorry, this black one is the only one we had," Russell said.

I had never seen anything so black against Russell's blindingly white skin.

"Why do I suddenly hear blues music playing in the background?" I said.

"Very funny," he said. "Just spread your legs."

I was laughing so hard, I couldn't even move. My whole face was screwed up in hysterics. I couldn't breathe. I was like an animal, gasping and snorting. I was helpless. And when it was over, I realized I hadn't had a release like that in a long time.

*Part Two*

# 100 Words or Less

# 20

In the cab on the way to meet Joy for dinner, I thought about the fight I'd just had with Russell. We'd taken Duncan to the Natural History Museum that day, and as we were leaving through the revolving door, Russell had one of his breakdowns. He couldn't fold the stroller so he started trying to jam it into the revolving door, his head bent way down, unseeing, blinded by insanity. I had already gone through the door with Duncan when I saw the people start to gather and the security guard approach.

I pushed back into the revolving door with Duncan and back into the museum, where, despite the security guard and the crowd, Russell was still trying to jam the stroller in and banging it over and over again on the marble floor.

"Is everything okay, ma'am?" the security guard said to Russell from behind us. This happened to Russell all the time because he was short and had longish hair. It had happened on our second date—the waiter had said, "Can I get you ladies a drink?"— and I had almost died laughing.

"Ma'am?" Russell said, looking up to show the guard his Saturday and Sunday beard.

"Oh, sorry. Sir. Are you having a problem here?"

"No, no, no, no, no, no problem," Russell sputtered hysterically, like a balloon with its air escaping.

I took the stroller from Russell and folded it in two seconds. A perfectly good time ruined.

We'd fought about it all the way home, right in front of Duncan, completely defeating the point of the day, which was to show Duncan what a happy, functional, cultured New York City family we were, as my parents had shown me, at least until I was twenty-five.

"Why does every day have to end with being stopped by security?" I screamed in the car. "Duncan is almost two years old. Why can't you learn how to fold the stroller? Every other father can fold the stroller. It's a *folding* stroller. It's an *umbrella* stroller. Do you even know how to work an umbrella?"

I thought about the father I liked in Duncan's new class who was always picking his son, Leo, up at school and videotaping him coming out of the school's blue door with the flowers painted on it. I was starting to think a video camera was the most attractive quality in a man. The world-famous photographer Annie Leibovitz had photographed the class for the school calendar, which was the kind of thing that happened at these fancy preschools—our class was August and had a gardening theme—and he had sent me an e-mail saying how cute Duncan had looked holding his little rake. "Good-looking boy you have there. So cute," the e-mail had said. Why was Leo's father writing to me? I wondered over and over. Was this how married people with children flirted?

All I did was spend my time thinking about other people's husbands. They were so relaxed and happy, working their strollers and video cameras. I remembered when I'd bought my Baby Bjorn. I'd stood in Buy Buy Baby and stared at the picture on the box of a gorgeous man and woman and their baby. In the picture, the man was the one with the baby strapped to his chest and I'd laughed to myself, knowing that the man I was having my baby with could never walk and carry a baby at the same time.

I couldn't believe it had been exactly a year since I had been laid off. Labor Day weekend had come and gone, and another 9/11, and the anniversary of the collapse of Lehman Brothers. I'd made no use of the outplacement services offered in my package or even called a single contact and really I missed work less and less. I took Duncan to classes with Gerde and planned his upcoming birthday party. I got Marilyn and Doris and Gert to take Aquacise with me at my gym and we always went to the University Diner after. Duncan had forty-five hand-knitted sweaters. Deirdre-Agnes had had her baby and I still hadn't given her back her crib.

I walked into La Lunchonette and saw Joy already at our table making notes in a diary. She was in town for the perfume expo at the Jacob Javits Center and had so many meetings booked, this had been her only opening.

"So tell me about him," Joy said.

"I don't know," I said. "I think it must all be in my imagination."

*The Seven Year Bitch*

"He bids on you at an auction after thinking about you for eight years. He's been calling you for a year. You look beautiful," Joy said. "This is good for you. You should sleep with him."

"No," I said, wishing we could stop talking about it. The more we talked, the less likely it all seemed. "Tell me about Africa."

"Chili and I are going to have a love that's deep and real," she said.

"What do you mean going to have?" I hadn't thought of love in the future tense like that since junior high school. I remembered that Chili was the name of one of the penguins that arrived at the family's house in the children's book I read to Duncan.

She checked her BlackBerry and then checked it again a moment later.

"He hasn't called or e-mailed in three days. But sometimes there's no wireless connection there, so I'm not going to worry. And his wife is fat," she said, "and just gets fatter and fatter. Dark, heavy, unattractive. She squawks like a raven. We go to this restaurant in the town to hear music—he makes us sit behind the restaurant so she won't see us—but she and her friends walked by, and it was like a black storm setting in. You should come there. Bring Duncan. You're not still breast-feeding are you?"

She gave my breasts a suspicious sideways glance, like they were plastic bottles I had discarded on the side of the road instead of putting them in the recycle bin.

Joy was very against breast-feeding. "Oh bullshit," she had said when I'd tried to explain the benefits to the baby.

"He's about to turn two, Joy, I stopped a year ago. His birthday is Monday. We're having his party on Sunday."

The waiter came and asked if we wanted to see a dessert menu.

"No," Joy practically screamed. He should have known better than to even ask after she'd shoved the bread basket back in his gut when he tried to put it on our table.

When I got home I took off my clothes and stood in front of the full-length mirror. The scar from my C-section was purple and jagged and numb to the touch. My breasts were lower than I had remembered them. Lately I'd blamed my bras rather than the breasts themselves but now I was staring right at the source. I had always hated the tedious jokes vulgar comediennes made about their southwardly pointing breasts—making miming gestures of picking them up off the floor and tossing them over a shoulder like a scarf—but now I was practically standing next to them at the microphone. My nipples looked tired and pale and inviting only to a baby.

But Gabe Weinrib liked me, I reminded myself. Even Joy had agreed.

Russell had been the only man to see me since my scars, and for the first time I wondered if I could really show myself to another man. Of course you could, I said to the mirror. Of course you could.

Ever since childhood, I'd always been able to see myself with a certain healthy amount of suspension of disbelief and optimism. Well into my twenties I still expected to grow taller. But now all I could do was turn my head away and do something I had never done before: put on a bathrobe.

When Russell came home I asked him to change the Poland Spring water bottle and he said, "Yes, sir."

"Did you just call me sir?" I asked. I had always hated being called "ma'am," but being called "sir" was another thing altogether. I didn't need to be insulted like that, and in a fury, I spun around in my robe—a long robe made of African cloth striped in greens and orange and pink that Joy had brought back to me from her Kenyan shamba—and took a fake swing at him. He flinched. And I did it again, swinging my arms and karate chopping at him but not really coming near him. I felt like I could pick him up and squeeze his puny body through the child safety bars and throw him out the window. "Hi-ya," I said, kicking the air around him over and over again and snapping my arms all around like a lunatic.

"Stop it," he said. "I won't take this abuse."

"Hi-ya!" I kicked.

"Izzy, stop it!"

"Yes, ma'am," I said to him.

Then I went into the bedroom and cried because I had become a monster. Joy was right. He had turned me into one.

# 21

I'm going to throw up," Duncan said from the backseat, when we drove upstate the next day for his big birthday weekend.

"He shouldn't have had all those pumpkin seeds," Russell said.

Then we heard the retching and the brave little sigh at the end.

"Stop the car," I said.

"I'm doing my best," Russell said.

Finally he stopped and I got up and sponged up the vomit with an old blue golf shirt that had belonged to Russell's grandfather before he died and some McDonald's napkins.

"There's a garbage can," I said, noticing one outside some strange deserted business. I balled up the dripping mess and got out of the car, and as I passed behind the car, Russell backed the car up and hit me. I screamed and fell, twisting and sliding with my right arm stretched out in front of me. I lay in the gravel too stunned to move. Russell had stopped the car but it seemed like minutes before he bothered to get out and see if I was all right.

"What happened?" he said, rushing slowly to my side.

"You ran me over!" I screamed.

"I didn't run you over. I tapped you."

"You just ran over me with our own car," I said.

"I thought you were sitting in the backseat with the baby," he said.

"But the door was open. You just back up without looking?"

"I'm sorry, honey, I thought you were in the car. Oh my God, I'm sorry, I'm sorry." He was doing this fake-crying thing he did when he knew I was really going to be mad at him.

"Stop crying."

"I'm not crying."

He tried to help me up, but I didn't really want to be touched by my murderer. "Don't touch me," I said. My right arm was badly hurt. I stood up and walked with survivor's determination over to the garbage can and threw out the vomit. I walked slowly back to the car and got in.

"Mama, what happened?" Duncan asked.

"Daddy hit Mommy with the car, but I'm okay now," I said.

"You're really overreacting."

"I was just hit by a car," I said. "I'm underreacting."

"Okay then," Russell said, looking at me and then at Duncan. "Is everyone in the car? Duncan?"

"I'm in the car," Duncan giggled.

"Mom?"

Russell always called me "Mom," and I really couldn't stand it. He made it into a two-syllable word and it always came out an octave higher than the other words he spoke. He said it the same way he said it when he called his mother every Sunday. "Hi

Mo-om!" he said into the phone, his voice dripping with upbeat pain, like a puppy barking. I couldn't stand to be called the same thing his mother was called. Whenever Russell called me Mom, I said, "Don't call me Mom. I'm not your mother."

"Don't call me Mom," I said. "I'm not your mother."

"Sorry," Russell said.

"But I can call you Mom, right, Mama?" Duncan said.

"Yes, Duncan, you can call me Mom."

*"What should we do* about Deirdre-Agnes?" I asked Russell in bed that night. "She's called five times for her crib."

"What do you think we should do?"

"I don't know!" I said. "Duncan's still using it. And she gave it to me. I even said to her when she gave it to me, 'Deirdre-Agnes, what happens if you have another child?' and she said, 'Oh, I'll never have another one,' and—"

"I know," Russell said, interrupting me. "You've told me that a thousand times."

"When she lent it to me, I mean . . ." I stopped, upset by my mistake. "No, not lent, gave. When she gave it to me . . ."

"Why don't we just give it back to her and we can buy another crib?" Russell said.

"Duncan is using that crib," I said.

"So, offer her money."

"But how much money? It's an expensive crib but it was used when she gave it to me. She got it used. There were like five babies in it before I got it."

"So offer her two hundred bucks."

*The Seven Year Bitch*

"Maybe I could tell her it was stolen," I said.

"Don't do that," Russell said.

"Why not?"

"Who would steal it? Someone would break in and steal a crib?"

"Maybe it got stolen on the street when we were bringing it downstairs to put in our car to take to our country house."

"That's ridiculous," Russell said. "Oh yes, I've read about him in the papers—the masked crib bandit—he roams the streets until he finds an old used crib, then slinks off with it. He leaves the baby, thank God, just takes the crib."

"I think someone could steal it," I said. "Like an NYU student or a homeless person."

"Sure, you see homeless people sleeping in cribs all the time, and NYU students."

I lay there perfecting the crime in my mind until I realized Russell was right and there was no way someone would steal a crib.

## 22

The next day, the morning of Duncan's second birthday, he went for a walk in the woods with Russell while I got ready for his birthday party. We'd decided to have it in the country, with my parents and Russell's aunt and uncle coming up from the city and some of our local friends who had children. Fall was the nicest season for a party. We had an apple tree filled with apples. Gra was doing all the cooking and I'd hired a miserable pony named Hustle to give the children rides in a circle on our lawn.

We'd hired Charlie to run yards and yards of extension cords down to the stream and we'd strung a small part of the woods with fairy lights. Russell's only job was keeping Duncan away from that part of the woods so we could surprise him and his friends by telling them that fairies had decorated the woods for them. I had gathered sticks and tied them into neat bundles with ribbon so the children could throw the sticks into the stream in a kind of contest. From a tree hung a piñata filled with $287 worth of little toys I'd bought online from the Oriental Trading

Company. There were tiny buckets of M&M's under mosquito netting, and Marilyn, Doris, and Gert had knitted little bunnies and pigs and bears for favors.

I was ecstatic. Duncan was two! I was the mother of a two-year-old. He wasn't a baby anymore. I had done it.

"Mama," Duncan said, running into the house. "We found something!"

"What?" I asked, in that famous Mom-voice, as if my whole being depended on finding out what it—a leaf, or salamander, or bird's nest—was.

"Look!" Duncan said, glowing pink with excitement.

He handed me an old DVD with the title *Hairy and Over Forty* printed on its label. Below the title was a faded photo of a black-haired woman with a proud expression on her face sitting with her legs spread on some kind of office swivel chair. She was pulling her panties aside to show off a healthy thatch of bushy black pubic hair.

"Isn't it beautiful?" Duncan asked.

"It certainly is," I said, looking at Russell, who had come in behind him followed by a completely filthy Humbert.

"It was just lying there in the woods. What can I say, my son appreciates nature," Russell said.

"For you, Mama," Duncan said, holding it up to me, my first gift from him. I imagined I would keep *Hairy and Over Forty* in a special box to be eventually joined by collages and beaded necklaces and ashtrays made out of clay.

*Later, when most of* the guests had left, Gra and I were cleaning up in the kitchen and Russell was serving drinks to a few of our friends who had driven up for the day. Duncan was asleep in his crib, his forehead covered in stickers, holding a dragon puppet he had received in one hand and the *Hairy and Over Forty* DVD in the other. I had taken idyllic photos of him, but I'd decided against a video after the one Russell had made the year before.

"I want you to sit down," I told a very pregnant Gra. "It's not good for you to work like this."

"I hate this so much," she said.

"What?"

"This." She made a sweeping gesture over her remarkably small stomach. "I want it out! I so uncomfortable."

"It'll be over soon," I said. "Here's what I owe you." I handed her eight hundred dollars in an envelope.

She took the envelope but kept hold of my hand along with it. "Do me big favor. I tell Charlie I only make half this for this job."

"Okay. I don't tell Russell what I do with my money either," I said, thinking of all I had spent on Shasthi against his will. "That's very American."

"I send rest of money to my father in Thailand. I own a orchard there. I allow him live there even if I hate him."

"Why do you hate him?"

"He held gun to my head when I was young."

I couldn't believe how good her English had gotten and she was already using everyday American expressions like "held a gun to my head."

"He put gun right here," she said, pointing to her temple.

"He tried to kill you?" I said, hoping Duncan couldn't hear from his crib.

"He held gun to my head and I say to him go ahead and kill me

*The Seven Year Bitch*

please, kill me, because you are nothing, and I come from you, so I am nothing."

"Why are you going to send him this money?" I said. She should be saving up for a one-way ticket back to Thailand, maybe go on some more chaperoned dates and start again with another husband, or for a studio apartment in Queens.

I thought of my nice father asleep on the couch in the other room with Curry Puff and Humbert asleep on his chest and feet, exhausted from building forts with Duncan, his biggest crime not paying for my third year of business school. My father had brought a Nerf football and spent an hour with him on the lawn throwing it to him and saying things like, "Good arm, son!" and "Yup, I think we've got another leftie." Now that was a role model for a boy, I thought, not a man who sat hunched over the *New Yorker* literally crying over a bad review.

I thought of Shasthi, constantly sending money home to Guyana.

"You have nice father," she said. "If father nice, you nice. If father scum, you scum."

I was so impressed she already knew words like *scum*.

"Actually that's not how it works here in America," I said. "It's the first thing you learn in therapy. Your parents are absolutely no reflection on you. That's how I was able to marry my husband. I have the worst mother-in-law on earth. I mean, she never held a gun to my head, but her voice is like a gun. But Russell is not his mother. He is not his parents. You are not your father."

"I think Izzy teach me a lot," Gra said.

I always loved a house after a party. I loved the exhausted feeling and the mess. I didn't want to clean it up. On the coffee table were enormous phalluses made out of Play-Doh that were hand-made by Russell's friend Ben, the exalted author of the great novel *Shoes and Socks*, the one who had filmed last year's suicide video. The balls were huge and rainbow-hued; he must have spent quite a bit of time forming them.

I picked up my digital camera and started looking at some of the photos. I had captured Duncan's face when he saw the fairyland, marveling in awe. I stood there looking at photos on the tiny screen, and then I stopped and stared at one.

It was of Russell, my husband, sitting on Ben's lap with his arms around his neck. The next five photos were all of Russell sitting on Ben's lap in a loving embrace. Ben was a good six inches taller than Russell and much bigger and more muscular. Russell, on his lap, looked like a girl. I felt disgusted. Why would he want his son to see him this way?

What would he do at Duncan's next birthday, I wondered, give Ben a blow job while shooting himself in the head on the national news?

Gabe Weinrib, I couldn't help think, would never sit on a man's lap.

I walked out onto the deck where they were sitting, giggling like schoolgirls, obviously drunk on scotch again.

"Why did you sit on Ben's lap?" I asked.

"I didn't sit on Ben's lap," he said.

"Yes you did."

"No, I didn't," Russell said.

"Yes, you did."

"No, I didn't."

Not only was he now gay, he was stupid. "I have the evidence!

*The Seven Year Bitch*

195

Someone took pictures of it!" I said. "Is this what you want in the family album?"

"It was just a joke," he said.

"Why did you feel the need to sit on his lap? On your son's birthday?"

I could hear Charlie Cheney talking loudly now to my father in the living room about how Gra wouldn't mind cutting his toenails right now if he wanted her to. Russell had managed to make Gra and Charlie's marriage look like Ward and June Cleaver's. They were happy compared to us! Gra was fulfilled, learning a language, starting a business. And so what if she had to cut Charlie's toenails? There were women who came to this country who had to cut a hundred toenails a day for less than minimum wage and she only had to cut his probably once a month at the most. And what was so wrong with Charlie asking her to? I myself hadn't cut my own toenails since business school. But why, the question still remained, would Russell actually sit on a man's lap and then lie about it? How would I ever, for instance, erase the image from my mind and, say, have sex with him *ever again*? How was I going to forgive this one? I thought. How was I ever going to forgive this one?


*I went into my* room and sat on my bed with a pile of essays. I had just judged a contest—In 100 Words or Less Tell Us Your Most Positive Aha Moment—for *O, The Oprah Magazine.* The winner got $100,000 and an all-expense-paid trip to Chicago to appear on Oprah's show. I'd gotten a hundred boxes of essays, earned $40,000, and gotten a call from a member of Oprah's staff who said that Oprah personally wanted to give me a bonus for doing such a great job. I'd waited anxiously for my "bonus" (what could it be—$5,000, $10,000, $25,000?—I wondered) until it arrived: a copy of the book *Live Your Best Life: A Treasury of Wisdom, Wit, Advice, Interviews, and Inspiration from* O, The Oprah Magazine. Shasthi loved it, even if I was less than thrilled.

And before that I judged Iron Baby Organic Formula—In 100 Words or Less Give Us Your Best Good New Mom Tip for Exhausted Moms. The $25,000 grand prize went to a woman whose husband was in Iraq and who suggested taking a "Baby-moon" when your baby was born—an at-home vacation where you take two weeks for just you and your baby. The first-prize winner's tip was to string lights in the woods behind your house for your child's birthday party and tell your child fairies had done it. Her husband was also in Iraq.

The new contest that had arrived in fourteen boxes was Lavish Cosmetics: In 100 Words or Less Tell Us Why You Want to Stay Forever Young.

I couldn't wait to lose myself in the essays.

**Helen Jacobson**
**Wading River, NY**
*For life is fleeting!*
*Oh I wish I could stay young,*
*Ravishing,*
*Ever beautiful.*
*Victorious, I would go to my 20th High School reunion.*
*Everyone would stop to admire me*

*Remarking on my*
*Youthful, glowing appearance. "Ha-Ha," you*
*Oldsters, I would say*
*Under my breath of course*
*Never once looking back at*
*Gerald Gerson, the boy who broke my heart.*

**Marni Flood**
**Oakland, CA**

*Young is a state of mind, not a physical state. As an*
*Aquarius I will always stay young, for my mind will*
*explore new things—music, dance, the arts. I will find*
*a man who always knows I am young and beautiful*
*even when we're forty-five. I want to stay young forever*
*because I don't want to die, but then again, whoever*
*really does? Please send me a free coupon for your*
*Lavish Lashes Mascara. I love it!!!*

**Bruce Hollandar**
**Reno, Nevada**

*I am a man writing this for my wife even though the*
*rules say you have to be a woman. My wife deserves*
*to win because she is beautiful. I'm in a wheelchair due*
*to an on the job accident and I told her you don't have*
*to be my girl anymore, but she said she'll always be my*
*ladyluck. She is young when she makes me laugh. We*
*laugh so much. I could not have a better wife. I haven't*
*written this much since High School.*

The phone rang in the kitchen and I got up reluctantly to answer it.

"Is that Izzy?"

"Oh, hi, Deirdre-Agnes," I said. She'd never called us at the country house before. Instinctively I looked out the window to see if she'd pulled up in our driveway and was calling from her car. "I've been meaning to call you."

"I need my crib back now!" she said. "My baby is three months old and I can't keep him in the bassinet."

"Well, something terrible has happened," I said. "There was a terrible flood in our apartment."

"A flood?" she said.

"The ceiling in Duncan's room fell in and crushed the crib. Everything was water damaged. It's just terrible! I didn't call you, because we were checking with our insurance company to see if it would cover the cost of the crib, but they don't cover floods."

"How is that a flood?" she asked.

"Well it was flooding conditions, it was raining. Remember that huge rainstorm last month?"

"No," Deirdre-Agnes said.

"Well, I'm sorry, we had to throw the whole thing out. Listen, I have to go because I have company." I thought of Russell sitting on the company's lap.

"So what are you going to do about it?"

"Well, we're having the ceiling repaired and repainted."

"That's not what I mean. What are you going to do about it?"

"What do you mean?" I asked impatiently.

"To replace my crib!" she said.

*The Seven Year Bitch*

"Well, Deidre-Agnes, what would you like me to do to replace your old used crib?"

"I'd like you to send me a check for fifteen hundred dollars so I can buy a comparable one."

"Fifteen hundred dollars!" I said. "For a used, scratched crib that you gave me. I suggest you go on eBay and buy one for about a hundred dollars, and I'll happily send you the money."

"A hundred dollars!" she said. "You better give me back my crib."

"It doesn't ex-ist," I said. Why had I made up this terrible story? I asked myself. I had never regretted anything more in my entire life. I didn't even want to see the crib again, let alone lay my son down to sleep in it. I had made a terrible mistake and there was nothing I could do about it.

"Well, then we'll see you in court," she said in her Irish brogue so it sounded like "caaaaaart" and hung up.

# 23

I sat on the couch in the lobby of our building watching Duncan stare in awe at the Christmas tree. Every year before I had a baby, I had resented this tree with its *Sesame Street* and Disney ornaments and its huge Elmo topper. I had grimaced at the super's wife when she appeared each year to assemble and decorate it, apologized for it when I led company past it, noted other buildings' more grown-up holiday offerings, which involved fairy lights and branches of berries and pots of poinsettia and velvet-ribboned wreaths. But now that Duncan loved this tree, I loved this tree. I even appreciated the building's nod to its Jewish residents: three little plush Hasidic man-dolls standing between a Santa-clad Shrek and Winnie-the-Pooh.

Duncan stood before this tree as if it were a shrine, only looking, never touching, filling me with pride. Other children attacked it while the doormen scowled.

A man I knew from the third floor walked into the building and approached the couch where I was sitting. I couldn't remember his name, but I knew him because he had put Humbert in a Jude Law movie, which was exciting even though Hum ended up on the cutting-room floor, probably because Jude Law had felt threatened by my dog's movie-star good looks and acting skills.

The man was with his son, the same age as Duncan, who walked right up to the tree and manhandled an ornament of a bear character I wasn't familiar with yet, Calamine pink with a rainbow on its stomach. I felt oddly grateful for every character I wasn't familiar with yet, as if it meant I was that much closer to my old self. If I didn't know SpongeBob SquarePants or let the Wiggles into my house, I wasn't completely lost. Similarly, I tried to hold on to my femininity by refusing to learn the names of the different dinosaurs. When I accidentally learned which one was the triceratops one day at the Museum of Natural History it was like unwittingly growing a pair of balls.

"Look, Dad," the odd little third-floor neighbor-boy said.

"No touching," Duncan said, like a little museum guard.

The man, whose name I didn't know and never would because now it was about three years too late to ask, sat down next to me on the couch. I was a little surprised because we'd never really talked, just smiled when we passed each other in the lobby. We hadn't even had the usual elevator pleasantries because he usually took the stairs. All I really knew about him was he wasn't married to his son's mother and she'd been in a documentary about giving birth in their apartment. I'd been there the night her labor began and the camera and lighting crews came.

I never understood why people wanted to do anything in their apartments. I didn't even want to eat dinner in my apartment, let alone give birth in it. In fact, if I could afford it, I wouldn't even sleep there. I'd do what Coco Chanel did and leave my apartment every night to check into a nice hotel.

As soon as he sat down next to me I felt he was available.

"Duncan's gotten so big," he said.

"So's yours," I said. "He's beautiful." I always said that no matter how strange-looking a child was.

"It's gone so fast," he said.

I hated when people said things like "It's gone so fast" because to me it had gone really slowly.

"I know," I said. "It's amazing."

The man suddenly stood, reached up to the light fixture hanging low over our heads, and unscrewed the bulb a little, turning it off. "That's a lot better," he said. The light hadn't bothered me but I was impressed when a man took charge of his environment that way. I wondered what it would be like to live with a man like that. If Russell was annoyed by a lightbulb, he would either live with it for the rest of his life or call Rashid up to fix it. Rashid was up at our apartment so often that once when Duncan had drawn a picture of our family he had included Rashid, a very tall, angular scribble standing between short, round Mommy and Daddy scribbles.

Despite the macho lightbulb incident, the man had always seemed slightly gay to me. Not gay really—I didn't doubt he liked women—but a little effeminate. He smelled good. He was very attractive, I thought, but he seemed like the type of man who might sleep in a nightgown or knit by the fire in his country house. I wasn't at all attracted to him. Not in a romantic-comedy-I'd-really-end-up-with-him-in-the-end way but in a real

I-wonder-what-the-woman-who-gave-birth-in-her-apartment-sees-in-him way.

"Working on any good movies?" I said.

"What? Oh, yeah, I have a lot going on," he said.

I knew from this he meant he was breaking up with his girlfriend.

"I hear ya," I said, with a funereal nod.

"No, I don't think you understand."

"Oh, I think I do."

"Things aren't working out for me and my girlfriend."

We sat and watched our children in silence for a minute.

"My girlfriend, Natasha, just isn't stable. She goes off on me for no reason. Rages at me. I can't take it anymore. One minute she's screaming at me that I'm not a man, and then she's fine but I'm not fine. We were supposed to go to Miami last week, and the day we were supposed to leave she was yelling at me that I had done something wrong, I had packed wrong, and the next minute she's holding the tickets and saying, 'Okay, let's go,' and I'm thinking, There's no way I would go with you now."

"That's awful," I said, thinking I had done the exact same thing to Russell the last time we had gone to Miami.

"I really can't take it anymore. I took an apartment in Brooklyn."

I couldn't say anything. Usually when someone told me he was getting a divorce I would say something glib like "That's great," or "You're lucky," or "Cheers, darling!" In fact I'd said all three to my cousin just a few weeks before—"That's great, you're lucky, cheers, darling!"—and held up an imaginary glass of champagne. But I couldn't say anything right then because it was suddenly too painful and fresh, as if he were still blood-spattered and holding the scissors he'd used to cut the umbilical cord in his apartment.

As he continued complaining about Natasha he could have been Russell complaining about me. It seemed that despite the fact that I wouldn't want to deliver a baby in my apartment, we were exactly the same wife.

"She sounds awful," I said. "You did the right thing to leave her."

"I know," he said bitterly, standing up. "You worry if you leave, you'll be lonely. But there's nothing lonelier than living with the wrong person. I gave her the apartment and some money."

"Ah, bailout money," I said.

"Right, I like that. Bailout money. Still, it's hard to know if I'm doing the right thing."

"It all depends on your appetite for risk," I said.

He called to his son, "Come on, Em, let's get you upstairs."

"You too, Duncan, let's go for a walk."

When we got to Washington Square Park, I noticed that the fountain was gone. It had been completely ripped out. I had heard they were planning to move it, but I hadn't imagined they would get rid of it altogether and put a new fountain in its place. Now, where my white fountain had been, there was an open grave. A terrible mastectomy had been performed.

"Mommy, move!" Duncan said, pulling me toward the playground.

But I couldn't. I had spent my childhood playing in that fountain and the rest of my life brooding in it. In B School, I had studied at it. When I was pregnant with Duncan, I had walked by that fountain thinking, I'm walking by this fountain pregnant

*The Seven Year Bitch*

with a son. We had played there together just the month before. But I hadn't taken his picture. I didn't have a single picture of the fountain and now I never would. Panic overtook me. I was going to be forty and I didn't want much. I didn't want a Mercedes or a tattoo or a Cartier watch. My crisis didn't even require an affair. I just wanted my same old fountain in its same old place. They were yanking my past from me and it was too late to protest. There wasn't anything to chain myself to, no wrecking ball to stop; all that was there was dirt, an odd sort of light brown dirt, an espresso color. Maybe New York dirt was different from country dirt. Although this didn't seem like New York. It seemed like Baghdad with the dirt and dirty headless snowmen all around.

For some reason I thought of Shasthi. Was I, I wondered for a moment, no better than the Parks Commission, moving my bulldozer into Shasthi's uterus? If she got pregnant, would it be the right thing? And if she didn't, after going through all of this, would it destroy her?

I went to the chain-link fence blocking off the construction, grasped it and started to rattle it. Duncan grasped it and shook it too with his little hands.

"This is fun, Mommy," he said.

# 24

A few weeks later, Shasthi took Duncan home with her to the Bronx to spend the night. Russell and I had had a wedding to go to. We drove through the Bronx to pick him up. It had been my first night away from him and I was anxious to get to him. And the wedding we'd gone to hadn't been worth leaving him for.

Shasthi had come the morning before and packed his little things and left with my son in her arms, duffel bag and folding stroller slung over her shoulder. "Here's one more extra shirt for him," I'd said, handing her the one that had "MOM" on it in a way that was meant to look like a tattoo. Her face had clouded over and I realized she didn't want the shirt that said "MOM" on it. She didn't want a reminder of "MOM." Maybe for that day she was his mom.

"I just think we should have checked out her apartment first," I said to Russell, who was always a wreck driving in other boroughs for some reason. Once when we'd been lost in Brooklyn one sunny morning, he'd almost had a nervous breakdown, sweat shooting out of his temples, terrified of our surroundings, while I pointed to the fat old black ladies smiling in their Sunday hats and squat white shoes and the sounds of joyous choir music pouring out of every church.

"It's okay," he said. "We'll just make sure to see it now, so we know if it's safe for next time. Jesus, we're really in the middle of nowhere," he said, practically shaking with fear as I watched two young children holding hands and running on the side- walk while their mothers pushed their empty strollers leisurely behind them. "If it's really bad, crawling with roaches or lead paint flakes everywhere, we won't let it happen again."

When we pulled up in front of her building, an ugly brown brick monstrosity with small windows, Shasthi was waiting, radiant, with Duncan smiling in her arms, his little legs wrapped around her, koala-style.

I looked at Russell. "Do you mind if I use your bathroom?" I asked Shasthi. I was determined to get upstairs to see where my son had spent the night.

She loaded Duncan into his car seat and he cried when she said good-bye. Then I followed her into her building and up one flight of stairs to her apartment.

When I walked in her door I couldn't believe what I saw. To my right was a small kitchen the same size as mine at home, immaculate of course, with a Poland Spring water cooler that, like ours, dispensed both hot and cold water. In the living room there was a fifty-inch wall-mounted Sony Aquos flat-screen TV between windows lavishly draped in red brocade with tasseled sashes. Along another wall, behind a baroque mahogany table with eight upholstered chairs, was a breakfront with beveled glass doors protecting a full set of china and other treasures, including the ones I had given her from our wedding. In the center of the table was a huge china-flower arrangement, a Capidimonte sort of thing, and in the corner was a Roman-Greco-style statue of a naked woman with swans at her feet. Everywhere, on end tables, were vases of vast china-flower arrangements. I hadn't seen anything so grand since we'd been to the Borghese Gardens in Rome on our honeymoon.

I was happy her life was so nice—it was what I had wanted for her—but for one tiny moment I thought of the sixteen thousand dollars I'd spent for her to go to Heiffowitz.

I had always felt sorry for her when she lifted her Queen Helene hand cream out of her purse, cheap drugstore stuff in an ugly brown bottle, but now, in her bathroom, as I pumped some on my exfoliated hands I saw that it was the finest cream I had ever tried.

"Where did Duncan sleep?" I asked when I came out.

"In bed with us," she said and showed me her room and its enormous king-size bed several feet off the ground covered in more brocade and tassels and a hundred perfect square pillows. An oval Rococo-style mirror faced the bed and a vanity held pots of creams and brushes and dozens of perfumes and eye shadow palettes. I could only imagine what splendors hid behind the closet doors; if I opened them skirts and scarves and sequined blouses would probably flutter out like parrots.

"He must have been very happy in there," I said.

"Oh he was!" she said. "But I didn't sleep, because I was so afraid he'd fall off of it."

*The Seven Year Bitch*

"Well," I said, laughing, when I got back into the car with Russell.

"How was it?" he asked.

"Let's just say I didn't see any roaches crawling around or lead paint chips."

"Well, that's good news," Russell said.

I sat in the backseat like a Hasidic woman, so I could hold Duncan's hand and look at him while he slept. It was hot in the car so I unzipped his sweatshirt and saw that he was wearing a new little T-shirt.

Written across him were the words "SOMEONE IN GUYANA LOVES ME."

Guyana, I thought, looking at the shirt in its garish red and orange Kool-Aid hues. Guyana. Where the mass suicide took place at Jonestown. Someone in Guyana loves me.

# 25

We have to decide who would raise Duncan if something were to happen to us," I said.

I was lying on the floor near the dining-room table, too tired to move. Russell was reading "Page Six" of the *New York Post*.

"Ummm hmmm," Russell said.

"It's not a joke in a post-9/11 world." I waited a moment and then said, "You're not listening to me."

"We have to decide who would raise Duncan if something were to happen to us. It's not a joke in a post-9/11 world. I'm listening," Russell said.

"Not your parents," I said.

"Of course not," Russell said, horrified at the thought. "Not yours either."

Then Russell got up, stepped over me, and walked into the other room. He just stepped *over* me, like I wasn't even a person. Like I was a dog or laundry or garbage.

"You just stepped over me," I screamed, still on the floor. Russell came back into the room.

"What? Sorry, you're just lying there. I had to go to the bathroom."

"So you just step over me!" I yelled at the top of my lungs. "You can't say, 'Excuse me, honey,' or just walk around me. You could have walked there, or there, or there, but you had to just step over me."

"I'm sorry, I don't know why you're getting so upset."

"I'm getting so upset because you just walked over me like I don't even exist."

I started weeping, in a heap on the floor. "I am a person," I sobbed. "I am a person. I am a person."

In just a few short weeks I was going to be forty. I couldn't believe it but it was true. Forty years old. And that sort of shone a spotlight on things, didn't it? At forty I didn't think I'd get walked over in my own home.

I remembered the essay that girl had written about the definition of *deserve*. How she said that she didn't know if anyone deserved anything. And I thought about how wise that was. I made a mental note to go through the enormous "no" pile and find her essay and put it at the top of the yesses.

I called my mother and told her what happened.

"I'm sure he didn't mean anything by it," she said.

I started to cry again. "I wouldn't even do that to Humbie," I said.

"Well maybe you should look for someone else," my mother said.

"What do you mean 'look for someone else'?" I said, infuriated. I knew she was just giving me the same advice her mother had given her, but it was so unrealistic and old-fashioned. "You don't just look for someone else. I'm almost forty years old," I told my own mother. "I had a C-section, Jesus! And I would never do that to Duncan."

"A happy mother makes a happy child. All I'm saying is I wish I'd left your father when you were a baby."

"That's because your father would have supported you!" I practically screamed. My parents and Russell's parents were always telling us what to do but would never dream of bailing us out even in an emergency, whereas *their* parents paid for every adult move they had made. Her father had sent her to Bennington and Cornell and Columbia and provided the down payment for her apartment. He would have sent her to Bennington a dozen times if she'd wanted. "We can't afford two households."

"Well, we'll see what my shrink says about this," my mother said. "She's still very worried that he hit you with the car."

"But this is somehow even worse than that," I said. "Somehow being stepped over is worse than being run over."

"I completely agree," my mother said.

I tried to explain what it felt like to be stepped over but it was one of those things you couldn't possibly know the pain of until you had experienced it.

"You wouldn't even step over a cockroach. You'd step on it," I said, nonsensically. "The cockroach would probably rather be stepped on."

"How do you figure?" my mother asked, agreeably continuing our conversation.

"Because it would mean it had been seen. It would imply some kind of passion."

*The Seven Year Bitch*

"Someone should step on *him*," my mother said.

I lay on my side of the bed thinking of Gabe Weinrib and how he called me every few weeks when he was back in New York. He wanted to have dinner with me but I said no, stifling my appetite for risk. I hadn't given him the hat that Doris had made for him. I'd picked it up from her and brought it right to my locker, wondering if I would ever really see him again. And if I did see him again, I finally decided, I couldn't really give him this hat. I was married and shouldn't be going around giving men hats. But I thought about it every time I read Duncan a book he loved called *Caps for Sale* and finally I brought the hat home and gave it to him even though it was too big. He loved it.

# 26

The following weekend we drove to the country to see Gra and Charlie's new baby.

"Oh, he's so beautiful," I said, looking at the baby asleep on his stomach on their bed.

Gra seemed to be in a very bad mood.

"You know you're not supposed to put him to sleep on his stomach," I said.

"That is bunch of bullshit," she said, continuing to astound me with her excellent English.

"Well, there were studies—"

"He will only sleep on his stomach! He sleep better that way!"

I suddenly wished I was the kind of mother who let my baby sleep on his stomach. Maybe if I ever had another one I would give that a try.

"How was your delivery?" I said.

Gra groaned.

"It wasn't good," Charlie said. "She was in terrible pain. I mean, it really hurt her. And it just went on and on and on."

"Was it twenty-four hours?" I asked, cringing. "Thirty?" I always acted extra sympathetic to anyone's labor story due to my C-section one.

"No," Charlie said. "Maybe three or four."

"Four?" I said. "Four isn't so bad."

"It was awful," Charlie said.

"I hate it so much!" Gra said.

"But you knew it would hurt. Didn't you?"

"I didn't know! No one tell me."

In a country where they teach their daughters how to play Ping-Pong with their vaginas, they neglected to mention that childbirth was painful.

"Finally after four hours she asked for a C-section. So they gave her a C-section and when the baby came out she didn't want to hold it or even look at it," Charlie said.

"No," Gra agreed.

"And the nurses all acted so *horrified*. I told them, 'Why should she hold it when it caused her so much pain?' They kept trying to shove the kid at her and finally I said, 'Will you get that thing away from my wife, she doesn't want to deal with that right now. I don't know that kid. I know my wife. I love my wife. She doesn't want to hold some stranger we don't even know.'"

I looked at him, completely shocked. There were many terrible things about motherhood, but seeing and holding your baby for the first time wasn't one of them.

"Why I have to have boy?" Gra asked me as if I had been the one to give him to her.

"Boys are wonderful," I said. That morning Duncan had said to me, "Mama, I like my penis. Where'd you bought it?"

"How did you decide on the name Fisher?"

"We needed an F for my sister," Charlie said.

"You're going to love having a boy."

"We're getting to know him slowly over time. I'm doing all the work. Feeding, changing—which let me tell you is the most disgusting thing I have ever done in my life—holding. We couldn't be happier."

"You do all work?" Gra said. "You have C-section or me have C-section?"

"My wife is a little angry," Charlie said. I hated when men called women "my wife" when they were standing right there next to them.

"Anger is the first stage of motherhood," I said. "So you're not nursing?" I asked Gra.

"Nursing?" she asked.

"Breast-feeding?"

She pointed to her breasts. "From here?" she asked, completely affronted as if she'd never even heard of that and I had been the one to invent it. "No!"

"You're going to feel better," I told her, thinking she must be the worst mother I had ever seen or heard of in my entire life. "You're doing a great job. He's so beautiful."

I sat down on the edge of her bed and reached over to pat her back. She burst into tears and crawled into my lap like a cat. "Where my scar is hurt so much. You know you wake up in the morning you want stretch. I can't even put my arm up."

"I have a scar too. It will feel better."

*The Seven Year Bitch*

"Really?" she asked, looking up into my eyes.

"Really," I said.

I looked down at the baby boy, the only Asian baby in Kripplebush, New York, or probably all of upstate for that matter. If he even survived all that sleeping on his stomach, what would become of him? I wondered.

# 27

I'm going to be forty," I told Shasthi.

"Really, Izzy?" she said, as if such a thing were impossible. I loved her for it.

"Next week. It's going to be my birthday on Friday."

"Happy birthday," she said.

I wondered what she was going to get me. She had a cousin who worked at Victoria's Secret, so maybe something from there or something modest, like a soap or flowers.

"I think we should get you a cell phone," I announced grandly.

"I told you, Izzy, I can't afford—"

"No, Russell and I talked about it and we want to put you on our family plan. You'll have to keep your minutes down but there're unlimited nights and weekends." Russell had said no to this, but I really thought he was wrong. It was for Duncan's safety. I had to be able to reach her in an emergency. I had to know where Duncan was at all times. And if I couldn't get her a baby, the least I could do was get her a phone.

"Okay," she said. "Thank you."

We walked together with the stroller to a phone store on Broadway and she chose the phone she wanted. I added her to our family plan.

"My own phone," she said, tucking it into its little case and then into her purse.

For a moment I hoped she wouldn't be one of those nannies who talked on it all the time while the child languished. But I shook the thought out of my head. I had done a nice thing. It wasn't that expensive. Shasthi had her own phone.

*On my fortieth birthday* I woke up depressed out of my mind. The phone was ringing off the hook, with its merry ring, but it wasn't mine. It was Shasthi's.

She was in the kitchen making a pancake and an egg for Duncan. I walked out of my bedroom shyly wrapped in my usual towel.

"Happy birthday, honey," Russell said. "Duncan, it's Mommy's birthday. What do you want for your birthday, honey?"

A little last-minute, didn't he think? "All I want for my birthday is not to be stepped over," I said. I was still angry about that.

Angry, I got into the shower. Shasthi hadn't so much as wished me a good morning. No Happy Birthday, no flowers, no soap. In fact we were out of soap.

As over-dramatic as I'd been about turning forty and as upset as I'd pretended to be about it, it didn't prepare me for how upsetting and traumatic it really was. All day long I had the feeling that the Grim Reaper was celebrating my birthday with me.

*Jennifer Belle*

220

At Aquacise, as I kicked in unison with the other old ladies, I thought he was the instructor standing at the edge of the pool looking down at us. And at lunch I could swear he was at the table with me.

At four o'clock I went for my massage. It had been a gift from my father, my stepmother really, right after the baby was born. I'd bristled with anger when I opened the envelope containing the gift certificate. I'd just had a baby via emergency C-section. I hadn't lain on my stomach in a year. The last thing I wanted to do was gallivant around a fancy dressing room in terry-cloth slippers, sit in a sauna, have my body touched by a stranger. But now, on my fortieth birthday, I was finally ready to give it a try.

When I was twenty-one I got a massage once a week for forty bucks in a guy's loft on the Bowery. Looking back, I wondered what I had to be so tense about. Over the years I'd gotten massages sporadically—in a hotel on vacation, or a Chinese place on the street, or some scary basement somewhere with hockey-puck Combat roach traps stuck to the walls—but it was the last thing I had wanted for a gift after Duncan was born.

When I got there, I checked in at a sort of phony reception desk and was given flip-flops in a bag and a locker key. I tried to convince myself that putting on a strange robe and flip-flops was luxurious and I should be enjoying myself.

I was shepherded into a waiting area where I sat on a couch next to a gigantic bowl of Gala apples. While I was waiting, I ate three, one after the other.

Tony, my massage therapist, came into the waiting room to collect me.

"Hi," he said, looking at me. "How are you?"

*The Seven Year Bitch*

Maybe he was the Grim Reaper, I thought. Wouldn't that be ironic if my appointment with Tony was an appointment for the ultimate Blissage, to be caressed by the hands of death. I had eaten apples, the fruit of knowledge, which were close enough to pomegranates, the fruit of death. At least, if he was Death, I could fuck him in the privacy of a massage room.

"Is there anything I should know before we get started?" Tony said.

"I don't want much pressure on my lower back, but you can go very hard on my neck and shoulders. I had a C-section, so don't touch my stomach," I said. "I have carpel tunnel, bursitis, and tendinitis in both arms and arthritis in both hips and in my spine. My whole sacrum was pushed out of place by the baby." I prattled on about my health problems, looking intently into his eyes. "I'd really rather not have creams or lotions put in my hair," I instructed. I'd just had it blow-dried straight. "I've been having a lot of headaches lately. I really have a big knot right here." I tried to show him where the big knot was through the enormous robe.

"Anything else?" he said, smiling at me.

I looked into his wide warm face, thinking he seemed pleasant enough. He seemed a little blissed-out but down to earth and handsome.

I followed him into the massage room and he waited outside while I took off the robe and lay down on the table, arranging the towel over me and my breasts under me for a few minutes.

I was starting to look forward to this. I just hoped he wouldn't talk. I didn't want to talk about the economy or my baby, or about what I did for a living or anything. And I certainly didn't want to know anything about him.

*Jennifer Belle*

"Ready?" he asked through the door. He came in and folded the sheet down, so my back was exposed. Then he pressed his fingers into the middle of my back.

In an instant my year of massages came back to me. His loft on the Bowery, his wife and newborn baby in the next room, his shiatsu mat and meditation cushion. My body remembered him, even though I hadn't.

"Tony?" I said. I twisted around to look up at him.

"I wondered when you would figure out it was me," he said.

It was my body that had been the one to figure it out. Since I was twenty-one I'd had many massages and been touched by many men. I couldn't help but wonder if my back would remember every touch it had ever felt, like shoe prints in wet cement, if everyone's fingers had made as strong an impression or if it was only Tony it would remember.

I just couldn't get over it. I'd sat in the waiting area, clutching my key and my apple cores, talking to him for ten minutes. I'd looked into his eyes, been told his name, heard his voice, answered his questions, but I simply hadn't remembered him until he'd touched me.

For the rest of the seventy-five minutes he massaged me the way he used to, and we reminisced. He was divorced and I was married.

"I've gained a little weight since then," I said, cringing at the thought of it, and the list of ailments in my lament to him, and the scars from two surgeries. Since I'd last seen him I'd had an abortion, a miscarriage, and a baby. What did his fingers remember of my body? I wondered.

"It happens," he said. "You're still totally beautiful."

*The Seven Year Bitch*

For the rest of the hour I was twenty-one again. My body was lighter, took up less space on the table. My hair was enormously big and curly, the bonding on my teeth was white and new, my arms didn't hurt at all. And my stomach! My stomach was round and smooth and untouched. I was perfect.

"My body was so relaxed back then," I said.

"What are you talking about?" he said.

"I was in such great shape. Young and pain-free."

"Are you kidding me? You had an ulcer. You were constipated. You had headaches and insomnia and TMJ. Remember your jaw? I never saw a jaw as tight as yours. Remember you had hives and eczema and you were constantly throwing up? You were just as tense right here." Again he touched the memory bank located between my shoulder blades.

He pressed his thumb into a painful spot along my spine that he'd once told me was fear. I flinched.

"So here we are after all these years," Tony said.

"It's my fortieth birthday," I said, my eyes filling with tears for the hundredth time that day.

"And you came to me on your twenty-first. Well happy birthday, Izzy. You can turn over now," he said.

I turned over onto my back and he rearranged the towel. He pushed his fingers into my scalp, ruining my blow-dry. My back, my legs, my feet, my arms, my hands, my neck, my shoulders, my face. Even my hair remembered him.

My body felt so good, I forgot about the Grim Reaper for a while. I left Tony with forty dollars folded into a tiny tip envelope, turned in my key and my flip-flops, and left. Then, at dusk, walking home past the playground on Thompson Street, I really saw him. He was sitting on a bench in his black hooded cloak with nothing but blackness where his face should be. I froze but then found my breath and continued walking. I wondered if I would kneel down on the ground in front of him and blow him right there on that bench.

I thought of Duncan and let out a single sob from somewhere deep within me. As if I were being pulled in his direction, I approached him, blinking my eyes as if trying to wake up from a dream. That's when I saw that he was just a black guy in a black sweatshirt.

"Sorry," I said, "I thought you were someone," and I walked home to my family as fast as I possibly could.

When I walked in the door, Duncan greeted me with a beautifully wrapped box. "Mama, Shasthi left something for you." I opened it to find an Indian top in bright magenta embroidered with tiny silver beads and sequins. I put it on and admired myself in the mirror.

"Now you look just like her," Russell said.

We went to dinner at Chanterelle, where we had been married. Russell turned off his phone. We walked there with our arms linked, which was nice, even if Russell always did it wrong, holding on to my arm as if I were the man and sort of leaning all his weight on me.

"Hey, isn't that Jack?" Russell said. "Jack? Jack?" he yelled. Jack was the loud, moronic, drunken waiter at a pizza place we sometimes went to in the Village and before I knew it Russell had invited him to join us.

*The Seven Year Bitch*

*At seven the next* morning, I lay in bed picturing Shasthi. At this very moment she was checking into New York Presbyterian–Cornell Weill Medical Center with her husband. They would do blood work. Then her husband would be brought into a room with a TV and given a porno video. He would jerk off into something.

I had taken five hundred dollars out of the bank every day for sixteen business days and I hadn't mentioned it to Russell. Then I'd given her the money in two manila envelopes and her husband had picked her up from work.

I looked at the clock. It could be now that the doctor was taking the sperm and putting it in her. I willed it up, past those fibroids, into her follicle.

# 28

"Why don't we share two panini?" Gerde said at lunch. It was the middle of May and we were sitting in a glassed-in garden. "You will have the St. Lyons de Rosette and Gorgonzola splashed with grappa, and I will have the *salume*."

"Okay," I said, even though I would rather have shared a pizza. "You should come to the country with us," I said, wondering if they would. I wanted them to, but I wondered how it would work, all of us crammed into our little house. "It's small. You and Rolph would have to sleep in the living room and Minerva could sleep in Duncan's room, or the three of you could take Duncan's room and Duncan could sleep in bed with us." I wondered if they liked us enough to come.

Since we'd had the house for the last few years, we'd invited people to come, but, with the exception of Duncan's party, no one ever did, which proved my point that no one liked the country. When we'd bought the house, before Duncan was born, we'd imagined the bedrooms, the living room, even the hammock

filled with friends, constant trips to buy more meat for the bar-
becue, and tours of the reservoir and local farm. We had come
to understand that "Come to Kripplebush" was not exactly an
invitation people couldn't resist.

"*Ja*, we would very much like to come," Gerde said. "We will
come next weekend. Don't worry, we will be prepared to rough it."

"Great," I said, a little let down. "We'll rough it in Kripplebush."

"Kripplebush is a German name, so it must be great," she said.

On the day they were meeting us up there, I bought six
pounds of meat for Hungarian goulash from Citarella packed in
an insulated bag with ice. By the time we got there the meat was
rotting. I slid it into the garbage, which we couldn't bring to the
dump until the next day.

I was nervous. "Can you please bring in wood for the fire," I
commanded Russell.

"You told me to change the sheets in our room," he said.

What if Russell and I couldn't keep it together? I thought.
What if we fought? We weren't fit to be hosts, I suddenly realized.

"I don't know why you're friends with Gerde," Russell said.

"Duncan and Minerva love each other," I said, but I didn't
know either.

They arrived late with apologies that they had been held up at
their friend's house in East Hampton because it was like heaven
there. Duncan and Minerva immediately began to argue and
then Minerva bit his face and he cried in pain.

"It's okay," I said to Minerva.

"Of course it's okay! Oh, my baby," Gerde said, scooping
Minerva up and rocking her.

Duncan's face was bleeding and starting to bruise. I went into

*Jennifer Belle*

the house to get him an ice pack and when I came back Gerde was rocking Minerva in a lawn chair, saying something to her in German.

"She always feels so bad when this happens. Every time she bites someone I feel so bad for her."

Grimly we walked into the house and I showed her around.

"It would be better if we slept in here, so Minerva can sleep in bed with us," Rolph said, standing in the doorway to our bedroom.

"Okay," I said.

He hoisted their bags into my room and all gathered in there. Russell and I listened to heated German being spoken behind the closed door. Gerde was chanting something that sounded like a nursery rhyme.

> *Hoppe hoppe, Reiter,*
> *wenn er fällt, dann schreit er,*
> *fällt er in den Teich,*
> *find't ihn keiner gleich.*

> *Hoppe hoppe, Reiter,*
> *wenn er fällt, dann schreit er,*
> *fällt er in den Graben,*
> *fressen ihn die Raben.*

> *Hoppe hoppe, Reiter,*
> *wenn er fällt, dann schreit er,*
> *fällt er in den Sumpf,*
> *dann macht der Reiter . . . Plumps!*

*The Seven Year Bitch*

"What do you think they're saying?" I whispered to Russell. He had studied German at college.

"I'm not sure. *Graben* means 'grave' and *raben* means 'raven.' Something about Jews falling into a grave and a raven swooping down I think," Russell said. "Can I ask where we're supposed to sleep?"

"We'll just sleep in the living room," I told him.

When they came out I told them we would have to go out to dinner.

"I don't want to do that," Rolph said.

"What about this great goulash I have heard so much about?" Gerde said. I explained that the meat had spoiled.

"What other foods do you have? Gerde could cook a casserole," Rolph said.

"Actually our oven doesn't work," I said.

"Maybe I can fix it," Rolph said.

"Jews don't usually let Germans go near their ovens," I said.

Everyone laughed, horrified.

It was like a children's book I had read to Duncan where a tiny mouse couple—a dentist and his wife—have to work on the cavity of a fox.

"Then perhaps we can eat something cold," Rolph said. He and Gerde discussed something in German, ignoring the fact that we were there. "Don't you have anything we can eat?"

Gerde made a pasta sauce with the vegetables that were meant for the goulash and half a bottle of ketchup and I made a salad, and we ate and drank in our screened-in gazebo. I began to relax. It was everything Russell and I had imagined.

"So are you two going to have another baby?" Rolph asked.

*Jennifer Belle*

"One's just fine for me," Russell said.

"We are already trying," Rolph said.

I wondered what it said about our marriages that they were and we weren't.

"I'll get another bottle of wine," I said, as if that was going to help them try right now. I went into the kitchen. They were moving on in life, expanding, proliferating if that was a word, and we the Trents were withering up. I was happy for them. I didn't know why I felt so shaken up. It had just taken me so much by surprise. I wasn't expecting it. But I couldn't expect my friend to consult with me before trying to get pregnant, like we were making a plan for tea.

"I don't know if a sibling is such a great thing in the after all," Rolph said. "My brother and I shared a room and I always hated him."

"I love my brother," I said. I even loved his wife. They lived in Seattle, so I almost never got to see them.

"I could do without my sister," Russell said.

"How did you come up with the name Duncan?" Rolph asked. "Are you great fans of the doughnut?"

"I wanted Duncan to be named Otto," Russell said, ignoring the insult. "Otto Trent."

I didn't say anything, but I had said no to Otto, because to me it sounded like the name of a Nazi guard. "No way I was going for Otto," I said. "Unless I was giving birth to a Nazi guard."

"*Ja*," Rolph said. "Exactly. My grandfather was named Otto."

"Did he ever kill any Jews?" I asked.

"Jesus, Izzy," Russell said.

"*Ja*, of course. He killed lots of Jews, thousands, of course. He was a Nazi *Geschwader* in the *Luftwaffe*," Rolph said.

*The Seven Year Bitch*

Russell and I looked at each other. I was thinking about my relatives in their graves in the Jewish cemetery and, I was almost certain, Russell was too.

Later that night, with Rolph and Gerde and Minerva snuggled up in our bed, Russell and I lay in an L shape on the couches in the living room. In a romantic moment, Russell had suggested we lie head to head instead of feet to feet.

"Why aren't we in our own bed?" he whispered.

"I'm not sure," I said. "It all happened quickly."

"Did you notice they didn't bring anything, not even a bottle of wine?" Russell said.

"I know!" I whispered.

"Can you imagine spending the weekend at someone's house and not bringing a bottle of wine? And people think Jews are cheap."

This was one thing I really loved about Russell, the negative spin he put on things. It gave me such a cozy, familial feeling, like I was a child talking to my mother after one of her dinner parties.

"Gerde did make the pasta sauce," I said.

"God, it was just *awful*. And I'll tell you why they didn't want to go out to dinner. They were afraid they might have to offer to pick up the check."

"I don't know," I said, thinking how I felt closer to him than I had in a long time.

"Well I know. It's great you're trying to make friends with the other mothers and all that, but did you have to bring home a couple of Nazis? I mean this is just god-awful. I'll sell the house if I have to. No *danke*. Never again!"

*Jennifer Belle*

I smiled.

"And I'll tell you another thing," he said. "The name Otto is out. If we ever have another son, I can assure you, he won't be named Otto."

In the morning Minerva bit Duncan again and again Gerde comforted her. Then Rolph bounced Duncan on his long leg and again said the German nursery rhyme.

"How does it go in English?" I asked, completely sick of them speaking German in front of us like we weren't even there.

"Let's see if I can say it in English," Rolph said.

> *Bumpety bump, rider,*
> *if he falls, then he cries out*
> *should he fall into the pond,*
> *no one will find him soon.*
>
> *Bumpety bump, rider . . .*
>
> *Should he fall into the grave,*
> *then the ravens will eat him.*
>
> *Should he fall into the swamp,*
> *then the rider goes . . . splash!*

"I guess it's not too cheerful," Rolph said as Duncan managed to climb down from his leg and run to me.

# 29

"Did you get your period?" I asked Shasthi when she walked in the door in the morning. The two weeks' waiting time was up from her third round of artificial insemination. If this didn't work we were going to have to decide whether or not to move on to in vitro fertilization, which would involve more daily hormone injections and general anesthesia and many more thousands of dollars. In which case, Dr. Heiffowitz had said, it would really make sense to consider having the myomectomy—the operation to remove her fibroids—first.

"No," she said.

"So you could be pregnant!" I said.

"No," she said. "I went for the test this morning."

"So, next time," I said. "It will work next time. Whatever we decide to do next." I felt crushed. Like a Las Vegas gambler losing eight thousand dollars. A year's tuition in preschool. How could Dr. Heiffowitz have failed me like this, I couldn't help but think.

"I worry I could be in menopause," she said and burst into tears. "I told my husband I wish we had gone to the doctor sooner. I didn't know this was happening to me."

"Wait," I said. I couldn't believe what I was hearing. Dr. Heiffowitz would have to do something. "Do you get hot flashes?"

"Yes," she cried. "Sometimes I get them."

"But you're only forty-one," I said, almost begging. My eyes had filled up with tears. I didn't know what to do. "It's still possible to get pregnant," I said tentatively. I tried to think of people I knew who had gotten pregnant after menopause but I couldn't think of anyone. It wasn't possible. It wasn't possible!

"You don't know if this is true," I said. "We'll ask the doctor. I'm so sorry. This is terrible." I felt flattened. Menopause. I was sick. Here he was, Shasthi's Grim Reaper, coming for her in my house. I wished I had left her alone and not gotten involved. Russell had been completely right. I had made it worse for her. This was my fault in some very real way. Having no blood was the bloodiest ending of all.

All day I had the strange, clutching feeling of being abandoned. When I got home I felt relieved to see that Duncan was fine, lining up tiny animals in a long parade. Shasthi was still there. Life had somehow continued.

"What are you going to do on your vacation?" I asked. We were going upstate for a week.

"My husband and mother-in-law and brother and I are going to Niagara Falls," she said.

I didn't know what I was expecting but I was surprised. Niagara Falls was where honeymooners went. It seemed like such a hopeful place. Such a long drive and for what? Just to have a loo-kylou. It seemed so pointless. "Oh that's nice," I said. "It's beauti-ful there."

"Have you ever been?"

"No," I said.

Shasthi took her envelope of cash from the table, zipped her pocketbook, and went to the door. "Okay, bye then."

I thought of her and her family, probably in her brother's cab, singing songs and laughing, talking about cricket, sleeping in a cheap motel, eating delicious food they'd brought from home.

I went to the door and opened it.

"Have a good time. Don't worry . . ." I started to say, but she was gone.

I stood there fighting the urge to run to the door and beg her to take me to Niagara Falls with her. I felt panicked, like I was straining against something, grunting with effort, like Duncan trying to break through the straps of his car seat. "Take me with you," I whispered.

There were sequins everywhere because I still hadn't gotten the vacuum fixed. I bent down and picked them up off the rug while Duncan watched me.

# 30

I can't," I said to Gabe Weinrib when he called and asked if we could meet the following week.

"Why not?" he asked.

"I'm going to Miami." Russell was going there on business and I'd told him there was no way I was going with him because I hated Miami and always regretted traveling with him because he acted so crazy in airports, and I'd just end up alone on the beach all day with Duncan and stuck in the hotel room all night while Russell was out with his client—but I didn't think I should get together with Gabe again.

"Well, I can meet with you there, m'dear," he said. "I'm going to be visiting my uncle in Boca."

"I'll be there with my son," I said. "I won't have any time—"

"I'd love to meet your son. Dustin?"

"Duncan."

"Duncan. It'll be a nice change from the geriatric set of Boca. Call me when you get there."

I felt my face get hot. I couldn't speak. I couldn't imagine it—me in a bathing suit? Me in a sundress? Jeans? How could I explain spending time with this man? Would he come back to my hotel room with me?

When I got off the phone I lay on my bed and imagined his weight on top of me.

The next day I had my own appointment with Dr. Heiffowitz. I'd had dozens of conversations with Russell that had gone nowhere about whether we should have another baby. Or not. And we always decided against it. We didn't have the room or the money. We were on the verge of divorce. All the more reason, I thought, if we were going to get a divorce, to have another baby. So Duncan would have someone to be shuttled around with. He wouldn't bear the whole burden. When we fought and I did my karate kicking, Duncan would have someone to cry and cower with, huddled together under blankets, big brother holding the flashlight.

When my parents got divorced I would have died without my brother, and I was twenty-five and he was twenty-one. We didn't huddle under blankets, but we did go out for sushi and toast the end of an era and that had been an enormous comfort.

Duncan needed a sibling.

Either way there was the matter of the medication I was supposed to be taking for my thyroid that I had stopped taking while I was nursing and I had to go to Dr. Heiffowitz to find out if I should start taking it again.

Seeing him made my heart pound. His white-blond hair and icy blue eyes looking sensitively at me over his rimless glasses made me close my eyes for a moment.

I loved Dr. Heiffowitz. There was no other way to describe it. He had given me my son. He was more powerful to me than God or the Grim Reaper. He had listened to me and figured out what was wrong. He had shown me my follicle when a lesser doctor wouldn't have bothered. He was a genius and he loved me too.

If I took off all my clothes, I thought, it would not surprise him. It would almost be the only thing to do, to climb on his lap and wrap my arms around his neck.

"So," he said, in that beautiful Israeli accent. "You had twins in September."

I laughed but he didn't laugh.

"No," I said.

He looked down at my chart.

"Yes, you had twins in September."

"No," I said.

"Are you being some kind of a joker?" he asked.

"No, I wouldn't joke about a horrible thing like twins. I had one son two years ago in November."

"That's not possible," he said.

"I'm sorry."

He looked at the chart. "Your name is Isabelle Brilliant?"

"Isolde Brilliant," I said.

"Your husband is David?"

"Russell."

He got up and stormed out of the room yelling for Scottie.

Five minutes later he came back with my chart.

"You had one son, two years ago in November."

"Yes," I said.

"Without the medication, half a pill in the morning and half

*The Seven Year Bitch*

at night, you cannot get pregnant. It would not be possible. With the medication you can get pregnant, but you would have to give it a few weeks. Your levels are all wrong now. To put it in medical terms, you're all out of whack. So I want you to start taking the medication, regardless of whether you're planning to get pregnant. We have to get you back to normal."

"So you're sure I can't get pregnant right now?"

"I'm sure."

"By the way," I said, "do you know what happened to Dr. Lichter?"

"Not really. I don't know for sure. I heard his mother died and he had a nervous breakdown," Dr. Heiffowitz said.

"His mother?" I'd heard it was a family member, but I had assumed it was his child or wife, not mother.

Reluctantly, I got up to go.

"Do you think I should have another child?" I asked. I looked at him meaningfully in case he would want it to be with him. "My husband and I are probably going to get a divorce and then we might have to live in two small apartments."

"My brothers and I shared a room," Dr. Heiffowitz said.

"How many children do you have?" I asked.

"Three," he said, writing something on a prescription pad. "But I wish we had had more."

When I left his office I looked down at the prescription he'd handed me, thinking it would say "Have 1 child a year for 3 years." But it was a prescription for the thyroid medication—half in the morning and half at night.

I stood on the street trying to decide what to do next. I hated myself when I did that, just stood there frozen, and I always noticed when other people did it. Duncan was with Shasthi. I had the rest of the afternoon to myself.

I hailed a cab and told the driver to take me to Fifty-sixth between Fifth and Sixth and then got out in front of the Norma Kamali store.

Standing in the dressing room, I examined myself in the mirror in a red ruched bathing suit. I imagined Gabe Weinrib looking back at me, wondering what he would be thinking when he saw me in it in Miami. The bathing suit was a size large, which seemed to mean that I must be a size large, something I had certainly never been before. But it really wasn't so bad. I had the same shape, just a little bit bigger. My hair looked great, maybe a little wild, my legs, my shoulders.

I'm not buying this bathing suit for Gabe Weinrib, I told myself. I'm buying this for the pool at the gym. But when I handed my credit card to the salesgirl, I knew I really had bought it for Gabe, because you don't spend $280 on a bathing suit to wear for six old ladies at the gym.

Afterward, with my Norma Kamali shopping bag on the seat facing me, I had lunch at La Bonne Soupe. I noticed a miserable-looking couple at the next table. The woman was in her fifties, with a nose and boob job, dressed in a suit with a hint of Goth to it. The man, well past his prime, looked uncomfortable, handsome, dumb.

"You're disgusting," the woman said to the man. "You're a reprehensible piece of shit."

"So then don't marry me," he said.

"Oh believe me, there's no way in hell I would marry you.

Why would I marry you? So you can take all my money? I don't think so."

"Fine," the man said, as if this were the most normal conversation. He took several bites of his soup with interest.

"You're a reprehensible piece of shit."

The woman caught my eye and I tried to give her a sympathetic smile, to show we were sisters in the war of love.

"Everywhere we go, people laugh at us," the woman said to the man.

He just ate and grunted. "God you're an insufferable cunt."

"What kind of man goes to his accountant and asks if you will save money on taxes if you marry me?" the woman said. "You know what kind of man? A piece of shit. A reprehensible piece of shit. What must he have thought of you when you asked that question? He must have just thought, What a reprehensible piece of shit."

I wondered what would happen if I turned to them and said, "I don't think it's so bad that he asked that question." But then I thought better of it and ten reprehensible piece of shits later, I realized something. They were still both sitting there. They were eating their meals with relish. Neither one of them was going anywhere. That was marriage. Theirs would be a more solid marriage than most.

Do you—Isolde Pearl Brilliant—take this reprehensible piece of shit—Russell Ellis Trent—to be your lawful wedded husband?

I do.

And do you—Russell Ellis Trent—take this insufferable cunt—Isolde Pearl Brilliant—to be your lawful wedded wife?

I do.

*Jennifer Belle*

I now pronounce you husband and wife. You may now give each other the finger.

*When I got home* I told Russell the good news that I couldn't get pregnant, and that night, with Hum by our side, we made love. Sex for sex's sake. At least for that night, not having a second child was not an issue. He didn't have to dig around in my underwear drawer for a condom, rip it open and put it on, and then carefully dispose of it afterward, so that Shasthi wouldn't see it.

# 31

Russell was not good at getting on planes. He wasn't afraid to fly, but something about the transition from being in the airport to being on the plane was too much for him. He couldn't handle taking off his shoes and going through the metal detector. Anyone who saw it would think he was harboring a bomb up his ass. "I'm doing the best I can," he yelled at the man behind him.

"Will you calm down!" I screamed at him. "You're acting like a lunatic."

"Just stop it. Leave me alone. I will not be attacked like this!" he screamed back, one shoe on, one shoe off, a hole in his fruity striped Paul Smith sock revealing his big toe. Where was Gra when you needed her?

"Is everything okay here?" the security guard said, approaching us with caution, the way he was trained to do.

It seemed being stopped by security was becoming a regular thing for us.

"You have to be married to understand," Russell said.

"Do you need my assistance here, sir?" the guard asked.

I imagined Gabe Weinrib easily sliding off his Gucci loafers, folding the stroller with one hand and scooping up Duncan with the other, taking off Duncan's shoes with David Copperfield finesse and putting them back on, all the while handling his carry-on bag and mine, and all of our millions effortlessly.

Duncan ran over to a garbage can and threw his new Oscar the Grouch doll, which I had just purchased for him, right into it. "That's very bad," I scolded Duncan, although when you thought about it, it was really very clever, putting Oscar the Grouch, who lives in a garbage can, into a garbage can.

"What's your name?" the woman who took our tickets asked.

"Duncan Trent," he said.

"And how old are you?" she asked. We had lied and said he was under two so we wouldn't have to pay for his ticket.

"I'm two, except when I go on an airplane, then I'm only one," he said.

*"We're in Miami,"* I told Duncan.

"I like Mommy's Ami," Duncan said.

"No, not Mommy's Ami," Russell said. "Miami."

"Daddy's Ami," Duncan said.

"Not Daddy's Ami," I said. "Miami."

"Mommy and Daddy's Ami," he said, already a little expert at solving our fights, I worried.

We checked into our hotel room at the Raleigh with its colorful batik pillows. Thinking of Shasthi, I showed Duncan the

*The Seven Year Bitch*

ocean for the first time. I felt terrible that we hadn't brought her, but it was supposed to be a family trip, my time to spend with Duncan. And, I thought, Gabe Weinrib.

"Let's go," he said.

"I'm surprised you agreed to come here," Russell said. He knew how much I hated South Beach, with its boob jobs everywhere you looked. Driving along parts of Collins Avenue was no different from driving along Queens Boulevard in Forest Hills.

"So what are you going to do when I'm working all day?" Russell asked.

"I don't know," I said. "Beach, pool. Maybe I'll have the hotel arrange a car service and I'll take Duncan to Parrot Jungle or something."

"I have a few hours," Russell said. "I'm going to take him down to the beach."

I changed Duncan into his blue bathing suit, with a bright orange pattern of starfish. Russell took off his pants and his striped socks and put on his bathing suit.

"I'm dex-cited," Duncan said, and they headed out together holding hands. "I want to push the button," I heard Duncan, fading, down the hallway.

I walked around the hotel room, noticing all the mirrors it had in it. I looked at myself in each one and I thought how few mirrors I had in my apartment. Just one, now that I thought about it, on the inside of a closet door, and around the fireplace was some old mirror, and over the fireplace, but that was too high to see yourself in, and of course the medicine chest in the bathroom. I made a mental note to buy a few and put them around the house.

It was important to see yourself. It had a grounding effect to see yourself every minute. I found it comforting.

I called Gabe Weinrib and got his voice mail.

"I'm in Miami," I said. "Or Mommy's Ami as Duncan calls it 'cause he thinks when I'm saying *Miami* it's really *My* Ami." Why was I mentioning Duncan? I wondered.

A beep interrupted me and a woman's recorded voice said, "To accept and send this message press one. To erase and rerecord this message press two."

I pressed two with the relief of a convict being released from death row.

"Hi Gabe it's Izzy, I'm here in Miami at the Raleigh, call me on my cell, bye."

I hung up and put on my red Norma Kamali bathing suit and looked at myself in one of the mirrors.


*That night Russell went* to a business dinner and Duncan and I ordered room service. Duncan sat in a dresser drawer watching *Bambi* on pay-per-view.

My phone rang. "So you're here," he said.

"Yes, are you?"

"Yes, m'dear. I'm in Bo-ca." He said it the way he said everything, in this sort of seventies swinging-single way.

"Okay," I said, sounding like Shasthi.

"Shall I pick you up tomorrow at your hotel? We could go to the beach?"

"Actually I promised I'd take Duncan to Parrot Jungle," I said.

*The Seven Year Bitch*

I didn't know why I had said that. I had absolutely no desire to go to Parrot Jungle but it had just nervously come out of my mouth. It was the only thing I could think of to get out of going to the beach with him.

"That sounds like fun," he said. "Parrot Jungle it is. My treat." The man had two hundred million dollars. He had to stop saying "my treat" all the time, for Christ's sake. Some things went without saying.

"Okay," I said.

"Shall we say eleven?"

"Sure," I said. He must really like me, I thought. I sat down on the hotel bed and smoothed my hair like a fifties housewife. If I'd had an apron I'd have smoothed that too. "Let's meet there, though. We have our cell phones, we'll find each other."

"Oh, okay," he said, knowingly.

"Oh, okay, what?" I said.

"Just okay," he said.

"No really, what?" I said, like a fifties housewife talking to a seventies swinger, like Lucy had somehow lost Ricky and somehow wandered aboard the Love Boat.

"Great," he said. "So I'll see you around the entrance at eleven."

I got off the phone completely bewildered.


*Everywhere you looked at* Parrot Jungle there were birds walking around eating garbage. There were parrots to pet and tortoises to photograph and a tiger named Champa, which Duncan got a huge kick out of because that was also the name of one of the other nannies in the playground, a friend of Shasthi's. There was every kind of preening, colorful male species.

The only thing there wasn't was Gabe.

Finally, when Duncan passed out in his stroller after ice cream, I called him.

"Sorry, m'dear. I got held up in Bo-ca."

"Oh, no problem," I squawked. "We were coming here anyway."

"I would have liked to have met your son. Next time I'll bring my son and we'll all go."

"What? You didn't tell me you had a son!"

"Didn't I? That's strange. He lives in France with his mother and her yoga instructor boyfriend who I support."

"Why do you support him?" I asked.

"Because he lives with my son and my son's mother and I want my son to be totally comfortable in every way. His name is Mathieu and he's eight. His mother is a French model who I had a short fling with. And now it's worked out very well. I spend half the time in New York and half the time in Paris with him and I couldn't be happier. But back then, when she told me she was pregnant, I thought it was the end for me. I begged her to get an abortion. I offered her millions of dollars. I threatened her, I said I would demand a paternity test, give her nothing. But she wouldn't even consider an abortion. So I have a son. And it's the best thing in the world. And I have you to thank for it, m'dear."

"What am I to thank for?" I asked.

"I met the mother of my son the day I landed in Paris, the day after I met you at Don Hill's. If you had come with me I wouldn't have met her. I wouldn't have Mathieu. You might not have Duncan. I'd love to have another baby one day, this time with a wife who I actually live with in the same country. Do you want to have more children?"

All the mothers in Duncan's toddler class were constantly asking each other if they were going to have another baby. It was so personal, so private, yet it was the first thing out of everyone's mouth and considered totally acceptable.

"Russell—my husband—and I aren't getting along that well," I said, which I seemed to be saying to men left and right lately. I didn't even know why I was talking to him at all. I had sat down on a bench without realizing it and tucked my legs under me. I felt like he was there watching me, but I couldn't see him. I felt like I was in a confessional.

"I'm sorry," he said. I didn't know what he meant by that. Why was he sorry, exactly?

I had come all the way to Florida for this, I thought. I had made a fool of myself, getting stood up by this man, almost exposing my *son* to him, risking my entire marriage, and he was sorry I wasn't getting along with Russell? I vowed right there and then to devote myself completely to Duncan. And to spend the entire next day on the beach with him looking at shells. His little tank top that Shasthi had gotten him that said "I'm the Boss" was covered in ice cream.

I felt duped but I had no one to blame but myself.

"You know," Gabe Weinrib said, "you have so many of the qualities I'm looking for in a woman."

"Like what?" I asked, wondering how to get off the phone.

"You're smart, and funny, and beautiful, and a wonderful mother . . ."

"I thought you liked models and redheads with great little bodies."

"I see you've been paying attention. But actually I like brunettes. Let me put it this way, you have so many of the qualities I'm looking for in a woman *I'd want to settle down with*."

"What do you mean 'so many' of the qualities? What qualities don't I have?" I asked.

"Well, you're married," he said.

"I should go," I said. "I have to take Duncan to the monkeys."

I got off the phone and stared at Duncan, wishing that he would wake up so I wouldn't feel so alone, and when he did I prayed he would go back to sleep because I had no idea how to pretend to be having a good time.

"Come on," I said. "I'll take you to the gift shop. My treat."

He looked sleepily up at me as if asking who the hell else's treat it would be. He chose a stuffed Champa the tiger. On our way back to the hotel in the car service, he threw it out the window.

*When we got back* to the hotel I was tired. Russell was waiting for us in the room.

"Let's go to the beach," he said.

"You go," I said. "I'm going to lie down for a little while."

A few hours later I woke up to find Russell staring down at me.

"You're taking a nap," he said.

*The Seven Year Bitch*

"So?" I said.

"So you haven't taken a nap since you were pregnant with Duncan."

"It's just a nap," I said. He just stood there continuing to stare at me, suspiciously. "I'm not pregnant, if that's what you're thinking. Dr. Heiffowitz said I can't get pregnant." My period was late. I thought of the unopened box of Tampax I'd thrown in my bag. After my last date with Gabe Weinrib I'd wanted to be prepared.

The next morning, driving back to the airport, Russell pulled the rental car over in front of a Walgreens and Duncan and I waited while he came back with a pregnancy test kit.

"You're being silly," I said.

"Do the test now," he said when we got to the airport.

"Let's wait till we get home."

"Test now," he said.

I waited on line in the ladies room with Duncan by my side because as a mother I was never allowed to pee alone. We locked ourselves into a stall. "Don't touch anything," I said.

I unzipped my jeans and sat on the toilet. I removed the pregnancy test from its wrapper.

"What's that?" Duncan asked.

"It's something for mommies," I said.

I heard a woman on line laugh. "It's hard to have boys," she said.

"Is that a toy for me?" Duncan asked.

"You can have this part," I said, giving him the wrapper and the plastic cap that went over the stick's tip.

"Mommy's making a poopie!" Duncan announced loudly.

I heard a couple of women laugh.

"No, honey, I'm not," I said, and before I'd even finished peeing, the stick said pregnant.

*In the morning I* got Dr. Heiffowitz on the phone.

"Doctor?" I said, after I was sure he knew which Brilliant I was. "I took a pregnancy test and it said I was pregnant. That's how messed up my body must be, how wrong my levels are, how out of whack I am. Maybe it's early menopause. I'm forty. I mean I know I can't be pregnant. So, what do you think?"

"I think you're pregnant," he said.

"But you said that would be impossible!" I practically screamed, like I was a teenage girl and Dr. Heiffowitz was my teenage boyfriend, not the most eminent reproductive endocrinologist in the world.

"I would never say that," he said. "I've seen sixty-five-year-old women get pregnant, women who had been in menopause for years, women with nonexistent levels, much worse than yours, women whose bodies were ravaged with cancer, women with just a sliver of one ovary left in them. So you see, I would never say such a thing."

Before I could say one more "But you said that" he had handed me over to Scottie.

*The miscarriage I'd had* before I'd gotten pregnant with Duncan and before I'd met Dr. Lichter was called a blighted ovum, which meant that the pregnancy had never really existed. There was nothing in the egg. Even though I had taken a home pregnancy test, several of them actually, and had had the pregnancy confirmed by an ob-gyn, been prescribed prenatal vitamins, stopped drinking alcohol and taking hot showers, vomited and fought exhaustion, and told every person I came in contact with for nine and a half long weeks that I was pregnant, they had the nerve to tell me that I hadn't really been. There was no heartbeat. It hadn't ever been real.

I had lain on the table staring at the sonogram screen, waiting to hear the heartbeat.

"That's funny," the doctor said, shoving the wand around a little more aggressively.

"What's funny?" I asked.

"I don't hear anything."

Even though I had to have a D&C to remove the egg, I had never really been pregnant.

And once, when I was eight months pregnant with Duncan, I prayed for a miscarriage. Russell's parents were visiting us at the country house. To make his mother happy we went to a crafts fair, which was not so much crafts as crap. Still his mother looked at everything—refrigerator magnets, Post-it notepads with flip-flops and suns wearing sunglasses on them, crappy clothes from India that you could buy at any street fair in Manhattan, and every manner of tote bag.

Watching his mother buying a sweatshirt for herself with Noah's Ark on it and the words "TWO BY TWO" puff-painted under it made my head feel like it was going to blow off my body. Her husband, my future son's grandfather, was nattering by her side. I welled up with bile. I was sick. I weaved behind them through aisle after aisle—his mother had now put on the sweatshirt, leaving the collar of her shirt peeking out over the collar of the sweatshirt—and I had to sit down on a chair made out of rope for a few minutes with my head down between my legs. *What have I done?* I wanted to yell out to the fertility gods I had once prayed to. *What is inside of me? Please God*, I begged, *rid me of this . . . thing . . . inside me.* I did not want to propagate whatever genes were in those people and now in me. I did not want to bring forth into the world another Trent boy child.

A security guard approached me and asked if I would like to be escorted to the first-aid tent, but I'd refused. I doubted they would give me an abortion in first aid between the face-painting booth and the guy selling the flamingo lawn ornaments.

From the backseat of the car, as we'd driven back to our house with Russell's father in the passenger seat next to Russell happily chirping questions at me about phantom bonds and Russell's mother chirping next to me about how everyone was meant to be a couple, I told Russell I felt sick.

"Two by two's pretty much how God intended it," his mother said.

"I think I'm going to throw up," I said urgently.

"Well that's pregnancy for you," his mother said.

Pain was shooting up my neck into my ears. I'd had one or two bouts of morning sickness in the very beginning but nothing like this.

"Russell pull over," I said.

"Okay, give me a minute," he said.

"*Ugh*," his mother said. "Did I ever tell you about the two times when I was pregnant with Russell that I got so sick?"

"No," I gasped.

*The Seven Year Bitch*

"Well, have you ever smelled the smell of *old mop*? Once I was in a supermarket and I turned a corner and I suddenly smelled that smell of really old, dirty, moldy *mop* . . ."

"*Oooooooohhhh*," I moaned.

"And I kept asking myself, 'What is that?' and I realized they must have mopped the floors with an old smelly mop, and well, I just lost my lunch right there in the produce aisle. And the *second* time . . ."

"No," I said.

"Oh yes. I was in the kitchen in the Cape Cod house, and I thought to myself, Well, it's time to make dinner, and I took a whole chicken out of the fridge, and I said to myself, 'You know, this just doesn't smell right.' You know that smell of rotting chicken, long after it's turned?"

"Russell, pull over!" I begged.

He swerved to the side of the road, and, with his mother rubbing my back in irritating little circles, I vomited and vomited out of the open car door, right in someone's driveway. I lay in bed for the rest of their stay with cold wet washcloths on my forehead, praying for death. God had punished me for thinking those thoughts about my baby.

*When I got off* the phone with Dr. Heiffowitz I was too stunned even to call Russell. I was pregnant! I was going to have another baby. I filled Humbert's water bowl but I forgot to put it on the floor for him. He didn't have any water for the whole day.

Shasthi came home with Duncan.

"Izzy, may I speak to you about something?" She handed me a pregnancy test stick in a ziplock sandwich bag.

"What's this?" I said. I'd taken a few more tests before calling Dr. Heiffowitz and I must have accidentally left one on the side of the tub for her to find.

"It's a pregnancy test," she said.

"So you know," I said. "I'm pregnant."

"You're pregnant?"

"Isn't that why you're showing me my pregnancy test?" I asked.

"No. I'm showing you mine. I'm pregnant. I did this over by Champa today."

"We're pregnant!" I said, and we both started jumping up and down. Duncan joined in.

"Why are you both so happy?" Duncan asked.

"Because we love you so much," I said.

# 32

As soon as I found out I was pregnant, instantly, it seemed, I got huge. This second pregnancy was nothing like the first. Everything was happening so fast I didn't have the luxury of sleeping enough or eating properly or dreaming about the baby inside of me. If it hadn't been for my enormous size and the fact that there was no possible position to sleep in, I would have forgotten I was pregnant altogether.

"Why am I so much bigger this time?" I asked the nurse.

"You're three years older," she said.

At the end of that summer, in the country, Russell got stung by a wasp. He had taken Duncan down to the stream and I had stayed up at the house. Even from inside the house, I heard the terrible, bloodcurdling screams. This was it, I thought to myself. Russell had been attacked by a bear. Wearing just my Crocs and my beige Old Navy maternity panties, I waddled as fast as I could down the hill, overgrown with tall ferns, to protect Duncan. The howls of pain continued and there was cursing, "Shit, fuck, shit, fuck." I was gripped with panic, thinking that it might not have been Russell, that it might have been Duncan who'd been hurt. I stood frozen for a second, wondering if I should go back to the house to call 911 or continue on to find them.

"Duncan, Duncan," I repeated over and over as I tore through the woods toward Russell's cries of anguish.

Then I saw them. Russell was doing a crazy dance like Rumplestiltskin, and Duncan was trying to calm him by trying to rub his back. Russell's skinny limbs were flying everywhere.

"Duncan," I yelled.

He ran to me. "Daddy said a *fucket* word!" Duncan called all bad words "*fucket* words," including words like *stupid.*

"What happened?"

"Daddy got sting-ed," Duncan said. "Hey, why are you naked!"

I took his hand and approached the insane little dancing man.

"I got stung by a wasp," Russell cried. "*Oooooooooh ooooooh.*" He showed me his calf with its small red patch.

"It's okay," I said. "Duncan, Daddy's going to be all right. Is this how you want your son to see you?" was how I began it. I was shaking in my Crocs. "You are teaching him that it's okay to be hysterical!" I screamed.

"It's okay, Mommy," Duncan said.

"No, Duncan. It is not okay. This is not how you should act if you get hurt. You have to be brave. Men are supposed to be brave. And mommies have to be brave too."

"It really hurts," Russell said.

"It doesn't hurt that much," I said.

"It does."

"Well, why don't you stay down here and cry and Duncan and

I will head back up to the house. When you come up I'll give you some Advil and an ice pack." I took Duncan's hand and we started back through the mud toward the house, the naked pregnant mother and the toddler.

"I'm sorry, I'm sorry," Russell stuttered, limping behind us. "You're right, I'll try to be brave next time."

My rage was more poisonous than a thousand wasp stings.

"Ow, shit. It just really hurts. It's . . ." He gasped for air. "A lot of pain."

"You don't know pain," I yelled. "You're complaining to a pregnant woman that you're in pain?" I continued the long uphill march to the house, uncomfortable being naked, even though that was why we had bought the house. "If you had to feel what I feel for one minute, you would drop dead." I was huffing and puffing from the exertion.

I should be comforting him, I thought, but his blubbering made that impossible.

"You should be a man," I said. "You're hurting Duncan by showing him this. Do you want him to act like this when he has a wife?"

"What you're doing hurts him far more," Russell said.

"No it doesn't," I screamed, even though it did.

"When I have a wife I'll be brave, Mama," Duncan said.

"That's good, sweetie," I said. "I love your daddy but he acts silly when he gets a boo-boo."

Finally I reached our deck, and Russell and Duncan went inside.

"I want a divorce," I said out loud. "I want a divorce, I want a divorce, I want a divorce." I looked down at my pregnant stomach.

*Jennifer Belle*

I thought the bitterest thought. I should have gotten an abortion. I did the math in my head. Four months pregnant. No one would give me an abortion now. I had missed my chance. I was too late. I imagined myself going to have the baby alone, checking into the hospital alone, filling out the birth certificate. I imagined the fetus doing Russell's Rumplestiltskin dance inside of me. This was bad, really really bad, this mess I had gotten myself into.

I knelt on the deck and I cried. And then I felt it, the wasp sting, like my leg was tied with the roughest rope and a slow and angry serum was being injected into me. Slowly, slowly, the pain grew. I stood up and watched the wasp that had stung me crawl down between two of the deck's floorboards. I went into the house.

"I was just stung by a wasp too," I said. "It hurts, but I don't have to dance around like a maniac. I just have to take some Advil."

The pain was climbing my leg like a boa constrictor.

And yet, it didn't warrant Russell's hysteria. Almost nothing would warrant that. So that was that, I thought. His and hers wasp stings had ended our marriage. Our marriage had started with bees painted on delicate white china cups Joy had given us for our wedding, and now it had ended with wasps. Cupid had pulled out his arrows and set these wasps on us instead. I removed the stinger and wondered if I should keep it as a memento, the way I had Duncan's tiny stump of dried umbilical cord like a bit of potpourri in the box that had held my engagement ring.

I would never get over this, I was sure of it. We would never overcome what had happened in our woods.

*The Seven Year Bitch*

I was too angry to speak. The phone rang and I answered it while secretly giving Russell the finger so that he would see it but Duncan wouldn't.

It was a friend of mine from business school. He worked as a consultant for *Sesame Street*, and he said Cookie Monster was doing a segment on happy families and Duncan, Russell, and I were invited to appear on the show.

"Oh," I said.

"Don't you want to do it?" he asked.

"What do we have to do?"

"Just be a happy family," he said.

I was silent.

"Is that going to be a problem?"

I looked at Duncan and I asked myself how I could deprive him of this. I couldn't stand in the way of his meeting Cookie Monster. I couldn't stand in the way of his having a father. A father he lived with, whose bristly cheek touched his every single morning and every single night. We would go on *Sesame Street* if it was the last thing we did. We would be the happiest fucking family on the goddamned street.

I took the information and got off the phone, and noticed my curse finger was still sticking straight up like it had a mind of its own.

*I was still angry* a few days later when we drove to Kaufman Astoria Studios and arrived promptly at ten. Russell had insisted on wearing a suit and tie—although he never wore one when I begged him to wear one—because he thought he was going to be meeting an agent after, even though they had told us to expect to be there all day.

As soon as we walked in, a wardrobe guy rushed over to us and said Russell would have to change.

"I didn't bring anything to change into."

"I told you," I said.

"Take off the tie and jacket," the guy said. Russell took off his jacket. He was wearing a plain white button-down shirt. "You can't wear white on the set. I'll get you something."

He came back several minutes later with some kind of shiny plaid leisure suit.

"What is this?" Russell said.

"I got it from Gordon's wardrobe. It's probably from the seventies. Here, follow me. You can use Bob's dressing room. He's in the commissary."

Russell trailed unhappily after the guy and the suit and came back wearing it, looking like he thought he was supposed to be on *The Love Boat*.

We were led out to the stage, and suddenly I was standing on Sesame Street. Cookie Monster was already there, sitting on the steps waiting for us. "Hello, me cookie!" he said.

Duncan looked very surprised.

"Hi folks," a man said, coming over to us. He introduced himself as the director. "So you know your line?"

"No," I said.

"This really smells bad," Russell said, making a face and trying to smooth down the enormous pointy collar of his shirt.

"This won't take long, folks. We shoot it twice with both families and then you're free to go."

*The Seven Year Bitch*

"Both families?" I said.

"Yeah, we always have an alternate family in case something goes wrong. But I'm sure you'll be great."

"But we get paid," Russell said. My friend had told me we'd get fifteen hundred bucks.

"The family we use gets paid," the man said, obviously starting to get annoyed. "Now you're going to walk over to Cookie on those steps, and Cookie's going to say to you, 'What do families like to do together?' and the dad is going to say, 'Family hug!' and you're all going to have a big hug with Cookie. Then Cookie's going to say, 'I know what families really like to do together,' and the mother's going to say, 'What, Cookie?' and he's going to say, 'Eat cookies!' Got it?"

They told us to stand a few feet from Cookie Monster.

"Pick up your son, what's his name, Dustin?" the director said.

"Duncan," I said. "Who should pick him up?"

"You. The father," the director said, pointing at Russell.

Russell heaved Duncan up into his arms. They both looked miserable and uncomfortable, Duncan's cheek pressed against the smelly polyester leisure suit and Russell's hands slipping a little so Duncan was sinking lower and lower.

"Can you pick him up a little higher?" the director said, moving behind one of the three cameras, pointing toward the spot. I saw the alternate family being moved in, shining nervously and perfectly dressed in not a shred of white. They were already sort of hugging.

"What do families like to do together?" Cookie Monster said to us.

"Hug," Russell said. He threw himself at me, practically knocking me over.

*Jennifer Belle*

264

"Ow," Duncan said. "Daddy, you're hurting me."

"Cut," the director said. "It's family hug. 'Family hug!' Let's try it again."

"Can you just try to do this one thing right," I said to Russell. The alternate family moved even closer together. The parents had their arms around each other, each with a hand on a shoulder of their perfectly behaved little boy.

"Okay let's try again," the director said.

"Family hug," I whispered to Russell.

"What do families like to do together?" Cookie asked.

"Family," Russell grunted and hoisted Duncan up a little higher, "hug." Then he threw himself at me again.

"Cut!" the director said.

"What?" Russell said. "Family hug! Family hug! I said family hug! I said it. Family hug!"

I secretly gave him the finger so that Duncan and Cookie Monster and the director and the alternate family couldn't see. All those years watching *Sesame Street* as a child I never imagined I would one day actually be standing on Sesame Street giving my husband the finger.

After a few more takes of Russell saying "Family hug!" like a complete lunatic, the alternate family was brought onto the stage and we were rushed out the door. I sat in the car seething.

"Well, that was fun," Russell said.

"I loved it," Duncan said.

*A few weeks later*, Gabe Weinrib called. "I'm going to a gala tonight for the Innocence Project. I bought a table and a few of

*The Seven Year Bitch*

my friends are coming out and I was wondering if you would join me. You might find it interesting. I'm excited for you to meet my friends."

Russell was in LA on business and our neighbor Sherry's daughter was available to babysit.

"I'd have to see if I could get a babysitter—"

He cut me off. "I'm on an airplane, Izzy, and I can't hear you too well. Come to Cipriani Downtown at six thirty for cocktails and the auction, and then dinner follows at eight. After, I'd love to take you home so I could say hi to Duncan."

"Okay," I said, meaning okay to the cocktails and dinner part but it seemed we had already been disconnected.

I looked at my apartment and even though I had no intention of inviting him upstairs to see Duncan, who would be asleep at that hour anyway, so there would be no point, I started to clean. The first thing I did was throw out all the piles of Russell's newspapers and old, old manuscripts he had already rejected, filling the garbage room so the door couldn't even close. Then I started with the toys. I had been so intent on worrying about Shasthi's inability to get pregnant, I hadn't noticed her inability to bend down and pick up a toy. But now that she was pregnant it didn't seem like the right time to ask her to start doing a better job with the cleaning. Not a single toy had all of its parts in one room. There were balls and puzzle pieces and dolls' limbs everywhere I looked. Lego and Lincoln Logs and Mr. Fucking Potato Head. A nanny's job was to pick up after the child! Tend to the nursery! I felt strangled by a dozen mangled Slinkies.

When Shasthi came home with Duncan, I was crouched down

gathering toys. I was sure she would rush to my side to help me but she didn't seem to notice anything unusual.

"Shasthi," I said. "Do you think there's any way we could keep these toys organized a little better? I mean, the whole family has to do a better job with it," I said, huffing and puffing a little.

"Yes, Izzy, everybody does," she said. I hadn't meant everybody, so much as her.

"Do you think you could put away some of these things?" I tried again. "I have a friend coming over later."

Her lids got heavy with anger. "You have to do your part you know," she said.

"Well I *buy* all these toys," I said. "And Duncan can't get any use out of them if the pieces are scattered through the whole apartment."

I continued to work silently. I crouched at the cabinet beneath the kitchen sink, which filled me with dread, searching for the Lysol toilet bowl cleaner, and then scrubbed the toilet. When I was finished, the apartment looked better. It looked—I searched for the word to describe the phenomenon—*cleaner*. It looked cared for.

I went into my room and put on a black Liz Lang maternity halter dress, which hid the fact that I was definitely showing. I accidentally lined my eyes with blue glittery powder, thinking it was black, and stuck an oversized Rafe clutch under my arm, like a pregnant star in a sitcom carrying a plant from room to room. Or a bloated Marilyn Monroe wearing black instead of white. If Gabe put his hand on my waist at any point, he would feel how round I had become. This wasn't a date, I tried to remind myself, so it was okay to be pregnant.

*The Seven Year Bitch*

Shasthi left with barely a word and Sherry's daughter came from next door. And out I rushed to Cipriani.

My name mercifully was on the list, although the woman with the clipboard hadn't understood that my last name was Brilliant and thought I was somehow insulting her. Even when I said my own name, I had a way of sounding sarcastic.

I couldn't see Gabe anywhere. I wandered around with my Coke trying to look like it was perfectly normal to be pregnant and all alone at a gala. I made my way to the silent auction tables and looked at the offerings with casual indifference.

I paused at a pair of $40,000 Renee Lewis earrings with an opening bid of $5,000. Then I saw what I wanted to bid on. Something for Russell.

When I was pregnant with Duncan and still working at the firm, in a moment of insanity I bought Russell a gold Cartier watch and had "For Timing Contractions" and our initials "RET & IPB" engraved on the back. I gave it to Russell for his birthday in front of his parents, who gave him a faux leather Dopp kit that reeked of a vile chemical smell.

Russell put it on, but it had a black alligator bracelet band that was loose on his wrist. It looked big on him. He wasn't used to wearing a watch and he seemed uncomfortable in it. The sentiment on the back seemed to make him nervous and ended up ironic, as I'd had an emergency C-section with no contractions whatsoever to time. He wore it two or three times before abandoning it on his bedside table for several months. Then, one day, I tried it on, and I loved it. I loved that it was a man's watch because it made me feel like a man. It was huge and round and gold. I felt like Apollo in it. Everyone I met said they didn't know what was different about me. But as soon as I started to wear the watch, Russell suddenly wanted to wear it. I told him he had never wanted to wear it before but he just said, "It's my watch," and took it from me. He wore it out that night and lost it. He hadn't even noticed he had lost it until I asked him where it was. It had slipped off his wrist and somewhere someone in New York had seen it glinting on the sidewalk and was the proud new owner of my ten-thousand-dollar 18k-gold Cartier watch.

"It was his watch and so it was his to lose," my mother's shrink had said, but I couldn't forgive him for it. Not so much for losing it and for not even noticing that he had lost it but for taking it from me when he knew how much I loved it.

I hadn't really given him a gift since, unless you counted Duncan, but this was just what he wanted. And his birthday was coming. I wrote my name on the bid sheet and the minimum opening bid, two hundred dollars.

"Bidding on something?" Gabe asked, coming up behind me. "These earrings?" He pointed to the beautiful earrings.

"No," I said. "This one."

> Vasectomy: Dr. Stuart Little (Sutton Place Physicians, NYU Hospital) will perform an outpatient procedure and all follow-up care.

"I think my husband will love it."

"I wouldn't put my ween in the hands of a doctor named Stuart Little," Gabe said. "Unless your husband has a very, very small ween. Small enough for a mouse to operate on."

"If it means not having any more children, I don't think he'll

*The Seven Year Bitch*

mind." I wasn't sure why I was talking about my husband or his ween.

"No? You're not going to have another one?"

"Well actually," I said. "I am."

"Oh! Well congratulations, m'dear," he said. His face had gotten serious. "I couldn't tell." I suddenly felt foolish for being there.

I followed him to a round table filled with couples and stood by as he introduced me, but the speeches were starting, so we took our seats next to each other and our salads were served.

"How long have you two been an item?" the girl sitting on my other side asked.

"Oh, no, I'm his investment consultant," I said ridiculously.

Alan Dershowitz took the microphone and explained that the Innocence Project used new DNA technology to free prisoners who had been wrongfully incarcerated.

Behind him were what looked like a police lineup of disgruntled-looking men, who then took the stage one by one to explain what they had been convicted of and how hard it had been to get a job once they were exonerated. One man had been in jail for forty years.

Gabe seemed to be ignoring me.

I was so hot, the room was spinning.

I excused myself and went to the bathroom. I wished I hadn't worn panty hose. I couldn't bear to wear them for another minute. That's when I had the idea that I could take off my panty hose and no one would know because my skirt was so long. I took off my black high-heeled boots and peeled off the panty hose that had already torn to spiderwebs between my thighs, and threw them in the garbage can. But when I went to put on my boots, I couldn't do it. They wouldn't go on my bare feet. Some-one was banging on the bathroom door.

"Just a second," I called.

I sat on the toilet and I pulled and pulled, but my feet would not slide into the boots. I was the opposite of Cinderella. I pulled and pulled and pulled and pulled but the boots would not budge. My feet had swelled in the heat of Cipriani. Finally I left the bathroom barefoot and sat on some marble steps and continued to try. I had no idea what to do. If it weren't for my clutch, which I'd left at my seat, I would have just run out barefoot and gotten a cab home. Every girl in New York had at least one coming-home-from-the-party-barefoot story.

I was practically in tears. It was bad enough I had shown up on my date pregnant, but now I was barefoot.

"Is something wrong?" a gray-haired man asked, appearing in front of me. I pulled the skirt of my dress down fast to cover my legs as best I could. To my horror, I saw that it was the con-vict who had just spoken who had been in prison for forty years and lost his wife, his house, and any way of making a living. The Innocence Project might have used DNA evidence to prove beyond a shadow of a doubt that he was completely innocent, but I was not convinced.

"I can't put my boots back on," I said.

"Do you have any lotion or powder or something?" he asked.

"That's a great idea!" I said. "I have some hand lotion in my purse but it's at my table."

"I'll go get it for you," he said.

"Wait," I said. It might seem strange for this ex-con to go up to my seat and walk off with my purse.

*The Seven Year Bitch*

"Look," he said.

By the door, the swag bags, black and shiny with Chanel printed on them, were being set out. He walked over and grabbed one—despite the dirty look he received from the girl who had thought I was calling her brilliant—and brought it back to me. I pulled out a deluxe sample of Chanel Precision, the very product I was supposed to be using for wrinkles.

He opened the jar and I slathered some on my feet.

"You have pretty feet," he said. "When my wife was pregnant all she wanted me to do was massage her feet. The only thing that would get her to quit complaining was a foot rub. You want help with that?"

"No thanks," I said.

"When are you due?" He asked the question like "How long are you in for?"

I quickly tried the boots again and they slid right on. I thanked him profusely and rushed back to Gabe's table.

"Sorry," I whispered.

"I looked everywhere for you. I was afraid you had slipped out without paying for your vasectomy."

We ate our meals and laughed. His friends were nice.

"This is who I would marry if I had to marry someone," Gabe announced, putting his arm around me.

"Why don't you?" a man across the table asked.

"She's pregnant with another man's child," he said.

"And I have a two-year-old," I said, which I liked to say as much as possible in case people wondered why I wasn't just a little bit thinner.

A woman standing at the microphone said the silent auction had ended and we should go to the back to pay for our prizes.

I stood up.

"Please allow me," Gabe said. "It's my treat."

"What? No! I can't let you pay for Russell's vasectomy."

"It would be my pleasure," he said. "Paying for a noble cause at a noble cause."

I tried to stop him but he walked off.

"Well," the woman sitting next to me said. "Gabe Weinrib finally falls in love and it's with a married, pregnant woman."

"I'll take you home in a cab," Gabe said when we'd gotten our coats and gift bags. I couldn't wait to give Shasthi the little gift bag of Chanel.

"Are you going uptown?" one of the other women who had been at our table asked.

There was an awkward pause.

"I'm going to take Izzy home in a cab," he said.

"No, that's okay. I live pretty close. I used to work right here and I'd walk home." I didn't know why I was rambling like that.

He hailed a cab. "Are you sure?" he asked as the other woman slid in.

"Oh," I stuttered. "Did you want to come up to my place?" I had no idea why I was saying this, except that I had worked so hard cleaning up. But it would be crazy. What would Sherry's daughter think, for one thing? The doormen? Duncan, if he, God forbid, woke up? There were sonogram pictures on my fridge. I was pregnant.

"No," he said. "It's late. Another time."

*The Seven Year Bitch*

"Okay," I said, nodding hysterically. I felt like a desperate fool. I thought of myself scrubbing the toilet, changing the sheets, throwing out newspapers. Why had I done all this? I wondered.

"Oh, I almost forgot, here's your vasectomy, and I bid on a little something else for you too. A small memento of this evening."

He reached into his jacket pocket and handed me a Renee Lewis jewelry box with the earrings inside splayed out on black velvet. They were dangling mismatched gemstones, a ruby and a diamond and an emerald and an amethyst.

"Oh!" I was completely shocked. "I can't."

"You're worried about what Russell will think?"

"No, I . . ."

"Just tell him there was a raffle. They'll look good with that dress. You of all people know I can afford it."

"Right," I laughed. He could. "Thank you. They're beautiful."

I put one on and then the other, unsure of how they didn't end up in the murky gutter. The cool gold on my earlobes reminded me how much I had loved to be kissed there.

"So things must be pretty good between you," he said.

"No," I said, surprising myself. "I didn't think I could get pregnant." I shouldn't be saying this, I thought. I shouldn't be explaining myself.

"You must love him," he said.

I must, I thought. Or I must have at one time. I felt drunk even though I hadn't had so much as a drop of wine. I must have loved him at our wedding. Taking the dancing lessons, choosing my ring. I must have loved him when I was pregnant with Duncan. I had wanted a baby so badly. I had loved him that winter weekend so long ago in the country when we stayed alone in Marlon's house—our first weekend away together. I'd lain upstairs in bed listening to beautiful piano music coming from the living room, then I'd floated downstairs thinking, If he can play the piano like that, then he really is a genius. I imagined the talent our future children would one day display. But the piano bench stood vacant, Marlon's hideous floral piano cover still in place like a giant tea cozy. It hadn't been him playing the piano, it had been the radio.

Without warning, I burst into tears. I choked back sob after sob. No matter how hard I tried not to, my tears kept coming. They betrayed me. And I betrayed Russell. No sexual act would have been more of a betrayal than those tears.

Gabe said something to the woman in the cab and she sped off without him.

He walked me home and we stood in front of my building.

"You sure you don't want to come up?" I said. What was wrong with me! "I have to walk my dog while the sitter's still there."

"I'd walk him with you, but I have a pretty early day tomorrow." I cringed in my earrings. "Thanks for the offer though. Well, thank you for coming, m'dear. And I'll call you to check how you're feeling. Take care of yourself."

"Yes," I said and walked into my building.


*Standing in my lobby,* I opened my clutch and looked at the time on my cell phone. It was only ten thirty. I ran back out onto the street and hailed a cab and made it to the New York Health and Racquet Club just in time. I handed my ID card to the girl behind the desk.

*The Seven Year Bitch*

"Gym's closing in ten minutes," she said.

"I'll just be a minute." I walked past her into the locker room and, hands trembling, turned the knob to the right, then the left, then the right again. 19-21-23. The happiest years of my life. I took off my earrings, put them back in their leather case, along with the gift certificate for the vasectomy, and placed them in the back of my locker.

Trying to get a cab home, I stepped onto a subway grate, and a gust of wind blew my halter dress all the way up. It fluttered up around my waist, leaving my bare thighs and panties and big round stomach exposed. I shrieked and struggled to hold it down around me, just like a pregnant Marilyn Monroe.

*Part Three*

# Run from
# Your Life

# 33

One day, when I was pregnant with Duncan, after I'd cajoled and cajoled, begging to know if it was a boy or a girl, Dr. Lichter had said, "I see a wee-wee."

"You mean . . ."

"It's a boy," Dr. Lichter said.

My whole life, I'd thought I would be the mother of a boy. I'd had a recurring dream since childhood that I was taking care of a small black boy.

I had a soft spot for boys. I loved them.

But now, with a wee-wee inside me, I thought there must be a terrible mistake.

I didn't know anything about dinosaurs. I knew about ballet and tea parties with the tea set I had saved from my childhood to give to my daughter and dolls. I knew about the Nancy Drews I had saved from my childhood to one day give to my daughter and Eloise at the Plaza and in Paris and in Moscow and at Christmastime, all saved from my childhood to one day give to my future daughter.

Cars, trucks, bulldozers, sports, pirates, Lego, boats, and trains—I would have absolutely nothing to talk about with this kid. I wasn't interested in anything he was interested in.

I wept on the table, naked from the waist down.

Dr. Lichter was unable to console me.

I called my mother from the cab home, crying. I couldn't even speak.

"What is it?" she said.

"There's a wee-wee in me," I said. "And now I'll never ever have anyone to have lunch with when I'm old."

My mother was silent because she knew it was true. I knew she wanted to say that she would have lunch with me but then she knew I would have to point out that she couldn't have lunch with me because she would be dead, so we both just silently, futilely, searched for a solution.

When I got home and told Russell, he was elated. He took it as some sort of personal victory. He had won and I had lost.

"You don't know anything about dinosaurs either," I said. And forget about sports. That was the one good thing about Russell: He didn't watch sports.

"Like hell I don't," he said.

"Name one thing."

"There are herbivores like the brachiosaurus and the bron-tosaurus, and carnivores like the *Tyrannosaurus rex*, otherwise known as T. rex. Dinosaurs became extinct at the end of the Cretaceous period. The stegosaurus, or old plate-back, as he was known by his friends, was an herbivore who lived in the Jurassic period. And I'll be sure to tell him about the pterodactyl who could fly." Russell spread out his arms and flapped them like a pterodactyl, running all around the room. "Forget it, you're outnumbered."

Even Humbert was a boy.

But no one was more disappointed than Russell's parents.

"Oh well," his mother said. "I wouldn't have been happy without a girl. We had two children, a boy and a girl, to replace ourselves."

Oh God, I thought, what a concept.

"But if Leslie had been a boy, I would have kept trying until I got a girl. I would have died trying! Maybe the doctor was wrong," was his mother's brilliant idea. "Ya never know—it just might come out a girl!"

But Dr. Lichter wasn't wrong, and one day, in the middle of a spirited sword fight with Duncan, I had an amazing realization. I loved sword fighting! And I loved talking like a pirate. *Arrrrrgh,* matey! Batten down the hatches, scalawag! I loved making Duncan walk the plank, and I loved when he made me walk the plank. And I loved sharks. Their crooked terrifying teeth and hideous nostrils and dorsal fins. And I loved roaring and screaming and running and discussing which was scarier, a fox or a wolf, or a witch or a dragon.

I walked to the boys' side of the Kidini clothing sale filled with excitement, proudly examining little plaid flannel shirts and tiny down jackets with the stoic determination of the mother of a boy. Pajamas that made him look like a little Hugh Hefner and striped socks just like his father's.

I loved when he wrapped his arms around me and mashed his hard skull into mine and said, "I love you, Isolde Pearl Brilliant."

*The Seven Year Bitch*

*Since Dr. Lichter had* bailed out on me, I had no choice but to choose a new ob-gyn. Dr. Sitbon was nothing like Dr. Lichter. He was French and young, no more than forty, and for nine and a half long months no matter how many times I asked him to call me Izzy, he called me madame.

It seemed absurd that I would wait for him, half naked on his table, pregnancy hormones coursing through my body, imagining him fucking me from behind against the dangerous wastes bin, and then he would enter and say, "Bonjour, madame."

The fact that I hadn't exactly had a bikini wax and had an enormous pregnant stomach and sometimes a rashy complexion didn't stop me from thinking that we really would fuck, long and hard, leaving all those other women to languish in the waiting room with their water bottles and swollen ankles and brochures for cord blood cell banks and doulas.

"You still haven't heard anything about Dr. Lichter?" I would ask in my disappointment with his professionalism.

"Ah, you still miss your Dr. Lichter. I am not good enough for you?"

Prove you're good enough, I thought, thrusting my huge stomach at him even more seductively.

"You're good," I said. But he never spent more than five minutes with me. We never had long philosophical discussions about what it meant to be a mother.

"What's that?" I asked, during one appointment, pointing to the Cartier ring that had suddenly appeared on his wedding finger.

"I got married two weeks ago," he said.

"Congratulations!" I said, my heart plunging. It was getting harder and harder to fantasize about him. Dr. Lichter had a tired old labor-and-delivery nurse for a wife, so riding him on the tiny round stool at the foot of the examining table was always a likely possibility. But Dr. Sitbon was a newlywed, just back from a honeymoon. "Where did you go?" I asked.

"China."

I hated people who took adventurous honeymoons. "Did you marry a nurse?" I asked.

"No, a doctor," he said.

"Are you going to have children?"

"I hope."

I had seen him once walking with a beautiful woman doctor up the circular driveway, talking heatedly in their respective lab coats, and I had burned with jealousy at the time.

"Ah, what is zis?" he said.

"The sex?" I asked.

"*Oui*, yes. Do you want to know?"

"Tell me," I said. "Do you see a wee-wee?"

"A what?"

"A wee-wee. That's what Dr. Lichter said."

"Ah yes, your precious Dr. Lichter. No, I do not see a wee-wee."

My heart soared with happiness. It was a girl. I was having a girl.

"However, I do see a penis!"

"Maybe you're wrong," I said, sounding like Russell's mother.

He circled something invisible with his finger on the sonogram screen. "I'm not wrong, madame," he said. "Do you see that?"

"No."

*The Seven Year Bitch*

"Well I'm afraid it's undeniable."

I tried to smile.

"Not what you were hoping for?" he asked.

I couldn't speak.

"My mother had two boys," he said. "I was her second son."

I let out an uncontrollable sob. And once that happened I couldn't stop crying.

"And then she tried one more time and had a girl. So it all could have a happy ending."

Crying, I told him that I loved boys, that I'd always dreamed about a little black boy, that I loved having a son. That I loved pirates and sharks and dinosaurs. Either way, I thought, I would probably have had some disappointment, mourned the one I wasn't having and would never have.

"Well the baby looks wonderful," Dr. Sitbon said. "He's totally healthy and perfect in there. It looks like he's having a very good time. So, are you okay?"

I was crying hysterically on the table.

"Aye, matey," I said.

"Aye, matey," he said back in his French accent. He held out his hand, which meant I was supposed to use it to hoist my enormous body up to a sitting position and also that my appointment was over.

"Thank you, ye old scalawag," I said.

"A pleasure as always, madame," he said and walked out the door.


*Going home in the* cab I called my mother, sobbing.

"What's wrong?" she said.

"There's another wee-wee in me."

*Jennifer Belle*

"It's okay," she said sadly. "It's great. A brother. A brother for Duncan!"

"But I'll never know now what it's like to have a daughter. No one will ever take care of me."

"But remember what my shrink said when you were pregnant with Duncan. She said she was jealous that you'd have all that boy-love. You'll have all that boy-love again."

"I don't live my life by what your shrink says, in case that comes as a surprise to you," I said, already starting to feel soothed.

We went on like that for the rest of the ride until I was pretty much all cried out.

*I'm having a boy,*" I told Shasthi when I got home.

"I'm having a girl," she said.

Then we both headed into the kitchen at the same time and bumped into each other because the kitchen was too small for our big stomachs.

*That night I had* dinner at Craft with Joy. "I'm only staying here for one night," she said. "I have to get back to the shamba."

"Why?" I asked.

"Things are just better with Chili when I'm there," she said. "It turned out his wife wasn't fat. She was pregnant. She gave birth to his daughter four months ago. But it's all fine," she said happily. "He was afraid to tell me because he thought I would leave him. I forgave him and he gave me a donkey which is apparently a very big deal and he sent both his wives away in disgrace."

*The Seven Year Bitch*

"Well, that's good," I said. "Both wives? I thought he just had one wife."

"He had another one in Mombasa, but he's done with that." She seemed thrilled. "I'm so happy, Izzy," she said. "You should leave Russell and move to Kenya with me."

"I can't leave Russell," I said. "In two days I'm having a birthday party for Duncan and then, in case you haven't noticed, I'm having a baby. It's a boy," I added.

"Oh, Izzy, that's great," she said. "I love being the mother of boys. I can't believe Duncan's already three."

We ordered and I ate the entire roll the waiter placed on my plate with his tongs, and then I ate another. Even Joy couldn't stop me from eating bread when I was pregnant.

"I just hope you're not going to do the whole breast-feeding thing again?" she said. "Really, don't come visit me until you're done with all that."

I laughed. "I'll wait for you to come here."

"There's nothing here for me anymore," she said. "With the exception of having my children, leaving Harry was the single best thing I have ever done. I mean, marriage is so distasteful really. Tell me, what is your definition of marriage?"

"Having good seats at the theater," I said.

"What are you talking about?"

"When I got married the first thing I noticed was that I could order tickets to something months in advance and know I'd still have Russell to go to it with. Before I was married I never felt confident enough to order them so I never had good seats."

"There's got to be more to marriage than that," she said. "I have no idea what you see in Russell. Frankly I don't even know what you see in New York anymore."

"The way you're talking, I'm worried I won't ever see you here again," I said.

"You probably won't. But you'll come to Africa."

"You'll have to come back to check on the store," I said.

"I'm not sure what I'm going to do about that."

We talked about her freedom and my captivity, but I couldn't help notice she was the one who seemed to be on a leash. She might live on a whole wildlife reserve and I might live in a cage, but at least when I went home at night I was the only wife having the only baby.

"How was your anniversary?" she asked when I hugged her good-bye on the street.

"Great," I said. "Russell spent the whole day and night at the Brooklyn Book Fair. We had a huge fight and I called him a fool and he called me a bitch."

"And it was your *seventh* anniversary?" Joy said, slowly nodding her head.

"Yes," I said.

"And *are* you a bitch?" she asked.

"Yes," I said sadly.

"You're a *seven year* bitch," she said knowingly. "But it's not your fault."

*The Seven Year Bitch*

# 34

"What are you doing tomorrow?" Gabe Weinrib asked when he called me on my cell phone the next morning.

"It's my son's third birthday," I said.

"I can't believe he's three already," Gabe said.

"I'm having a party for him."

"That sounds fun," he said.

"It's just a kids' party. It's too bad your son isn't in New York," I said, relieved that he wasn't. The last thing I wanted was for Gabe and Russell to pound the same piñata with the same stick. And I didn't want Gabe to see me that pregnant.

"Mathieu is in New York," he said.

*The next day Russell* and I tied green streamers around trees in Central Park leading from the West Eighty-first Street entrance to the Swedish Cottage Marionette Theatre, which I had rented out for all the kids in Duncan's preschool class to see a private showing of *Peter Pan*. When we had tied the last streamer on the last tree, a security officer from the Parks Commission came in some kind of cart and made us take them all down. No matter what we did, we were always being approached by security.

Shasthi helped me put down Peter Pan–green tablecloths in the cottage and cover them with pirate and fairy favors. All twenty parties Duncan had been to that year had a pirate-and-princess or pirate-and-fairy or pirate-and-ballerina theme, basically the child equivalent of a college pimps-and-ho's party.

When I finished setting everything up, my eyes filled with tears. Marionettes from past shows watched me from the walls—Pinocchio, the witch from *Jack and the Beanstalk*, the queen from *Snow White*. I was the mother of a three-year-old. According to Dr. Lichter, I had made it to the other side.

"What should I do?" Russell asked, standing dumbly in the doorway like one of the marionettes waiting to go on.

"Let people in and take their coats and give them a treasure map," I directed. "When the show starts, go with my father to get the hot dogs and the pretzels and start opening bottles of wine. And just please try not to ruin this day for me," I further instructed. I felt like Jack's mother sending him off to sell the cow. He had ruined Duncan's first and second birthdays, and I couldn't help but wonder bitterly what he had in store for the third.

When the children began to arrive, I got to work tracing each child's shadow on a long roll of butcher paper. I gave the girls fairy wings, and the boys hooks for hands.

"Okay, lie here," I said to the next kid. He was older than the other kids and I didn't recognize him. "You must be the brother of someone in Duncan's class," I said.

*The Seven Year Bitch*

"Actually, I'm nobody's brother," he said philosophically, with a French accent, like a little René Descartes.

"Oh, you must be Mathieu," I said shyly.

"I would like my shadow done too," he said. "But please make it as accurate as possible."

I moved my green grease pencil around his body, his new American jeans, and French shoes, and expensive button-down shirt. I traced his profile—his father's nose, his soft brown hair, the spikes on top. He was a beautiful boy.

"My father is in there," he said, pointing to the theater, his rolled-up shadow tucked under his arm.

When the show was about to begin, I took a seat on a bench by the door to watch. Duncan sat in the row in front of me next to Mathieu, and they were chatting very seriously about something, the older boy looking down kindly at the younger one.

"Hello, m'dear," Gabe whispered to me as soon as the house went dark. He had climbed over the bench behind me to sit next to me.

I looked around but no one seemed to notice anything. Everyone was already enthralled with the show. I sat stiffly on the bench with my legs spread like a man on the subway to make room for my enormous pregnant stomach and to keep from toppling over onto it.

"Nice party," he said. He took off his sweater and the shirt under it rode up, exposing a flat, hard stomach.

I felt a gush between my legs and for a moment I was terrified that my water had broken. What if my water had broken and it was Gabe Weinrib who took me to the hospital and helped me give birth? I was afraid to stand up.

*Jennifer Belle*

"Which one's Russell?" he asked.

"I don't know," I whispered. He was probably walking to the park's entrance to get the hot dogs.

Everyone in the room sang "Happy Birthday" to Duncan, including the Pippi Longstocking marionette who the puppeteer quipped was now an out-of-work actress waitressing in SoHo.

"I'm so glad we finally got the boys together. Duncan's a great-looking kid," Gabe said. "I've been saying they should meet for so long."

"I don't know why. Mathieu is a good sport for being here. He's so much older than Duncan."

"I just thought they'd like each other," he said.

I leaned forward and whispered in Duncan's ear. "Do you like it? Do you like your party?"

"Mom, no talking," he said.

I heard children laughing and the sound of applause, but all I could think about was the man sitting next to me and the wetness between my legs.

I wished I hadn't dressed thematically in a too-tight pirate shirt. They didn't make pirate maternity wear, so a glittering skull and crossbones stretched across my stomach, leaving a gap above my maternity pants. Except for my stomach, and my son, and twenty-two three-year-olds and their parents, this could be a date.

"I have some stocks I want you to take a look at," he whispered.

"Maybe we could meet next week," I said, confused again. Everything I was feeling between us was just in my own mind.

"You know, I'm going to India in January to look at buying some factories. I wish I could get your take on it. I was planning

*The Seven Year Bitch*

to turn it into a vacation in Mumbai. I wish you could come with me. Staying in the best hotels. My treat."

"Gabe," I said. "I'm having a baby in December."

"I know you can't come. I said, 'I wish.' There're a lot of great investments there."

"I can't do that," I said.

"I think the boys are getting along great," he said, nudging me with his arm.

To my astonishment, Duncan had slipped his hand into Mathieu's and they sat like that until it was time to applaud again.

On the stage three mermaids danced on their strings like embryos. Then the lost boys sang to Wendy, "Be our mother, be our mother."

"I have to go make sure everything's set up," I said and slipped out of the theater and into the party room. A moment later he followed.

"Wow," he said, looking at what I had done with the room. "You know, m'dear, if I were ever to finally settle down, I'd want it to be with someone exactly like you."

"But you only date models," I said mockingly.

"I do date a lot of models, but I like that you're not so tall. When I'm in bed with a woman who's taller than me I always feel like a baby gorilla in his mama's arms. You have so many of the qualities I am looking for in a woman."

"So you've mentioned," I said, sounding annoyed. Suddenly, I felt irritated. He knew there was nothing I could do about any of this. The jig should have been up, I thought.

I resisted the urge to hike up my pants and prayed they wouldn't drop lower. The baby kicked and, looking down, I saw the skull and crossbones change shape, like my stomach was a real Jolly Roger blowing on a high mast over a stormy sea.

"I wonder what qualities I don't possess," I mused bitterly, hiking up my pants and coming this close to asking him if he thought I was fat.

"You possess them," he said. "You're beautiful and smart and funny and sexy." He started singing a Bee Gees song in a high-pitched voice.

*Let me be the things you are to me and not some pup-pet on a string.*

"Very nice," Russell said, standing in the doorway. "Hi, I'm Russell, Izzy's husband, father of the birthday boy." He put out his hand to Gabe and Gabe shook it.

"This is Gabe Weinrib," I said.

"Don't worry, Izzy, you can't accuse me of ruining Duncan's birthday this time. My new friend Abdul the hot dog guy is going to wheel his cart right in here. I worked out a great deal."

"I think I'm the one ruining it with my singing," Gabe said. "Thank you, m'dear." He walked back into the theater, leaving me alone with Russell.

"M'dear?" Russell said. "What a putz."

"That in there is a lot of bullshit!" Marlon said at the top of his lungs, staggering into the room. "You sure you want to feed those kids that Peter Pan fairy crap? Take them to the opera, something of quality, not that Peter Pan suck-my-cock, be-my-mommy bullshit. This could be my last day on earth and I had to listen to that."

*The Seven Year Bitch*

"Marlon, could you keep it down, this is a kids' party," Russell said, fluttering around Marlon as he always did.

"Those kids know it's a bunch of b.s. I'll tell you, some of those girls in there are lookers. The little blond one in the front with the fairy wings . . ."

"Marlon, they're three," I said.

"Let me help you get a cab," Russell said, steering Marlon to the door. "Maybe I did ruin the party," he said, looking at me apologetically.

*At the end of* the day, when all the kids had gone and we were packing up Duncan's mountain of presents, I saw that one of the kids had left his shadow, rolled up on the floor of the theater. It was Mathieu's. I rolled it back up and tucked it into my bag, and a few days later, I put it carefully in my locker, taking my sneakers home to make room for it.

# 35

Another contest arrived, and I slit open a cardboard box and took out the instruction sheet and the first rubber-banded group of essays.

**Mashees Organic Baby Food Cravings Contest:** In 100 Words or Less Tell Us About Your Pregnancy Cravings.

**Mary DuCloth**
**Homestead, FL**
*My neighbor has a grapefruit tree and I stare out the window at it. I don't know what gets over me, but I just have to have one of those lucious round orbs dangling from those branches. So one day, I get a ladder and climb over our fence and get as many as I can, my heart racing, not in fear of getting caught, but in anticipation of tasting that sweet, sour, fragrant fruit. I also*

*want to eat the tender leaves. I peel the first grapefruit*
*right there in my neighbor's yard and bite into the pink.*

**Wendy Moldonado**
**Riddle, ID**
*I have not really had any cravings but what I have had*
*is aversions to certain foods such as chicken. If I even*
*see some chicken on TV I have to go into the bathroom*
*to puke. Eggs and meat are also quite noxious.*

I had plenty of cravings and aversions myself, and I stopped
reading for a while, wishing I hadn't agreed to judge this one. In
a way it was the most intense. The women would have written
in, even if there wasn't a prize—a new kitchen makeover to get
ready for baby. Their yearnings rose from the pages like steam.
They wanted to tell—anyone really—what they craved.

**LuRaine Cryer**
**Buckhannon, WV**
*I am almost embarrassed to tell you this, but what I am*
*craving most is dirt. Black rich soil in the park, in my*
*garden, in the potted plant in the waiting room of my*
*OBGYN. Yesterday when I was there, I scooped just*
*a tiny morsel of the velvety white-specked black dirt*
*onto my two fingers when I thought no one was look-*
*ing and placed it on my tongue like the finest caviar.*

*Aaaaahhhhh. I think it will be okay if I eat a little dirt every day. I can't help myself. Nothing will stop me!*

**Samantha Clark**
**Diamondville, WY**
*Dunkin' Donuts crullers and custard filled doughnuts, mint chocolate chip ice cream (has to be green), coffee ice cream, ho ho's, oreos, jelly bellies, sour patch kids, licorice (red only), rice pudding, pasta salad, chocolate, cotton candy, swiss roll from Monty's bakery, salami and cream cheese sandwiches, Coca-Cola, heavy cream, Cheetos, Stauffer's chicken pot pies, BBQ potato chips, McDonalds every single day, peanut butter, sugar cubes, and preferably all at the same time!*

I turned to the next essay and looked at the name on top as I always did.

**Isabelle Brilliant**
**New York, NY**

I couldn't believe what I was seeing. It was the woman who Dr. Heiffowitz had thought was me. We had sat in the same chair, lain on the same table, been touched by the same man. I felt as if I knew her.

*Being pregnant again only one year after having twins isn't easy. Your husband works at a job he loves, the*

*nanny takes the babies to the park, you get so tired*
*buying a wedding present in Williams-Sonoma you*
*actually ask for a chair and have to sit down. I want my*
*old self back. I want my husband back, our life, sex, fun.*
*I want my 20's back. I crave going to our friends' wed-*
*ding wearing high heels instead of hideous footwear.*
*I crave my old life and a different future. There is no*
*greater craving than that.*

I read the essay five more times. I wasn't sure if the Mashees executives would agree with me, but as far as I was concerned, we had our winner.

Each contest asked for one winner and a different number of runner-ups, usually with my ranking written in a circle in the top right corner. When I was done reading the essays, after I'd divided them into my piles of "yes," "no," and "maybe," I took the yesses and carefully applying the formula of percentages listed in the contest rules—originality and creativity, appropriateness to theme, sincerity—I arbitrarily picked the winner and ranked the runner-ups.

This time, with thousands of essays left to read, I took my Sharpie and wrote the number one in the top right corner and circled it. My heart was pounding. I had nothing to worry about—it wasn't like I was committing insider trading—but I had broken the contest rules. And it was stupid because our last names were the same and we lived in the same city, which might send up a red flag to the final judges if they noticed it. I could throw her essay away, simply remove it from the pile, and it would never be missed from the boxes they picked up from me at the end of every contest to store in their warehouse in New Jersey. But she was my winner. Just please, I thought, don't let anything stop them from sending me essays. I had to have them, like my own secret lifeline.

*The next day I* stood outside Duncan's preschool with the other mothers, waiting to pick up Duncan. I was due any day, and I was exhausted.

"Would Duncan like to come over for a playdate?" Gerde asked.

Lately I'd tried to keep Duncan as far away from Minerva as possible because she was always putting him in princess dresses as soon as we walked through their door.

"We have to do an errand, I'm sorry," I said.

"What is your errand?" Gerde asked.

I tried to think of something. "We have to go to ABC Carpet." I hoped we wouldn't have to go to ABC Carpet now that I'd said it, because it was the last place on earth I wanted to go.

"We will come along," Gerde said.

We collected the children and trudged unhappily to ABC.

"You carry this," Minerva demanded, handing Duncan a doll and a pocketbook.

"Duncan's a boy," I explained to Minerva.

"*Ja*," Gerde interjected, "that's why we got him blue nail polish to put on. Blue is for boys." She pulled out the bottle of nail polish at a stoplight.

"Duncan's not allowed to wear nail polish," I said.

"You don't think you are being ridiculous?" Gerde asked me. "You have to let him be who he is."

*The Seven Year Bitch*

"I am letting him be who he is. He's a boy." Lately, Gerde had been calling me ridiculous quite a lot, I noticed.

Duncan started crying and then Minerva started crying.

"Duncan, I wouldn't let you wear nail polish even if you were a girl," I lied. "Makeup is for grown-up women, not children."

"Nail polish isn't makeup," Gerde said.

"If it's sold at makeup counters, it doesn't go on my son," I said.

Gerde glared at me. I was all for letting Duncan have dolls, but I drew the line at dresses and nail polish. If it were up to Gerde she'd have him strapped into some kind of bra-and-panty set.

We walked along in tense silence.

"Are you ready for the baby?" Gerde asked.

"Tomorrow I'm getting a manicure, pedicure, and a bikini wax," I said, which after I said it, did sound like a strange way to get ready for a baby.

"I don't think you should have a C-section," she blurted out.

"Well, it's the safest thing since I had one before," I told her. "And besides, my stomach's already ruined but my vagina's still great."

She'd had the worst labor story I'd ever heard of. She did it with no drugs with a midwife and had forty hours of back labor before they figured out that the baby was breach.

"*Ja*, but you will not experience the joys of childbirth," she actually said. "For instance," she said, "Rolph and I still talk about when Minerva was born."

I looked at her in disbelief.

"Don't you think Russell and I still talk about when Duncan was born?" I asked, shocked at her insensitivity, that she actually thought that because we'd had a mere emergency C-section, we'd forgotten all about it. It was just another day not worth remembering.

When we got to ABC, since I had no real reason for being there, I agreed to go to the toy department so the kids could run around for a few minutes. They spotted a huge plush rocking horse and ran to it, but Minerva beat Duncan there and climbed onto its high back.

"Oh, no!" Gerde whispered when Minerva climbed down again quite a while later. "What should I do?" She pointed at the horse, whose brown fur was matted with shit.

"You don't have her in a Pull-Up?"

"She likes to wear her new princess panties," Gerde said. She nonchalantly looked at the price tag dangling from the rocking horse's silky ear, terrified they might have a you-shit-on-it-you-buy-it policy.

"Five hundred dollars," she gasped. "Do I have to buy this big ugly equine? It's out of the question." There was a big brown wet spot on the back of Minerva's white sweater dress. She was about to climb on an even more expensive camel. "I don't really want to buy it."

"Especially now that it's covered with shit," I said.

"What would you do if you were me?" she asked.

"I'd get outta here," I said. And I'd put that princess in a Pull-Up, I added silently to myself.

"Quick, you get the children, and I will buy this," she said, grabbing a blue velvet dress from a rack.

I herded the children to a basket of animal pillows while Gerde bought the dress. Then she grabbed Minerva and headed to the ladies room for a guilty quick-change operation, leaving the besmirched horse and any unsuspecting child who sat on it to his own demise.

"It was nice meeting you," Gerde said when we were in front of my building.

"Nice meeting you," I said and hurried into my lobby.

# 36

I sat next to Russell in the cab on the way to the hospital while he talked about how he hadn't seen some neighbor or other and he wondered if she had moved out.

I started to get angry.

"Who cares?" I said. "We're going into the hospital to have our baby! Our baby! It's not normal to talk about some neighbor, some neighbor I don't give a shit about!" If he were the one having surgery in less than an hour he'd be gripping my hand and boo-hooing all about it.

"Sorry," he said nastily. The driver eyed us through the rear-view mirror.

Guiltily, I thought about Gabe.

Gerde's voice was marching around like a Nazi in my head. It was like any other day. We weren't even excited.

"I just think you would be a little more excited."

"I'm excited," Russell said miserably. "This is great," he said, taking my hand, his mouth formed into a frown.

"And let's try not to fight when we bring the baby home," I said.

We'd had a huge fight when we'd brought Duncan home because Russell's only job was to buy Tylenol for me at the drugstore and when he'd come to pick us up he'd proudly handed me the box of regular-strength Tylenol. "Regular strength!" I'd shouted through my tears. "Regular strength. Do I look like I'm in regular-strength pain to you? Who would even buy this? If you're in regular pain why take anything at all? I've been in regular pain for nine months, now I'm in extra pain." I'd ranted like that for a while and then slam-dunked the unopened box into the garbage can.

"We won't have a fight," Russell said, unconvincingly.

"I hope our son never asks what it was like when we went to the hospital to have him," I said.

*"I have a difficult* back," I told the anesthesiologist.

"Yes, you do," he said.

"Where's Dr. Sitbon? I need the doctor here to help me." I missed Dr. Lichter more than I had ever missed anyone in my entire life. "I can't do this without Dr. Sitbon," I warned, but the needle slid right in with no pain.

Then Russell was let in wearing his scrubs and Dr. Sitbon joined us. "Madame," he said.

"Please, call me Izzy," I said.

And before I knew it he was holding my baby up over the partition but this time all I saw was legs.

*At New York Presbyterian–Cornell* Weill Medical Center, a private room in the maternity ward is $950 a night. I was given the bed by the window. I didn't have a roommate yet. My parents came and Russell's aunt and uncle. Russell's parents called on the hospital phone.

"So, do we have a name?" his mother asked, even though we had already told her we had chosen Rhys.

"It's Rhys," I said. "Rhys Samuel."

"Rhys?" his mother sneered. "What kind of name is Rhys? I never thought I'd have a grandson named Reeses Pieces. Oh weh-ell. I assume you're done."

"Done?" I asked.

"Yes, done. Through having children."

"For today," I said.

"Don't tell me you want more."

"I don't know," I said.

"Well, I'm surprised they didn't just tie your tubes while you were there on the table."

I handed the phone back to Russell.

When visiting hours were over and my parents and Russell went home to be with Duncan, she was wheeled in, a fat blond woman wearing a pink baseball hat with the word *Bitch* on it, written in rhinestoned script. She was accompanied by her minutes-old baby and her seven other children, the eldest of whom, I figured out, was retarded. The youngest was a beautiful little boy Duncan's age whose name was James.

*The Seven Year Bitch*

The nurse yanked the curtain closed and I listened to her struggle out of her wheelchair and into the bed.

"James," she screamed, when he and his retarded brother came over to my side of the room for the third time and gaped at my catheter and my naked breasts, "if you don't get over here right now I'll kick your ass all over this room! Stupid!"

"It's okay," I said through the curtain. "He's adorable."

"He's a little shit," she said. "If he bothers you I'll smack him."

The little boy's chin was shaking and all I could think was how carefully we had handled this transition for Duncan, how hard we had worked to make the new big-boy bed special and the closetful of big-brother presents we had waiting for him. I had brought a framed photo of him to put by my bed when he came to visit the new baby in the hospital and packed my suitcase with more presents. I wanted to give one of them to James but there were all his siblings who might be jealous. We had even thought of Humbert's feelings and bought him seven-dollar carrot bones and Russell had already brought a receiving blanket home to him so he could get used to the baby's scent. When we brought the baby home, we would all meet first on the street as we had with Duncan, and then we'd go up to the apartment, so Hum could lead the way home and invite the baby into his den.

I laughed nervously. "What's your baby's name?" I asked.

"I haven't decided so we just calling her Stinky Mama," she said through the curtain.

"Stinky Mama," I said.

"Don't touch Stinky Mama!" she yelled at someone on her side of the room.

At nine p.m. a woman came and took my roommate's children

home, and she got on the phone with someone she called Mimoo, who I thought might be her grandmother.

"I don't care if you give me a drawer full of con-domes," she said, "it ain't gonna do nothing to help me. I gotta get me a man, Mimoo. I gotta get me a man." Then two visitors came for her and she got off the phone. The visitors, who I noted with indignation had arrived at nine thirty, were a man and a woman who brought a big bag of McDonald's, and for the next two hours she flirted tirelessly with the man.

"Look at you, if you eat all that you gonna be big as a house. And you already big," the man said to her.

She giggled and flirted. "Well I know you like all of this," she said.

"He's ready to make another baby witchu right now if you're not careful," her friend said.

"I'm ready anyplace anytime," the mother of Stinky Mama said.

I was shocked. Scandalized. My baby, who was rooming in with me in a plastic bassinet, was listening to this.

This was New York Presbyterian–Cornell Weill Medical Center—the best labor-and-delivery hospital in the world—not a rent-by-the-hour hooker hotel. What kind of woman would try to pick up men hours after having a baby?

Finally at midnight they left, and I thought I could get some sleep, but yet another man came to visit her.

I'd had a baby. I'd had surgery. My painkillers weren't doing the trick. I was starving and nauseated, and I had a headache from the spinal.

"Hey, sweet baby," the man's voice slurred from the door.

*The Seven Year Bitch*

"Hey, bab-e-eee," my roommate said back. "How'd you get in here?"

"I told them I was the daddy."

"Maybe you is."

"That baby don't look nothin' like me. I ain't had no Chinese baby."

"She ain't Chinese!"

"She looks fucking Chinese."

I lay stiffly in my bed listening to the sounds of kissing and soft moaning.

Just then I heard yet *another* man's voice say, "Knock knock."

"Come in," the mother of Stinky Mama said.

This was too much! Jesus, I thought, who now? How many men were going to show up here? It was like giving birth in a brothel. It was like giving birth in the parking lot at Coney Island. It was like having a baby on a stoop at Forty-second Street and Tenth Avenue. It was after midnight. "Um, visiting hours are really supposed to be over," I said sharply. "I'm going to have to call the nurse."

"Don't be hating," she said.

"Look, I'm sorry but you've had men here all night," I said.

"The visitor ain't fo' me," she said. "So you should be minding yo' own damn business."

And Gabe Weinrib was suddenly standing by my bedside. He looked gorgeous in a black knit hat and pea coat, which he took off and put on a chair. He went to the bassinet. "Look at him!" he said, gazing down at my beautiful baby. "Oh God. Oh God, look at him."

I had no idea what to say. I had no idea what I must look like, stuck to an IV pole, wrapped in a totally unflattering white hospital gown with a black geometric print.

"Hi," I said, smiling. I pulled the skimpy white cotton blanket up over me. "How did you get past the guards at this hour?" I asked.

"I actually used to date a doctor from here, and she gave me this." He held up an ID hanging from a cord around his neck with a picture of a doctor who looked nothing like him. "I just had to flash it and they let me right in. Is it okay that I'm here? I didn't want to come if, uh, everyone was here and I figured you'd be up. I wanted to see you and Rhys. I'm leaving for Paris in the morning."

"Bitch!" the man said from Stinky Mama's side of the curtain.

"Whoa," Gabe said, standing stiffly as if he were getting ready for a fight.

"Tell yo' husband to be minding his own damn bidness," the man said.

"That ain't her husband," Stinky Mama's mother said. "Her husband was here before."

"So what she talkin' about you have all these men and she got mo' men than you?"

"Actually she had more men," I said. "I just had one, she had two."

"You had yo' husband and now him. That's two. We tied, two fo' two," my roommate said.

She had a point, I thought. I was no different from her. We were up to exactly the same thing.

"Whatchu mean you had two men? You had another man here, bitch?"

"Okay, take it easy," Gabe said.

*The Seven Year Bitch*

"You take it easy," the man said.

Luckily, the nurse came in and handed me two white pills in a paper cup. "Time for your Percocet," she said. "I'll give you all a few more minutes, and then you really should be leaving. Husbands aren't allowed to stay overnight in a semi-private room."

"That's not/ain't her husband," Stinky Mama's mother and I both said at the same time.

The nurse frowned. "Well gentlemen, two minutes and everyone out."

"I'll let you get some sleep," Gabe said. "I think it's an incredible thing you've done and I respect you for it. Bringing two children into the world. Mother of two."

"You gonna give that baby yo' tittie and let me watch?" the man said on the other side of the curtain.

"Gentlemen," the nurse said.

"I brought you something to eat," Gabe said.

"She's only allowed clear liquids until she passes gas," the nurse said.

"Whoo, I don't want to be here when that shit happens," Stinky's visitor said.

My cheeks burned with embarrassment.

"It's clear chicken consommé. Jean-Georges made it for you himself. But keep me posted about the gas."

He took my hand and kissed it.

"You have a beautiful son," he said, grabbing his coat. And then he left.

A few minutes later the nurse came back in. "You're changing rooms," she said to me.

"Why!" I said, not wanting to. I hated my roommate but I had grown to love her too. We had already been through so much together and now I would never know what happened tomorrow, who would show up, who would be Stinky Mama's daddy. Tomorrow they were going to make me stand up and walk, and I would be able to drag my IV past her bed and see through the gaps in the curtains. Now I wouldn't even get to see Stinky.

"Why does she get to change rooms?" Stinky's mama said.

"Don't be hating," I said. "Ask them to move you to the window side."

Two more nurses came and shifted me onto a gurney and transported me, clutching my soup and my baby, to a private corner room with its own bathroom and refrigerator and windows looking out at the river.

"Why do I get this room?" I asked.

"Because your boyfriend just handed over a ton of cash. Now I've really seen everything," she said.

If I were to write an essay in one hundred words or less giving my best tip if you're about to have a baby, it would be: Spring for a private room.

*The next morning was* blissful despite the pain. I was alone with the baby until Russell showed up. I held him and nursed him, and I thought, This isn't so bad. I could get used to feeling this much love. My mother came with Duncan, and Duncan ran all around the private room and then settled in a big chair to hold his baby brother for the first time. "I've decided to call him Pubba," he said. The nurse got me up out of bed and it wasn't as painful as the last C-section. Walking hunched over, I

*The Seven Year Bitch*

wheeled my IV all around. I visited the snack cart several times and carried my own pink plastic pitcher over to the crushed-ice dispenser and Poland Spring water cooler.

Russell and I decided it would be better, despite the chair in the private room that opened into a bed, for him to be home with Duncan, and I was enjoying being alone with Rhys.

I breathed in his faint smell of burning sugar. I had read somewhere that Buddhists believe that our cremation began at birth and that we spend our life slowly burning.

Dr. Sitbon came to visit me. "Madame?" he said. "How are you feeling?"

I wished more than anything it could be Dr. Lichter there instead, in his suit and tie that he wore for rounds, with his interns trailing him like an ermine cape. I missed the way he held my hand, looked at my scar and called it art. I missed his advice about parenthood.

I told Dr. Sitbon I was feeling fine.

"You looked disappointed to see me. Perhaps you were expecting someone else? The nurses told me you had a visitor late into the night," he said, which sounded even more clandestine in his French accent.

"Would it be safe, Doctor," I said, "to travel with the baby right away?"

"You have a trip planned?"

"No. I was wondering if a trip to a place like India would be safe."

"Well, I certainly would not advise it," he said. "Can it wait a while?"

I smiled and shrugged, and he examined me in the politest of ways. "This doctor you married," I said. "What's her name?"

"*His* name is Steven," he said. "He's a man actually."

Then I laughed, thinking about how I had lusted after him for nine months. I laughed so hard I hurt my incision and had to be given more Percocet.

With my baby in the crook of my elbow, I lay back and closed my eyes.

"Izzy," a man's voice said.

I opened my eyes and, to my complete astonishment, found Dr. Lichter standing over my bed, looking right down at me.

"Dr. Lichter," I said, practically jumping up, forgetting my baby and my incision.

"I couldn't let you have a baby without coming to say hello. I looked at your chart. Everything seems perfect."

He took the baby from me and held him up, the way he had once held Duncan. "You make beautiful babies," he said.

I was overjoyed. He had come.

"Are you working here again?" I asked. He wasn't wearing a lab coat or a suit and tie for that matter. He was dressed the way I had seen him in Kripplebush, in jeans and a Red Sox hat.

"No, I'm practicing upstate in New Paltz now. Let's just say I came to clean out my locker."

I thought of my locker with its beautiful earrings and vasectomy gift certificate in it.

"So, Dr. Lichter," I said, as if I were talking to a ghost. "What's going to happen now?"

"You're going to be a wonderful mother to your two sons. Two

*The Seven Year Bitch*

makes everything twice as worthwhile. Everything you do for one will benefit the other. You are going to love it."

I beamed with happiness.

"The Seven Stages of Motherhood only apply the first time. Now you should go back to work."

"I don't know," I said.

"You have to work. I just don't see you as a stay-at-home-mom type. Have you thought about who's going to do the circumcision?"

"I don't know," I said. "Doesn't Dr. Sitbon do it?"

"He's gone now for a few days and it should really be done today or tomorrow."

"I want you to do it," I said.

Russell had suggested a bris, but for me that was out of the question. And according to the mohel Russell had talked to, the bris would have to take place exactly eight days after the birth, which would put us at Christmas, turning Christmas into Brismas.

"I don't think so, Izzy. I don't think they'd take too kindly to my performing a procedure here."

"Please," I begged. "If you couldn't deliver him, the least you could do is give Rhys the same circumcision you gave Duncan. What if we bring him to New Paltz?"

"You're very sweet," he said, stroking my hair for a minute. Then he took my hand and we just sat that way silently for a little while. My heart was pounding and I thought of the Fleetwood Mac song he had once sung to me.

I started to cry with gratitude for this man who had helped me become a mother and was now here when I was becoming

*Jennifer Belle*

a mother again, but then I thought, it was Russell I should be grateful to.

"You're going to be fine," he said, sitting on the side of my bed and putting his arm around me and sort of holding me. He was half-lying in bed with me and I felt incredibly comforted despite how strange it was.

"I'll do it," he said after a few minutes. "Walk with me down the corridor." He put out his hand and I struggled up out of bed. Then, pushing Rhys in his bassinet labeled *Baby Brilliant*, we walked inconspicuously down the hall and through one set of double doors and then another until we were in the NICU.

"Wait here," he told me, lifting Rhys into his arms, and several long minutes later he came out again with the baby screaming and tucked him back in his bassinet.

*More exciting even than* my wedding had been the day Russell had driven me to Westchester to get our marriage license. It was raining, and I thought, I am sitting next to the man I love. We are going to be married. I got out of the car completely covered in Humbert's fur. I had never been so happy.

Now, when Russell was able to tear himself from his Black-Berry, we filled out our new son's birth certificate: Rhys Samuel Trent.

It was time to take him home. My mother was waiting with Duncan and we'd invited everyone over for deli sandwiches later.

"Look what I got you," Russell said, handing me a brown paper bag. I opened the bag to find a box of Extra Strength Tylenol.

"See?" he said. "Everything's going to be fine. Now, you ready?"

*The Seven Year Bitch*

Solemnly we walked out, Russell struggling with the bags. I held Rhys swaddled in the blanket we had taken Duncan home in and Russell's mother had taken Russell home in.

I waited in the lobby for Russell to get the car, and then, in the hospital's circular driveway, we had our hugest fight. Russell's only job had been to get the inside of the car cleaned and have the baby's car seat installed. I had bought the seat. All he had to do was get Rashid to install it.

Russell opened the back door of our car, and there was the seat. But it wasn't installed, and the car was far from clean. We might as well have put the baby in the trunk.

Aside from the fact that the seat wasn't installed, there were old McDonald's hamburgers on the floor, empty milk containers, old bottles, a million filthy toys. There was what might have been vomit crusted on the seat.

"You couldn't do that one thing!" I screamed, clutching my bundled-up baby to me as passers-by looked at us and shook their heads. "I married a moron. Stupid. Incompetent."

Another couple was also leaving with their baby girl in a pink furry snowsuit with dog ears on the hood. The father tucked the baby into her safely installed car seat in their gleaming SUV. The mother slid in next to her. There were family members, flowers, balloons. I could practically see a college fund bulging in the father's pants.

"Don't look at them," Russell said when they'd driven cautiously and safely off. "We can get it installed," he stuttered. "I, I, I, I, I thought it was in right."

"In right? Look at it!" I yelled. "It's not in at all!"

"Is there a problem here, folks?" a security guard said, walking over. "You can't leave the car here."

"The car seat isn't installed," I told him.

"Those things are tricky," he said.

"This is our second child," I said to the guard. "He's had plenty of time to figure it out. Taxi!" I yelled, holding my baby with one arm and sticking my other arm as far up as I could without screaming from the pain from my incision.

"Don't take a taxi," Russell said.

"Taxi!" I screamed, even though there were no taxis.

"Do you want me to try to get you some help, sir?" the guard said.

"Taxi! Taxi!"

The guard looked at the car seat. "Those straps ain't right. That baby's way too big for those straps. You really have to move the car."

In a complete rage I got into the filthy backseat with the baby on my lap, and, with the vacant car seat next to me, Russell wordlessly drove us home.

"I hope our son never asks what it was like when we brought him home from the hospital," was all I could manage to say to Russell for the rest of the day.

*The Seven Year Bitch*

# 37

On New Year's Eve, with my newborn son in my arms, Duncan asleep in his big-boy bed, and Russell lying on the bed next to me watching *New Year's Rockin' Eve*, I pined for Gabe Weinrib like a red-hot teenager. I mooned over him. I looked out my bedroom window at the lights and glistening tinsel rain and New York's signature black umbrellas. What time was it in Paris, I panicked. What was he doing and who was he sleeping with, and how did I get myself into this mess?

If I couldn't go to India, at least I could go to Paris, I thought, over and over again. But it wouldn't be so easy now with the baby. And what about Duncan, I thought. He'd be jealous if I brought the new baby. And if I left the baby home, what about nursing, I thought bitterly, as the baby latched on to me. My cheeks burned because I knew I was a fool. But I couldn't help it.

The claustrophobia of nursing was getting to me. Rhys depended on me to feed him every hour. I couldn't go to a movie, let alone Paris. And he was gigantic! I wouldn't even be able to handle the Baby Bjorn.

"What are your New Year's resolutions?" Russell had the nerve to ask me, as if having a baby wasn't enough and now I had to resolve to do something better.

"Cows don't make New Year's resolutions," I said.

*In the morning there* was an e-mail from Gabe, written just after midnight: "I'm leaving for India on Jan 8th. You can still come with me if you want to."

I got in the shower, turning my stomach away from the water because my scar was swollen and sensitive. I grabbed the bar of Dove and scrubbed at the black surgical tape on my chest and arms and stomach. What was this! I wanted to scream. Why wouldn't it come off?

For fifteen minutes I scrubbed with a washcloth but the residue from the tape wouldn't budge. I laughed and cried at the same time. What a joke! I was going to go to Mumbai with a man with my swollen stomach and black surgical tape and enormous milky tits and a baby. I was so fat, when I got out of the shower the towel wouldn't even go around me.

I was almost forty-one years old. I was married. I had a three-year-old son and a newborn baby. And even all of that couldn't ward off stupid lovesickness and heartache.

I didn't want to be forty-one, but I didn't want to be thirteen again either! I was in pain. Was that how things were going to be for me? I'd be ninety-five years old, on my deathbed with my loving family all around me, and I'd be longing for some hot new eighty-year-old who'd checked into the home the week before. As I looked down at my baby, who Dr. Sitbon had proclaimed "the most gorgeous baby I have ever seen, madame," I wondered what it would take for me to be happy with my life.

When I talked to Joy about it she just harangued me to leave Russell and told me all the incredible things that were happening to her. She wrote me long, long e-mails describing her nights with Chili under the mango trees, or sometimes it was cashew trees, and her newfound orgasms, and I would shoot back a quick "Africa is Africa so you better use protection!" Frankly I was getting a little fed up with it. She didn't have to send me these long e-mails when, as far as I was concerned, everything there was to say could be said in one hundred words or less.

When I talked to my mother she said, "Go to India."

"What!" I said, enraged. "I'm nursing!"

I imagined the trousseau I would pack: nursing bras and pads, my jazzy Medela pump with plug adapter for India that was designed in a smart-looking shoulder bag, maternity pants and nursing tops with the unfortunate brand name of Boob that I had gotten at a store that was actually called the Upper Breast Side.

"Just go," she said. "This might be your chance for love."

"I have to get off the phone. The baby's crying," I practically screamed.

I went to the crib and looked down at my son sleeping peacefully on his back in Duncan's old footed pajamas and then I wrote back to Gabe Weinrib, "I'd love to next time," and hit send.

What would Shasthi have thought, when she came back from

her maternity leave, to find me in India? I wondered. Her baby had been born the day after Rhys.

I wanted to call a friend but I couldn't think of anyone else I could confide in. I wished I could call my roommate from the hospital, but I didn't even know her name. I wondered how old Stinky Mama was doing.

There was someone, someone I could tell anything to, but I just couldn't put my finger on who I was trying to think of. How can you forget your best friend? I wondered. And then I remembered who this best friend was. It was Russell. But I couldn't very well tell Russell that I was depressed because I wanted to go to India with another man. Then I thought maybe I could.

I went to him at his desk. "I'm depressed," I said.

"Why, honey? How can you be depressed with that beautiful baby in there?"

"Because I want to go to India with Gabe Weinrib."

"What?" Russell said.

"He invited me on a trip of a lifetime."

"I thought our honeymoon was supposed to be the trip of a lifetime. Aren't we still paying it off on our credit cards?"

"This is a better trip than that in a better lifetime."

I went back into the bedroom and lay on the bed and Russell actually left his desk and lay on the bed with me.

"Oh honey," he said. "It's going to be okay."

"No it's not," I said. "I can't get this stuff off me." I showed him the black lines from the surgical tape. "How can I go to India with a man? Look at me!"

"I think you look good enough to go," he said. "I think you

*The Seven Year Bitch*

look beautiful. But you just remember one thing. Gabe Weinrib didn't give you those two beautiful boys."

He held me in his arms and I cried on his chest.

"Maybe you can go another time," Russell said.

And then I kind of laughed even though I was still crying.

# 38

I got to school for pick-up fifteen minutes early so I could slip in quickly and get Duncan all buckled into his stroller before Gerde showed up. She was always the last mother to arrive and my plan was to be blocks from the school already by the time she even showed up. But by the time I had helped Duncan into his sweater and signed out *The Runaway Pickle* from the book basket and signed up for what homemade snack I would be providing for the bake sale—bottled water—Gerde was standing there. "Shall we walk together?" she asked. "Can you wait for us?"

I tried desperately to think of a way to get out of it but I couldn't. If I tried to make up another errand, she'd just find a way to come with me. The only thing I could think to say to her was "No fucking way."

"Sure!" I said.

I waited while she peeled Minerva from the reading rug, and got her into her sweater, and signed out a book from the book basket, and signed up to bring homemade "cupcakes" to the bake sale, which I knew, from the one I had purchased for three dollars at the Halloween fair, were sugar-free, flavor-free multigrain muffins.

We began our walk home, two strollers side by side, the children in them arguing the whole way about which one of them was the rightful owner of something. "What toy are they fighting over?" I asked Gerde.

"No," Gerde said. "It is not a toy. They are arguing over the island of Manhattan. Minerva says New York belongs to her and Duncan is under the impression that New York is all for him." Gerde said something to Minerva in German. "I just told her they can share the city."

No, they really can't, I thought. "You certainly can," I told them over their stroller canopies.

Their argument continued, and at University Place and Twelfth Street they both struggled out of their restraints and ran into the lobby of a building.

Gerde and I stood helplessly with grimaced smiles on our faces. What fun! Walking our children home from school! A few minutes later Minerva came running out of the lobby talking wildly in German.

"There is poop," Gerde said.

"What do you mean?" I said.

"They were playing a bathroom game apparently and Duncan pooped on the floor."

"What!" I said, totally shocked. Duncan had been pooping in the potty for a year. There had never been an accident. I left Gerde with both strollers and ran into the lobby, where Duncan was standing frozen in a sea of liquid shit. There was shit covering every inch of the white tile floor, from the door to the elevators. I had never seen anything like this. His little chinos had a small wet spot in the front but there wasn't any shit on them. He must have pulled down his pants and then managed to pull them up again.

"Did you do this?" I asked, confused.

"Yes," he said. He looked like he was going to cry.

"It's okay, everyone has accidents."

A man got off the elevator and said, "Jesus Christ," as he hopped on the few stepping-stones of clean white tile to get through the shit storm to the front door. He stood just outside the doorway to see what I was going to do, as did a driver who had been leaning against a limousine but now had come to the door of the lobby. "Oh yeah, he did it all right," the driver said. "Look at his pants. They're all wet."

I took Duncan by the hand and we traipsed through the shit and out onto the street. Gerde stood her ground with the smile grimace plastered on her face. "I'll get napkins," I said and brought Duncan into the Vietnamese restaurant next door.

"We've had an accident," I said to the woman who greeted us with menus. "May we have some napkins?"

The Vietnamese woman pretended not to understand what I was asking but I persisted until I emerged from the restaurant with a small stack of white napkins that were not much bigger than playing cards.

"Look at his pants, they're soaking wet," the driver said to the man from the lobby. With Duncan next to me, I walked back into the lobby and sopped up the wet shit with each napkin. Shit got on the tips of my fingers.

*The Seven Year Bitch*

"Did you do this?" I asked Duncan again, suddenly realizing this was like no shit that had ever come out of him before. It was slowly dawning on me that if this wasn't his shit, I could at this very moment in my life be mopping up the shit of a homeless person with tiny napkins.

Duncan nodded miserably. "I did it," he said, like George Washington.

When I had soaked up what I could with the last of the napkins, we left the lobby even though the job wasn't nearly done. It had been nothing more than a token effort.

I carried the yellow napkins for a whole block to deposit them in a garbage can and then walked back to Gerde, Duncan, and Minerva at the strollers.

"Done!" I said brightly. There was shit on the bottom of my skirt.

"Okay, good!" Gerde said even more brightly.

"Wait. What's that?" I asked, seeing a beige smudge on Minerva's leg. "How did Duncan's poop get on Minerva's leg?"

"I don't know!" Gerde said.

Minerva was wearing an angelic Bu and the Duck dress in sage and white.

"Shall we go?" Gerde said.

"Wait. What happened exactly?" I said, more to Minerva than to Gerde. Minerva just looked at her mother. "A bathroom game?" I persisted.

"I don't even want to know," Gerde said. "Best not to even ask."

A piece of newspaper blew by and I spread it on the stroller seat so Duncan could sit on it. We walked to our building silently, no longer fighting over whose New York this was.

*Jennifer Belle*

As soon as we got upstairs I brought Duncan into the bathroom and carefully peeled off his pants, afraid of what I would find in his Claesen's pirate underpants. But what I found was nothing. Just the little damp spot and nothing else. It wasn't his shit.

"Duncan, you weren't the one who pooped in the lobby," I said.

"Yes, I was," he said. "Minerva said we should both do it."

That night I checked repeatedly for an e-mail from Gerde apologizing—*Oh my goodness, it wasn't Duncan. It was Minerva. I'm so sorry you cleaned it up!*—but none came. I imagined her getting Minerva to the bathroom and discovering the mess.

In bed, I told Russell what had happened.

"You cleaned her shit! You cleaned her shit!" Russell kept repeating, almost screaming. "That's it, Duncan is not to see that girl again!"

The next morning when Shasthi showed up with Louisa Isolde in her own Baby Bjorn I told her what had happened. "She always does that," Shasthi said. "She did it all over a swing in the playground and Gerde didn't even clean it up. Gerde knew Minerva was the one who did it."

"She couldn't have," I said. "She wouldn't have let me clean it up by myself."

"She knew," Shasthi said. "It's happened so many times. She poops all over the playground. Believe it. It's not normal."

That afternoon, standing outside the school waiting to pick Duncan up, I watched her approaching, her long German stride bringing her closer and closer.

"Hi!" she said brightly.

*The Seven Year Bitch*

"Hi," I said. I waited.

"Shall we walk together? Can you wait for us?" she asked.

"You know, that wasn't Duncan's shit," I said.

She paused for a moment as if she were trying to figure out if she could get away with a lie.

"I know!" she said, her voice going up an octave.

"You must have seen when you took off Minerva's underpants. They must have been completely filled with shit." There was a long silence between us as she continued to smile down at me. "Duncan's still upset about it," I said. "Why did you let him take the blame?" Her mouth widened and tightened and the sides of her eyes crinkled in a way I had never seen.

And then she said the only thing she was going to say by way of an apology: "Sorry about the shit, *ja*?"

The school doors opened and she dashed inside as *sorry about the shit, ja* played itself in my head over and over and over.

"Sorry about the shit, *ja*? Sorry about the shit, *ja*?" Russell ranted that night at dinner. "I'll show her who's sorry about the shit, *ja*!"

We were sitting at the table eating Indian takeout and seemed to be making an evening of talking about the shit.

"I know," I said.

"I mean you cleaned her shit, touched her shit, wiped up her daughter's shit with your own hands. Would you ever stand there and let someone else clean Duncan's shit?"

"Never," I said.

"Of course you wouldn't!"

I suddenly remembered another incident and swallowed

my food too quickly in my excitement to tell Russell. "There's another thing."

"What?" Russell asked, rapt with interest.

"I remember Gerde told me that Minerva pissed on the floor at Moss in SoHo and the sales staff was really angry about it."

"In Moss! They must have loved that. Unbelievable! What did she do?"

"She just left without cleaning it up."

"Of course she left, because you weren't there to clean it up for her. They're lucky it was just piss. I just can't believe it. Sorry about the shit, *ja*? Sorry about the shit, *ja*?"

"Sorry about the shit, *ja*," I said.

Later that night Russell and I both got terrible diarrhea from the Indian food. The dinner special included a choice of appetizer and a choice of entrée, and we'd both chosen mulligatawny soup and chicken tikka masala.

"Jesus," Russell said from the bathroom. "Forget rice and condiments, they should just send a free roll of toilet paper with your order. 'I will have the mulligatawny soup, the chicken tikka masala, and the Quilted Northern.'"

I lay on my bed and laughed, and then ran to the other bathroom.

*"A woman on the* subway thought I molested her," Russell said, coming in the door the next day. He set down the day's mail without looking at it.

"What?" I said. After seven years of marriage, if Russell did something wrong, I got the sinking feeling that I had done it too. I suddenly felt as if I had molested a woman on the subway.

What new aggressive act was this? I was sure it was a beautiful black girl he had done it to. He'd always had a thing for black girls.

"I was reaching my arm out to grab the pole and my arm brushed against her tits and I said, 'Sorry,' and she said, 'Don't let it happen again.' And I said, 'You've got to be fucking kidding me.' I said, 'Don't flatter yourself!' and everyone around me laughed. I felt really good. Enough already. Everyone practically applauded. I was like a hero."

Russell seemed genuinely proud of himself.

"It's always the ugliest girls on the subway who think you're trying to feel them up. *Ooooh.*" He shuddered dramatically. "Disgusting."

"Well, I'm sorry the woman you molested wasn't more attractive but I'm glad you had a good day," I said. I tried to remind myself not to compare him to other women's husbands. I'd just have to be happy with mine's big achievement—getting away with molesting a woman on the subway. Maybe it didn't exactly put money in our pocket, or was as wholesome a hobby as golf, but it made him happy and that was what counted.

"Why is Daddy a hero, Mommy?" Duncan asked. I paused for a moment because "He molested a woman on the subway" didn't seem like the right thing to say even if it was the true thing. "Did you save someone?" Duncan asked.

"Yes I did," Russell said. "I saved all the men on the subway from a very mean woman."

"You mean like a witch or somethin'?"

"That's right," Russell said.

As Duncan reenacted his own version of the story, proudly playing his father, I remembered that I used to have a vision for myself. I used to be able to see myself with a girl and a boy and a handsome husband, his briefcase lined up neatly next to mine by the front door, ready to grab on our way to our jobs as managing directors at our respective firms. Then my mother had explained to me, incorrectly I believe, about what her shrink had said about magical thinking. According to her shrink, you couldn't wish something to happen. And I think that was the moment that I had stopped wishing, even though I had been wishing for so long I didn't even know I was doing it, like stretching my legs when I brushed my teeth in the morning.

I started to slowly panic, trying to wish for something again. I felt time ticking, my birthday candle burning down, my cremation having begun at my birth.

I thought of the dead bird hanging outside of Marlon's house, and I realized I had been that bird, dead in my own nest, and maybe I didn't have to be anymore.

"Is this a treasure?" Duncan asked his father, holding up an old bent straw that he'd folded into his pirate chest.

"It is if you want it to be," Russell said. "It might not be a treasure to another pirate, but if it's important to you then it is a treasure. We treasure what we care about most."

"This is my treasure," Duncan said, putting his arm around Rhys. "You and Mommy and Rhys are my treasures."

"You and Mommy and Rhys are my treasures too," Russell said.

The phone rang and I let the machine pick up, waiting for

*The Seven Year Bitch*

the angry voice of Deirdre-Agnes to come through. But it wasn't Deirdre-Agnes, just an author of Russell's. Now that I thought of it, I hadn't gotten a call from Deirdre-Agnes in a long time. It could have been months even. I hadn't noticed her absence in the same way, I realized, that I hadn't noticed that I really loved Russell again.

To my surprise, Russell didn't run to the phone, despite his author's whimpers. He just picked up his sword and made Duncan walk the plank.

# 39

"We need you to do us a favor," Valerie, from the contest company, said. I was very surprised to get the call from her. It was eleven at night and I was pumping milk to leave with Shasthi the next day. It was a strange offering, like something out of a Grimm's fairy tale, handing my own milk over to Shasthi every morning. Even stranger was when I'd nursed Louisa once when she'd left her with me and taken Duncan and Rhys to the deli. I had ended up a wet nurse for my nanny after all. I could barely hear Valerie over the pump, a whirring noise that always somehow sounded like words—*feed him, feed him, feed him, feed him*. I watched the pump stretch my nipples to look like penises. Nature was strangely imperfect.

I turned off the pump. "What's the favor?" I asked.

"We're doing a giveaway for Coca-Cola. We need a judge, but it doesn't involve reading essays. It has to be done tomorrow at the Woodbury Commons Mall in Harriman, New York, and the judge who was supposed to do it had an emergency. We know it's very last minute, but it has to happen tomorrow morning at ten a.m. and we're hoping to avoid having to fly someone out from here. I thought of you, because you're always so nice on the phone."

I felt very touched when she said that because I always tried so hard to be nice and I didn't think people always thought of me that way.

"You would get paid, of course," she said. "The job pays five hundred dollars for less than an hour's work."

"What would I have to do?" I asked, thinking there was no way I was going to do it whatever it was.

"It's fun actually. Coca-Cola is giving away cash prizes, fifty thousand dollars, ten thousand dollars, five thousand dollars, and ten one-hundred-dollar bills. All you have to do is meet the Coca-Cola representative at the mall and walk around randomly deciding who gets the money."

"What?" I said, my heart starting to pound for some reason. "What do they have to do to be picked?"

"Nothing, you just surprise them. You just walk up to someone who looks nice and say, 'Congratulations, you've been chosen to win fifty thousand dollars in cash by the Coca-Cola Company.' Then the Coke rep will hand you a case with the cash in it, and you'll hand it over. It's better if there's a little diversity, you know, a young African-American man, a white old lady, if there's anyone Hispanic, that sort of thing. And it's better not to approach couples, even if they seem married. There can't be any confusion about who is the actual recipient of the prize."

"And then what does the winner have to do?" I asked.

"Nothing. Oh, and just make sure you don't know the person

and that the person doesn't work for Coca-Cola or any of its affiliates."

"Let me just look in my book," I said, looking down at the half-filled bottle of milk. "I can do it," I said.

"Oh, that's great, Izzy. I've MapQuested from your address, and it takes about an hour, so we'll have a car service pick you up at eight thirty if that's okay."

"I have a car," I started to say but then changed my mind. "Actually a car service would be great."

"Thanks, Izzy." She told me where I'd be meeting the man from Coca-Cola and that he'd have some papers for me to sign, stating I was an independent judge and that I would be completely impartial.

I got off the phone and resumed pumping. I had helped to give Shasthi a baby, and now she would have fifty thousand dollars in cash by ten fifteen tomorrow morning.

*In the morning Russell* called the garage and told them to bring up our car and he went to get it. Shasthi got the children ready. My mother arrived on time to babysit, and from where I was in the bathroom, I could hear Duncan enthusiastically grilling my mother. "Are you old, Grandma?" he asked.

"No," my mother said.

"Yes you are. Will you always be old?"

At eight thirty, Shasthi and I went down in the elevator silently and walked out of the building. Shasthi got into my car, next to Russell, and I watched them drive away. Then I got into the back of a black BMW that had been provided for me.

*The Seven Year Bitch*

*At the Woodbury Commons* mall, the man meeting me from Coca-Cola turned out to be a very nice young girl accompanied by two intimidating-looking armed guards holding three metal briefcases. "These are the hundred-dollar bills," she said, waving a fan of envelopes at me that had the Coca-Cola logo on them. "And the big bucks are obviously in there. Isn't this so fun?" she said. "I love when we do this! Do you mind wearing this?"

She handed me a stiff Coca-Cola baseball hat and I put it on, thankful it helped me to look nothing like myself.

"Do you need a cup of coffee or something?" she asked.

"No, let's just get started," I said.

"Well, where should we start? Here is a map of the mall and I was thinking . . ."

"Actually I know my way around," I said. "My country house isn't too far from here. I think the best place would be there near the Carter's outlet."

"Okay," she said. I looked at her and saw she could be pretty if she wasn't trying to look professional. "Let's go." We started walking toward the Carter's.

"So you're a hedge fund manager?" she chatted.

"I used to be," I said miserably.

"Oh wait, you have to sign the contract."

We all stopped walking and she handed me the document that stated that I was not related or in any way familiar with any of the prize recipients. And I signed it. Then we started walking again.

"Let's do the big prize first," she said. "Fifty thousand dollars. Take your time. Then just choose whoever you think deserves it!"

Outside of Carter's were two white moms with babies in strollers. A young girl with a Carter's name tag was smoking a cigarette, the pack of Yours clutched in her hand. Where was Shasthi? If Russell messed this up, I thought, I would never forgive him.

"Maybe we should start with the smaller prizes," I said.

"We like to start with the big ones so we're not walking around with so much cash," the Coke girl said.

"Izzy?" I heard from behind me. "Is that you?" I, and my strange entourage, turned to find Gra and Charlie, with Fisher toddling in front of them.

"Hi, Charlie. Hi, Gra," I said.

"What are you doing up here on a Tuesday?" Charlie asked. "Where's Russell?"

"Actually, I'm here on business," I said. "Coke is doing a cash giveaway." I pointed to my cap.

"How much cash? We'll take some of that," Charlie said.

"I'm not allowed to know the person," I said.

I turned my head and looked for Shasthi but she wasn't there.

"You don't know us," Charlie said. "Who the fuck are you?" He turned to the security guards. "I've never seen this person before in my life. My name isn't Charlie, and her name isn't Gra. What the fuck kind of name is Gra? Who's named Gra? How much fucking money is in there?"

"Stop it," Gra said. "He drunk. It's sister-birthday today."

"Your anniversary!" I said.

*The Seven Year Bitch*

"YOU DON'T KNOW US!" Charlie yelled. "What sister? I don't have a sister!"

"I'm going to have to ask you to step away from the lady," one of the guards said, tapping Charlie on the arm.

"Get your fucking hands off of me," Charlie yelled. "Give us our prize and we'll be on our way."

"I'm sorry. I can't," I said.

Then I saw Shasthi walking quickly toward the Carter's. She looked just as she had the first time I'd seen her. "I pick her," I said to the Coke girl.

"Which one?" she asked, and I realized the place had filled up with people, mostly moms.

"The girl with the long hair and the sequins," I said. "She looks Indian."

"Perfect!"

"Hey, go fuck yourself," Charlie said and stormed off with a pissed-off-looking Gra following behind him.

I walked up to Shasthi.

"Excuse me," I said brightly. "Coca-Cola is giving away money today and you've been chosen to win our grand prize."

"Okay," she said.

"Fifty thousand dollars!" I said.

"Really?" she said, and then she started to cry. I was startled by this and had to fight back my own tears. We'd practiced it in my living room and she hadn't cried there. She'd just taken Duncan's Diego backpack from me and pretended to be excited. "That's it, in there?"

The guard had come over to her and handed me the metal case, which I had handed to her.

"Congratulations," I said.

"I can go now?" she said the same way she said it each day at six o'clock.

"You can go." I shrugged.

And then she hugged me. She threw her arms around me and pressed her whole body into mine. And I realized that even though she had bathed and wiped and dressed my children, and seen me in every stage of undress, and used my hairbrush and borrowed my socks and my clothes when Duncan had peed or thrown up on her, and made my bed, and washed my underwear, and wiped up spilt breast milk, been pregnant with me for nine months, and held my children when they cried, and watched me fight with Russell for more than two years, she and I had never even touched each other.

"We just need your name," the woman from Coke said, taking a small pad and pen out of her jacket pocket.

Shasthi shot me a nervous look. I smiled widely. A small crowd had gathered around us.

"Just tell that woman your name," I said slowly. "And then you can go."

"Shasthi Dawabhar," she said. She spelled it.

The Coke woman wrote it down. "Pretty name," she said. "And what do you do?"

Shasthi paused and looked at me again. "I'm a nanny," she said.

"Great," the woman said.

And Shasthi left with the money, walking to the parking lot, where Russell was waiting to drive her back to our apartment.

"Now where should we go?" the Coke woman said.

A couple was walking toward me with a kid and a baby in a

*The Seven Year Bitch*

stroller. The woman looked familiar, something about her. The little boy was stepping from side to side the way boys did when they had to pee. She bent down and said something to him, then took his hand and headed in the other direction to the bathrooms, leaving the man to wait there with the stroller. Then I saw that there was a sticker of a shamrock on the stroller and I realized who it was. It was Deirdre-Agnes. I had never sent her the money for the crib. I turned around as quickly as I could. But then I remembered that I had never actually met her husband. He wouldn't know who I was.

For a quick minute I weighed my risks. I knew where the bathrooms were and how long it would take to walk all the way there with a child and all the way back. They would pass all kinds of things that would be of interest to the boy.

"Let's give out another prize," I said quickly. "I pick him."

As fast as I could, I walked over to Deirdre-Agnes's husband and said, "Hi, Coca-Cola is giving away cash today and you've been chosen to win ten thousand dollars."

"Oh my God," he said. "My wife just went to —"

"That's okay, she doesn't have to be here. Congratulations! Just quickly tell that woman your name." *That should pay for your damn crib,* I thought.

"Uh, okay," he said. "My name is Brandon O'Leary. This is incredible. Is this real?" he asked in his Irish brogue.

The Coke woman and the guards came over to us and the guard handed Brandon his ten thousand dollars. Before he could even say thank you, I said, "I'm ready to give out the next prize. Let's go this way."

I just started walking in the opposite direction from the

bathrooms, praying that they would follow me. I heard Brandon say, "We've fallen on some hard times, my wife and me. This is our baby boy, Colin, and my elder boy, Brandon Junior, is with my wife . . ."

Wait, I thought. Deirdre-Agnes's son wasn't named Brandon Junior. He was named Patrick Junior. Deirdre-Agnes's husband was named Patrick. Then little Brandon Junior started running toward us with his mother behind him, but it wasn't Deirdre-Agnes.

I handed out the rest of the money in a sort of daze and, in the car home, did what any mother of a three-year-old and a newborn baby would do under the circumstances, fell quickly and deeply asleep.

# 40

I stood in front of Joy's tiny perfume shop on Mulberry Street and looked at the sign on the door that said it was closing. She was bailing out of the perfume business, closing her three stores and her factory, and shipping everything she owned to Africa.

I walked in and said hi to the salesgirl and picked up the tester of Joy's newest fragrance, Shamba. I sprayed some on my wrist and before I had even lifted my wrist to my nose my eyes filled with tears. I sprayed it on my other wrist and oh the scent! I breathed it in, holding as much of it as I could inside me, before exhaling. I breathed it in again and again, spraying it on my wrists and then burying my face in them.

"Don't you love it?" the salesgirl asked. "It's musky and fresh at the same time. It's got a hint of wheatgrass. It's got such a homey smell, almost like crescent rolls or something."

With my eyes closed I was as good as standing at the changing table. It was uncanny. There it was, that fresh-baked buttery bread smell. Hot and sweet. With just a slight hint of vanilla.

"Joy called this morning and said you should take as much as you want from the store. And she wanted you to have this."

She handed me an old bathroom scale that I stood awkwardly holding.

"She had a scale in the store?" I asked.

"Yeah. She always liked to weigh herself right after lunch," the salesgirl said. "I miss her."

"I miss her too," I said, but I knew I would visit her wherever she was.

"What's happening with this space?" I asked. Joy had put so much into making it beautiful, I couldn't believe she was just going to close it like that.

"I don't know," the salesgirl said. "Probably nothing. It's so small, there're not a lot of businesses that could go in here. The landlady was just in here complaining that it'll probably just sit empty."

I walked out of the store and looked at the store-closing sign while the salesgirl packed as much Shamba as she could for me into five shopping bags. Then I took out my cell phone and called the landlady.

*The next day,* with my business plan in hand, I went to talk to Marilyn and Doris in front of the senior center. I explained what their investment would have to be in order for us to be partners, what our expenses would be, and what profits we could expect. A children's clothing consignment shop—new hand-knitted wares and gently used garments. What Duncan had outgrown alone could fill the shop.

*The Seven Year Bitch*

We walked to the Waverly Diner to discuss it.

"We could call it Is Old's," Marilyn said. "Get it? Isolde's."

"Or As Is," Doris said.

I thought of how Duncan always told people I was a hedgehog manager. "We could call it Hedgehog," I said.


*That night Russell and* I made love. I took my nightgown all the way off. When he said, "Do you want to turn over?" I said, "Yes," and he fucked me from behind. When he said, "Do you want me to come?" I said, "No, not yet. I don't want to stop." We ignored Humbert's crying and scratching from where he was locked in the bathroom. I kissed Russell. We kissed for a long time. It was different from kissing the wide, furry, flappy, wet lips of my dog, which was what I was used to. I would have to get used to it, but I liked it. I didn't think of Gabe Weinrib or Dr. Lichter or Dr. Heiffowitz or Dr. Sitbon or the father I liked in Duncan's class or anybody else but Russell.

"I love you," he said.

"I love you too," I said.

"And I love our children."

"I love them too."

"I love them so much."

"Me too."

"But I don't want to have any more," he added.


*In the morning Shasthi* said she didn't want to work for us anymore. "I want to stay home with my baby," she said.

We were sitting next to each other on Duncan's captain's bed with Rhys between us holding a fistful of my hair in one hand and a fistful of Shasthi's in the other.

"Okay," I said, glad it was ending like this at least, with stacks of Duncan's clothes at our feet, size 2T and 3T now history, along with Rhys's size 0–6. In a small way, it was almost a relief. I knew how tired she must be. How hard it would be to leave her baby in the morning and arrive home after she was asleep. I realized I had been waiting for this.

"Well, you won't be far away," I said. "You can visit us, and we can visit you in the Bronx."

"Yes," she said, but I knew we wouldn't.

I went into the living room to talk to Duncan. "Shasthi's not going to be your nanny anymore," I told him. "She loves you, but she has to stay home to take care of her baby."

"Okay," he said. "Dude," he added.

"What?" I said.

"Okay, dude." I looked at my three-year-old in disbelief. "It's okay, Mommy, it doesn't mean 'doodie.'"

"So you're not upset about Shasthi leaving?" I asked.

"No," he said. "I love Shashti, but she's not in our family. As long as no one in our family leaves I'm not upset."

Shasthi stood by the door. She hugged the boys and put her keys on the table. And then she left.

It felt strange being home alone without Shasthi, so Russell suggested we go for a walk. Pushing two strollers in tandem, we walked through SoHo to look at the store and then continued to Washington Square Park. Without thinking, I started to walk around the perimeter, when Russell pointed out that the park

*The Seven Year Bitch*

was open. I couldn't believe what I was seeing. Duncan scrambled out of his stroller and ran to the fountain, which was going full force. The cobblestones were smooth and seamless, the plants and flowers—rosebushes even—were incredible. Everywhere on the grass, people sat smiling. I had never seen anything as beautiful.

We laid out the baby blanket I had purchased from Marilyn and sat. Duncan made friends with another little boy and they played on the benches.

Suddenly Duncan ran past me screaming, "There's a monster coming! Run from your life! Run from your life!"

He collapsed into my arms, completely terrified by his own game.

"You mean run *for* your life," I said.

"No, run *from* it."

"You run for your life."

"No, Mommy. If you're scared you run from your life. To get away from it."

And that's when I realized I wasn't scared and I didn't want to run away from it anymore.

I could see all that we had and all that I wanted to protect. I could see five years into the future. In fact I could see fifty years into it. I could see Duncan and Rhys attending elementary school and then college and medical school. I could see us at their graduations, meeting their fiancées, dancing at their weddings. I could see my grandchildren, all boys of course, Russell and I taking turns changing their diapers.

As we sat laughing with Duncan and flipping through that

week's *Irish Echo* that we'd picked up at a newsstand, I could see my life instead of my death. Like that park, my marriage had closed and now it was reopened. And I loved it. I loved everything about it.

# Acknowledgments

Jennifer Rudolph Walsh, who willed this book here, Anna DeRoy, Lauren Whitney, and everyone at WME. Megan Lynch, Geoffrey Kloske, Susan Petersen Kennedy, Matthew Venzon, Kate Stark, Rick Pascocello, the entire hardcover marketing, paperback marketing, publicity, hardcover sales, and paperback sales departments, and everyone at Riverhead—I hope you all know how grateful I am. Craig Burke for four books and fifteen years of publicity and friendship. Tina Bennett, Julie Grau, John Ashbery, David Kermani, Erica Jong, Jennifer Weiner, Ulrich Baer, Debra Rodman, Penny Arcade, Robert Steward, Kit McCracken, Beck Lee, David Khinda, Michael Ruocco, Sonia Jacobson, Evelyn Horowitz, Eric Schnall, and Kim Kowalski, for continuous inspiration and enormous generosity. Melinda Chu and Tony Cheng for giving me their magnificent, empty loft on Wooster Street to write this book in. All the writers I have ever worked with, especially Jon Reiss, Erin Hussein, Stacey Lender, Michael Sears, Juliann

Garey, Bronwen Hruska, Desiree Rhine, Renee Geel, Elin Lake Ewald, Amy Perrette, Meryl Branch-McTiernan, Aaron Zimmerman, Marilyn Rothstein, Merrye Schindler, Emily Axelrod, Robin Swid, Heidi Brod, Dinah Prince Daly, and Gray Lippman. Everyone at the Olive Tree Café and the Rosendale Café, where I love to write, and Donna Brodie, who brought me back to the Writers' Room. My family, Jack Herz, and my mother, Jill Hoffman, for endless editing, praise, and pots of cabbage soup. The booksellers who have sold me, the readers who write to me, and Andy, who still takes me as I am, in this, our seventh year of marriage.

© Jeff Chenault

# About the Author

**Jennifer Belle** is the bestselling author of *Going Down* (for which she was named best debut novelist of the year by *Entertainment Weekly*), *High Maintenance,* and *Little Stalker.* Her stories and essays have appeared in *The New York Times Magazine, The Independent* (London), *Harper's Bazaar, Cosmopolitan, Ms., Black Book, Mudfish,* and many anthologies. She lives in New York City and Olivebridge, New York, with her husband and their two sons.

Printed in the United States
by Baker & Taylor Publisher Services